WHERE IS LOVE?

*

Barbara Cartland

Where is Love?

'I'm seeking Love,
Where is he hiding?
I'm seeking Love,
Where can he be?

ARROW BOOKS

ARROW BOOKS LTD
178–202 Great Portland Street, London W1

AN IMPRINT OF THE  HUTCHINSON GROUP

London Melbourne Sydney Auckland
Wellington Johannesburg Cape Town
and agencies throughout the world

*

First published 1947 as *If We Will*
Arrow edition 1971

*Made and printed in Great Britain
by The Anchor Press Ltd.,
Tiptree, Essex*
ISBN 0 09 004730 3

Michael Fielding walked slowly up the wide marble steps, feeling while he did so that his feet were going slower and slower as they echoed his reluctance to reach the top of the steps and touch the big, highly polished silver bell.

As he waited, Michael turned round and looked back down the quiet street where there were few passers-by, but where many important-looking official cars were parked.

'I wish this was over,' he said to himself, and then smiled, for it was unlike him to feel so apprehensive before going into action.

It was many years since he had felt that queasy, uncertain feeling in his stomach and a slight dryness about his mouth. He had faced death so often without fear and certainly without this sickening sense of apprehension, yet now he was definitely and genuinely afraid.

However, it had to be done, and as the door opened Michael squared his big shoulders and turned his thin, sunburnt face towards the butler standing there white-haired and impassive.

'I want to see Miss Cynthia Standish.'

'Yes, sir. What name, please? Is Miss Standish expecting you?'

'She told me to call this afternoon—Wing Commander Fielding.'

'Very good, sir. I will see if Miss Standish is at home. Will you come in?'

Michael stepped into the marble-floored hall. It was cold and rather dark and he felt himself react to the atmosphere of gloom.

'My sense of humour must have taken its day off,' he thought whimsically as the butler preceded him up the broad carpet-covered stairs and opened the door leading into a long, sunlit drawing-room.

It was a beautiful room and was typical of what could be achieved by the lavish expenditure of money. The furniture, the pictures and the carpets were all show pieces, works of art which would delight the heart of any connoisseur.

Michael, however, took little note of his surroundings. As the door closed behind the butler he went across the room to the window and stood looking out over the small paved garden in the rear of the house and beyond it to where the trees of Green Park were like an oasis after the heat and dust of the London streets.

But he did not see the loveliness of the green branches, the clear blue of the sky or the languid floating of the Royal Standard above the roofs at Buckingham Palace; instead he saw the hot arid plains of India, he felt the tropical heat burning its way through the dry thirstiness of his body, and heard again, as he had heard so often before, David's voice saying:

'You will go and see her if anything happens to me, Michael, won't you? You will tell her that I loved her . . . always and unceasingly . . . loved her with every breath I drew . . . even the last of all . . . you promise?'

'Yes, David, I promise. But don't talk like that, you are not going to die!'

'Who knows? Who cares out here? Jenkinson yesterday, Pat the day before! We shall miss Pat, Michael. I wonder if anybody would miss us if . . .'

'Oh, shut up, David! We are going to come through together, you and I. There is a lot of living and a lot of loving for us to be doing before our number is up.'

Michael spoke roughly because some strange uncanny sense within him had at that moment whispered surely and clearly that David would not come through.

And Michael's presentiment had been a true one. David had died, as many other fine young men had died before him; but . . . there had been something unusual about his death . . . something which had made Michael swear with a bitter, vehement anger drawn from the very depths of his being that the person concerned should suffer by learning the truth.

'Is that why I am here?' Michael asked himself now, 'or is it because of my promise to David?'

He had no time to formulate the answer because the door opened and Cynthia Standish came in. She stood for a moment framed against the ivory-and-gold panels of the door; and as Michael turned and saw her he understood for the first time why David had talked almost incessantly of her during those hot, arid nights, why he had been unable to forget her, and why—yes, why, because of her, he had gone to his death.

She was lovely, arrestingly and spectacularly lovely. Her dark hair was swept back from a perfect oval-shaped face; her eyes were unexpectedly and vividly blue beneath eyebrows delicately winged like the drawings on an old Chinese etching; her mouth was curved and full.

There was something so utterly feminine about it and the lissom grace of her figure that no man could look at Cynthia Standish and forget for one moment that she was an utterly desirable woman. Yet to Michael, standing there grim and stern, she was evil and bad and he hated her.

She moved across the room towards him holding out her hand with a friendly gesture which he ignored.

'You are Wing Commander Fielding?'

'Yes!'

There was just a flicker of surprise in her eyes at the tone of his voice and her hand dropped to her side. Then

7

with a gesture she indicated chairs on either side of the high ornate mantelpiece.

'Won't you sit down?'

She sat herself in a high-backed, tapestry-covered chair, but Michael remained standing. There was a moment's pause and she looked up at him half wonderingly, half questioningly, as though his silence was as unexpected as his attitude.

He was certainly extremely good-looking, she noticed. His features were clear-cut and there was something noble in the breadth of his brow, something strong and determined in the sharp line of his jaw. She guessed that the lines which ran from his nose to his firm lips had been etched by experience rather than age, and she liked the level directness of his eyes even while the steely expression with which they regarded her was puzzling.

'You asked to see me?' she prompted.

'I wrote to you.'

'Yes, I know. You were a friend of David?'

'Yes, a great friend of David.'

'I was sorry to hear of his death.'

'Were you?'

The question came like the report of a gun. Cynthia started, and her long fingers were linked together.

'I had known David for many years.'

'And he had loved you ever since I can remember.'

Now she was still and Michael saw that she drew a very deep breath. There was a long silence, a silence in which even the ticking of the clock on the mantelpiece was hardly audible.

'Is that what you have come here to tell me?' Cynthia asked at last.

Michael moved impatiently, almost resentfully.

'No,' he answered, 'I have come because David asked me; because he had talked of you so often and always he had made me promise that if anything happened to him I would come and see you and that I would tell you he had loved you always . . . up to the very last moment of his life.'

Cynthia's hands fluttered, and her head was turned away from Michael towards the window.

'Thank you for telling me,' she said at length, but her voice was not gentle as it should have been. Instead there was another note—a note almost of fear.

'Would you like to hear how he died?'

There was no mistaking now the antagonism in Michael's voice.

'There was quite a long account of it in the paper,' Cynthia replied. 'Was it incorrect?'

'It did not mention the one thing that was really important,' Michael said.

'No?'

'You know what that was.'

'Do I?'

She was fencing with him, but they both knew that the advantage was with him. He was striking at her, well aware that she had no defence.

'Yes, you do know; but perhaps you would like me to put it into words. David died the day he received your letter.'

'Oh!'

The exclamation came from her almost like a deep cry.

'Yes, the day he received the letter in which you told him you had no further use for him.'

'That is not true!'

Cynthia jumped to her feet. Now she was no longer afraid, no longer acquiescent. There was a fire in her eyes and steel in her voice which matched Michael's.

'You did not write a letter saying that?'

'I wrote a letter telling David that I did not love him. He had known it before. I had told him that often, but he would not listen. He wrote me wild letters from India, letters which presumed many things; and I thought it both unwise and unfair to let him go on living in a fool's

9

paradise of his own making. I told him the truth—that I did not love him, but that I was always anxious to be . . . his friend.'

'Charming and conventional,' Michael remarked sarcastically.

'What else could I say?' Cynthia demanded angrily.

'I have no idea, Miss Standish. I only know that after David received your letter he went out on a particularly difficult mission from which he did not return. I have the feeling that he was glad to go and that he knew he would not come back.'

Cynthia opened her lips as if she would answer him, and then she turned away suddenly and walked towards the window. She stood there with her back to him, silhouetted against the sun outside. She looked very slim, almost fragile, and yet Michael was conscious of a strength and resilience in her.

He had half expected tears, half expected her to crumple up at his accusations and put forward some pitiable defence that she could not help her own attraction. But instead, when at last she turned to face him, he saw that she was still angry.

'This is my answer to you, Wing Commander. I resent both the accusations you have made and your coming here at all. I do not believe for one moment that my letter to David sent him to his death. You believe it did, but then doubtless you were prejudiced by David himself, who was always prone to exaggeration.

'Having known him for so long, I claim to have known him better than you, even though you lived and fought beside him through the war. David loved me, it is true; but in a jealous, selfish way which was not really worthy of the name of love . . .'

'Stop!' Michael stepped forward and put his hand peremptorily on her arm. 'I won't have you say such things. David was my friend. He was as fine and as honourable a man as ever I have been fortunate enough to know. Who are you, living here in softness and security, to know what a man can suffer when he is far away? In Burma David was magnificent; in India he did a splendid job, and would, I believe, be doing it still but for your letter.'

'If you believe that,' Cynthia said clearly, 'you are more of a fool than you look.'

For a moment Michael gasped. Then the impulse rose within him to take her fiercely by both shoulders and shake her. There was something in the beauty of her face as she looked up at him defiantly which made him see red.

He stood very still and his eyes narrowed a little. He stared down at Cynthia, striving to master her by sheer will-power, striving also to keep control of himself. There was a vibrating tension between them so strong, so magnetic that it was as if the air around them was charged with electricity.

Michael was conscious that his breath was coming quickly, that all his hatred and resentment of this woman, fed by the years which he had passed abroad since David's death, had come to a culminating point at this moment. There was a fury within him so fierce and primitive that only conventionality kept it from breaking forth untrammelled . . . unrestrained. . . .

He looked into her eyes; they were deep wells of darkness; he knew that she, too, was breathing quickly. But she was not afraid of him. His own anger was so devouring, so consuming, that he was surprised that she was not scorched and singed by it; but . . . no . . . she was not afraid. She faced him defiantly even while her breasts moved beneath the thin silk of her dress.

'I could kill her,' he thought, and felt some part of him ready for action, ready to translate the poison of his thoughts into deeds.

Then the cloud which had weighed down on him for

a long, long time lightened—why he did not know—he was only aware of its passing.

Suddenly Michael was conscious that he was gripping Cynthia's arm so tightly that the skin was white on either side of his fingers. He released her, saw the marks which his fingers had left, but he would not apologise.

'There is nothing more to be said?'

His voice seemed to him to come from a long way away—so much had happened since he last spoke—or had it?

'No, I think not,' Cynthia replied.

With an effort, Michael put his hand into his pocket and drew out a little parcel.

'I brought you these,' he said, 'but if you don't want them I can take them to David's mother.'

Cynthia made no attempt to touch the parcel or to take it from him; instead she asked:

'What are they?'

'Photographs of you and some letters of yours.'

'Including the last one?'

'No, he took that with him.'

Cynthia looked down at the small parcel and then up at Michael again.

'I don't want them,' she said; 'but I don't think David's mother would want them . . . she has suffered enough.'

For the first time since the conversation had begun her voice was soft as she spoke of David's mother, but Michael did not notice it. He slipped the parcel back into his pocket.

'Very well then. I have fulfilled my promise, Miss Standish; now I will go.'

'There is just one thing before you do,' Cynthia said quietly. 'I understand, from the newspapers of course, that you have left the Service. I hope now you have come back to civilian life that you will try in your contacts with ordinary people to be more just and more under-standing than you have been with me.'

She spoke with a goading bitterness which made Michael feel his temper rising again.

'It is kind of you to take so much interest in me, Miss Standish.'

'I was not thinking of you,' Cynthia answered, 'but of the many people to whom you are a hero, almost a legendary one.'

For the first time Michael looked embarrassed, and as if Cynthia saw her advantage she added:

'People expect better things of you, Wing Commander, than that you should give judgment without evidence or condemn people without giving them the opportunity to speak for themselves.'

Michael looked uncertain.

'If I have . . .' he began, but Cynthia put up her hand as if to silence him.

'I make no pleas for myself. I would not stoop to argue with anyone so pig-headed, so utterly and completely biased as to the righteousness of his cause; but in the future you may do harm. I am only thinking of that. Good-bye!'

She dismissed him with an inclination of her head which was dignified and yet in its own way insolent. Michael was well aware that the advantage had passed from him to her. Now Cynthia was in command, and he felt not foolish but irritated, because here was something which he had not anticipated and which he did not un-derstand.

For a moment he contemplated asking her for an ex-planation and then he remembered the memory of David's stricken face after he had read Cynthia's letter and the dumb misery in his eyes as he said, 'She has made it pretty clear this time that she does not care for me. She is through, Michael, and so am I,' so he har-dened his heart and said gruffly:

13

'Good afternoon, Miss Standish. It was kind of you to see me. I hope in the future that you will remember that people can be easily hurt, especially those who are foolish enough to love you.'

A faint smile twisted Cynthia's lovely lips.

'That at least is plain speaking, Wing Commander.'

'Which is what I meant it to be,' Michael replied.

He walked to the door feeling that he could stand no more and yet somehow he was reluctant to go. He felt that he had not pressed home his advantage. He had come with weapons which he felt sure would utterly annihilate this woman who had destroyed his friend. Yet she stood there slim and utterly sure of herself.

'Damn her,' he thought, 'what she wants is a good beating. I would like to see her dishevelled and in tears. I would like to break her and know that in being broken she might have the chance to start again as a decent person.'

As if Cynthia half read his thoughts, the faint smile on her lips grew more mocking and the gleam in her eyes waxed brighter. But she said nothing and after a momentary pause Michael crossed the room. He stretched out his hand towards the door, but it was opened suddenly from the other side. A young man stood there wearing glasses and the harassed expression of one who is perpetually driven almost beyond endurance.

'I say, Cynthia,' he began, 'they tell me downstairs that you have got a Wing Commander Fielding with you.' He saw Michael and stopped speaking and ejaculated suddenly, 'Good lord!'

'What is the matter?' Michael asked.

'It is you then. I could not believe it when they said you were here.'

'Why?'

'Because we have spent the last two days trying to get in touch with you. The old man heard you were in England and wants to see you. We had no idea where you

14

'were and we have been simply scouring the place for you, and now of all places I find you here in the house. It is really too much!'

'What does my father want him for, Toby?' Cynthia asked.

'Lord knows!' Toby Dawson replied. 'He may want to offer him the editorship for all I care. But he wants him and we couldn't find him—which has been enough to drive us all crackers.'

'Well, I am here now,' Michael said uncompromisingly.

'And thank God for that,' Toby Dawson replied. 'Come upstairs. I ought to get an increase in salary after this.'

'I will come with you,' Cynthia said.

Michael looked at her. He had half a mind to say something sarcastic, then changed his mind and in silence he and Toby Dawson followed her as she led the way into the lift.

The *Tempest* was a forceful newspaper with both power and influence. It had been built up, sustained and invigorated almost entirely by the personality of one man —its founder and owner.

As the lift travelled swiftly upwards Michael tried to recall all he had heard about Lord Melton; but he could remember only that the woman beside him, whose fragrance percolated through the lift, was his daughter.

They reached the top floor of the house, the lift gates clanged to behind them, and Toby Dawson threw open the door of the big sun-filled sitting-room, announcing, like a conjurer producing a rabbit out of a hat:

'Wind Commander Fielding.'

Cynthia went into the room first and Michael, following her, was conscious first of all of almost blinding sunlight and then of the familiar, much-caricatured face of Lord Melton, staring at him from the one corner of the room which was in shadow.

15

He was sitting in a great armchair and beside him on a table were at least a dozen telephones. He appeared in no way surprised at their appearance. As they moved across the room towards him he merely raised his thick eyebrows a little and asked:

'Well, Cynthia?'

'Toby said you were screaming for Wing Commander Fielding, and as he was with me I came up to see what it was all about.'

'Does it interest you?'

The question was sharp and searching.

'In a way,' Cynthia replied. 'He is one of the most unpleasant young men I have ever had the misfortune to meet and I wondered what use you were going to make of him.'

Now at last a smile twisted the corners of Lord Melton's lips and he looked up at Michael.

'My daughter's recommendation is not very favourable, Fielding?'

'I am content that it should be so,' Michael replied grimly.

The situation seemed to amuse Lord Melton, but he made no comment and merely waved Michael to a chair in front of him, while Cynthia, pushing some of the telephones aside, perched herself on the edge of the desk.

'We don't want you, Cynthia,' Lord Melton said without turning his head.

'But I want to stay.'

'It would be better if you didn't. Fielding is obviously on edge because you are here. I shan't get the best out of him in such a mood.'

Michael could not help but be amused by a conversation which was conducted as though he were not there, but which he felt at the same time was obviously calculated to intrigue him. Cynthia looked irresolute.

'Let me stay, Daddy?'

'I would rather you didn't. Besides, if he is all you say he is, why worry yourself?'

'There is a good deal more I can say about him,' Cynthia said getting down from the desk, 'but you are right. It is a mistake to worry over one's enemies.'

'So Wing Commander Fielding is an enemy?'

'Most certainly! War has been declared.'

She spoke lightly, but there was nothing light in the look she gave Michael. Then without another word she turned and moved across the room. The door closed behind her and Michael was alone with Lord Melton.

There was a moment's silence and Michael felt that he was being inspected. Instinctively he resented it. They were a strange pair, this father and daughter, and he was sure of one thing: that he disliked them both.

'I have been trying to get hold of you,' Lord Melton said at length.

'So I understand,' Michael answered. 'I am sorry if it was difficult, but I am only in London for a few days.'

'And then you will be going down to Melchester?'

'Perhaps.'

'I don't think there is any uncertainty about it. They will adopt you.'

'You think so?'

Michael was surprised at Lord Melton's knowledge of his movements, but he was not prepared to say so.

'They would be very silly if they didn't. You are exactly the type of young man they want to represent them in Parliament.'

'Thank you.'

Lord Melton smiled.

'You understand that I am speaking not so much of your politics as of you personally.'

'Again I can only say thank you.'

'When I heard you had arrived back in England, I thought you were just the person we needed for the *Tempest*—to write a series of articles for us.'

'I don't think I should be able to do that, sir.'

'Why not?'

'To begin with, I am not a writer and consequently I do not think people would be particularly interested in what I have to say.'

Lord Melton smiled.

'Must you be so modest? You have got a pretty big reputation, you know, for what you did in the war. Besides, there is not a schoolboy in England who does not know the story of that particular act of gallantry in Burma and that you refused the V.C. because the twelve other men who were with you could not have it too.'

'I don't want to trade on that.'

'Nobody is asking you to. I am merely proving that the public would be interested in what you have to say. Anyway, to put it bluntly, Fielding, I want six articles from you. I can commission them now at 100 guineas each, and they should be entitled "Why Britain is Losing Her Grip".'

There was silence for a moment and then very decidedly Michael got up from the chair.

'Thank you, Lord Melton; it is very kind of you to offer me the chance of writing for your newspaper, but my answer is no.'

Lord Melton's dark eyebrows shot up.

'No?'

'No!'

'And why?'

'To begin with, as I have already told you, I am not a writer, and secondly I do not like your subject.'

'You do not think it is correct?'

'Most decidedly not.'

'That is interesting. Most people would, I think, agree that Britain is losing her grip on the world.'

'Most people cannot see an inch beyond their own noses.'

'But surely?'

'Lord Melton, may I speak frankly to you?'

'Of course!'

'Then I would like to say that I deprecate both the tone of your newspaper and of many others. They are too busy telling us that things are wrong, they are too busy showing us the mistakes we have made in the past and pointing out the mistakes we are making now.

'People need something in which to believe. They do not want to be told they are on the wrong path; they want to be shown the right; they require something constructive, not the everlasting destructive criticism they are being given.

'Give a man an ideal and he will work and die for it. I found that in the war, and I know it is true of all men. What the *Tempest* is doling out every day is Death. I want to give the people Life—something to live for, something to aim at, something to achieve.'

Michael spoke with fire and there was something extremely virile and magnetic about him. As he spoke the sun behind him touched his hair with a golden glow. From the shadows Lord Melton answered him:

'It all sounds very well, my boy, but the British people are a tired people. Newspapers are merely mirrors; they reflect what is in the hearts and minds of the people who read them. What you are reading in the *Tempest* is the truth.'

'It is not!'

Michael almost shouted the words.

'In this uncertain, difficult world,' he went on more quietly, 'I am certain of only two things—my faith in God and my faith in the British people. We have an instinct for what is right and for what is true. It has never failed us in the past and it will not fail us now.'

Lord Melton shrugged his shoulders.

'I hope you are right.'

'I know I am right. That is why I came out of the Service. I think I can serve this country better in politics.'

'A great many people have believed that they could find their way through the mess and the machinations of a political world,' Lord Melton sneered, 'and a great many have been disappointed.'

'If I fail, there will be others who will succeed,' Michael replied quietly. 'Good-bye, and thank you for your offer.'

'One minute,' Lord Melton said. 'I would like you to reconsider that. From what I hear of you you are not rich. You will need the money. Why not try the articles? You can twist them round to your way of thinking.'

Michael stood very still in the sunshine and then he laughed.

'Why are you laughing?' Lord Melton asked.

'Strangely enough,' Michael replied, 'I was thinking of a certain episode in the Bible.'

A faint smile altered Lord Melton's expression.

' "And the Devil took Him up on a high mountain . . ." ' he quoted.

'Exactly,' Michael answered.

'Very well, then,' Lord Melton replied. 'Go to the devil your own way. You will find it less comfortable than mine.'

'Probably,' Michael replied, 'but I will take the chance.'

The two men shook hands. It was difficult to know whether Lord Melton was annoyed or not. He had lost too many battles in his life to bear malice now. He pushed a bell on the table beside him and the door was opened instantly by Toby Dawson.

The lift carried Michael down to the ground floor. He went through a small lane which led him into the Park. There was a faint breeze to offset the heat of the sun, and when at length he found an unoccupied chair in the shade of a big tree he sat there smoking and thinking.

The afternoon drew on, children who had been playing on the grass were taken home, picnickers gathered up the remains of their teas, dogs chasing one another were whistled for and put on their leads. Still Michael sat on, a faint frown on his brows, until the sun sank and the London twilight became blue and luminous and slightly mysterious.

At length he got to his feet and walked slowly through the Green Park, across the Mall into St. James's Park and on to the Embankment. Beneath the shadow of the grey bridge he paused. A barge, heavily laden with timber, was passing up river. He watched it go and was just about to move on again when something attracted his attention below.

To his left there was a flight of steps leading down to the water with locked gates at the top. On the steps, low down, someone was crouching. For a moment Michael imagined he was mistaken and that it was a piece of wood or bale of merchandise, and then as there came a movement he thought it was a boy.

He looked down again, and now he was certain. With an instantaneous swiftness of action which comes only from men who have lived with danger, he vaulted the iron gate at the top of the stairs and ran down the remaining steps.

He caught the boy's arm as he was about to spring forward. The impact of his hold and the movement forward coincided so that the body he touched slipped and fell in a crumpled heap on the steps, his legs in the water.

'You can't do that,' Michael said, and his words were a command.

In answer there came only an agonised sobbing as from someone who, keyed up to commit an action and failing at the last moment, is overwhelmed by a desperate and almost instantaneous reaction.

'Now stop that,' Michael said, 'and I must get you out of this. The police may be here at any moment.'

He lifted the boy up by the arm and started to drag

him up the steps. It was only then that he realised that he held not a boy, but a young woman. At the top of the steps a street light fell on her face and Michael saw that she was very young and her face was ashen pale.

She was in a state of collapse. Picking her up in his arms he climbed over the iron gate and on to the pavement. He put her down, propping her against the balustrade.

She sank against him and he saw that her eyes were tight closed, but the tears were streaming down her cheeks. She made no attempt to wipe them away, her arms hanging limply.

'Stop crying,' Michael said.

Surprisingly she obeyed him. He waited a moment and finally she opened her eyes and looked at him. She looked desperately white and frightened and he could see that she was very young.

'Now tell me what is the matter,' Michael said quietly.

'I can't,' she answered. 'I can't. Oh, why did you interfere? I thought no one would see me.'

'If I had not seen you, someone else would have,' Michael replied. 'If you want to die, this is not the right place to do it.'

'But I do want to . . .' she said. There was something so petulant in her cry that Michael could hardly forbear from smiling.

'What is the matter?' he asked.

'I can't tell you. Let me go.'

'I'm not going to let you go,' Michael answered, but his tone was kindly and friendly and somehow infinitely reassuring. 'You are wet and you are overwrought.'

He looked down at her feet as he spoke and at the puddle of water which was gradually growing around her. She followed the direction of his gaze and said wonderingly:

'I'm wet.'

'Yes, I know you are,' Michael said, 'but you might have been much wetter.'

It was as if his words reawakened her resolution and she gave a cry.

'Oh, please let me go . . . ! Please let me go!'

Her face turned in a haunted manner towards the river.

'Now listen,' Michael said, 'if you want to kill yourself there are far better ways of doing it than jumping into the river; and if I don't rescue you the police will, in which case you will find yourself in very serious trouble. Now I am going to take you home to have a hot drink and change your shoes and stockings. Then we can talk things over. Is that all right with you?'

For answer she started to cry again. Michael looked at her and then without another word put his arm round her shoulders and led her forward to the edge of the pavement. Standing there, he waited to signal a passing taxi.

2

In the taxi the girl sat for several seconds staring ahead
of her, then she covered her face with her hands. She
was crying, but not so desperately or with such utter
abandon as she had cried a few moments before. Michael
said nothing, feeling that the tears in themselves might
bring some relief

They drove on through the darkness for some way until at last the girl spoke, straightening her shoulders and
making what appeared to be an almost superhuman
effort at control.

'Where are you taking me to?'

Her voice was low and educated.

'To someone who will help you,' Michael answered,
'someone who has mothered not only me all my life
but hundreds of other people. She is a very sweet person and you will feel quite safe with her.'

'But why should you do this?' the girl asked, and
Michael noticed that there was fear in her voice.

'Suppose I ask you a question,' he replied. 'What is
your name? Don't tell me if you would rather not.'

'My name is Mary Rankin,' she answered.

'And mine is Michael Fielding. Now we are formally
introduced.'

He spoke lightly and easily, but she gave a little gasp
as though he had hurt her.

'What must you think of me?' she said. 'I don't

know what came over me, but I just felt that I must escape. Everything was too much—too . . .'

Her voice broke.

'Don't think about it,' Michael said soothingly. 'It is all over now. We all have desperate moments in our lives, and in this case there is no harm done except that I'm afraid you are going to catch a frightful cold.'

Mary Rankin looked down at her wet feet, then raised her eyes to Michael's face, which she could dimly see from the passing street lamps.

'I am so ashamed of myself,' she said, and there was something childish and rather pathetic in the words.

Michael smiled at her.

'Forget about it.'

'I wish I could.'

'Can't you?'

'You see . . .'

She hesitated as if the explanation were difficult to put into words.

'Yes?' he prompted.

'I've . . . I've been such . . . a fool!'

'Aren't we all at times?'

'I don't know,' she said helplessly. 'I am afraid I know very little about other people, but a great deal about my own foolishness.'

The taxi stopped for a moment in a traffic block and Michael could see her quite clearly. Her profile against the window was delicate, her features well formed and pretty in a somewhat indecisive manner. He could see a little pulse beating in her throat and the quivering of her fingers as she interlaced them nervously together.

Her breath was coming quickly, and he noticed for the first time that her clothes were of good material and were doubtless comparatively expensive. At the same time Michael's kindness prevented him from being too curious. He felt only a surging sense of pity for this poor waif for whom life had become too big and too frightening.

He saw her lips trembling as she sought for words to explain herself, so he said quickly:

'Don't try to talk. You have had a nasty shock. Try to relax; think about something quite different.'

'But I want to tell you,' she insisted. 'You are only a stranger and so I can talk to you. Perhaps if I had had somebody to talk to I should not be here at this moment.'

It was the eternal cry of loneliness and Michael could not help but respond to it.

'Tell me,' he said gently, 'we have got quite a little time ahead of us. The person to whom I am taking you lives some way away, but I will explain about that later.'

'I lived in Devonshire . . .' Mary began, and Michael knew that she was determined to give him her confidence.

In war he had known it happen often enough for a man who had been through a tremendous shock to lay bare his innermost feelings to anybody whom he could find to listen. As Mary went on speaking, Michael knew that to her he had no personality but just a lay figure to whom she could speak of the fullness of her heart.

'I have not travelled much and I have been away from home very little,' Mary said. 'My father is dead. He was in the Navy; and as he died soon after he retired my mother and I had grown used through the years to being alone and being sufficient in ourselves. We had friends, of course, in the village but not very intimate ones, for we were very poor and could not entertain much.

'Then three months ago the most amazing thing happened. A film company started to make a film along the coast. We got to know some of them and amongst them was a man called . . . Charles Marsden.'

Mary drew a deep breath and Michael thought grimly that here was the villain of the piece.

'Charles was not an actor,' Mary went on. 'I think he called himself a producer, although he was not producing that particular film. Anyway, he was very important and had a lot to do with the running of it. He often used to drop in for an evening at the Cottage and sit with my mother and me.

'You can imagine how fascinating it all was and how exciting for me. At last, when the film was nearly finished, he told my mother that he had a proposition to make. At first neither of us could believe our ears when he said that I had the making of a film star. He wanted me to come to London and he would give me my chance. He told my mother that he was certain that within a year I should be famous. Can you imagine what this meant to us?'

Mary made a gesture with her hands as she spoke, and then for a moment raised them to her eyes.

'I have a good idea,' Michael said; 'won't you go on?'

'It was like a bombshell,' Mary continued, 'and yet at the same time it was so exciting, so astounding, that we could hardly believe our good luck. For a long time my mother and I had been wondering what I could do to earn my living. I had learnt shorthand from a correspondence course and I could type, but nobody wanted a secretary in our village and I think we were both too shy and apprehensive of failure to suggest that I should go further afield to look for work.

'But this was different; this was a ready-made opportunity; here was an easy road to success. By the time we had taken in exactly what Charles meant the whole village knew of his suggestion and were almost as thrilled as we were.

'I don't think until that moment we knew how many friends we had. There was hardly a soul in the village who did not contribute something to my trousseau. They all realised that on the tiny pension on which my mother lived she could not provide the proper clothes for me to go to London.

'Even the school children hemmed me handkerchiefs

in their spare time, and when I left home a fortnight later I did so amidst such a shower of good wishes that I might have been a bride going away on her honeymoon.'

Mary paused a moment and then she repeated in a dull voice:

'Yes, a bride! That is what I might have been.'

There was a moment's silence before she went on.

'We came to London. Perhaps you have already guessed the end of the story. I was so stupid, so dense, that I did not understand, not even after Charles moved me out of the lodgings to which he first took me into a flat which he said was owned by his sister, who was away.

'It was true he gave me a few film tests, but I am quite certain they were hopeless even if he bothered to look at them. There was only one thing he wanted, and that was not connected with the films.'

'You were not in love with him?' Michael asked.

Mary turned her face towards him and he knew that her eyes were wide and surprised.

'. . . In love with him?' she repeated. 'Such an idea never entered my head. To begin with he seemed to me awfully old. He was bald and slightly pompous in his manner of speaking. It was interesting and exciting to listen to him, but I never thought of him as a man . . . not in that sort of way.'

She shuddered, and Michael guessed the shock it had been to her when she learned that Charles Marsden was very much a man, and a particularly unpleasant one at that.

'At first,' Mary went on in a flat voice, 'I did not understand what he was talking about. But he laughed at me and said I might be innocent, but not as innocent as all that. He accused me of knowing what he wanted all the time, and when I said that I would have nothing to do with him he said that I would soon come round to his way of thinking. He banked, you see, on my being too ashamed to go back to the village . . . and how right he was! I am ashamed . . . too ashamed . . . to go home and admit what a fool I have been.'

She gave a deep sigh that was almost a cry and then said:

'I have fought him for a whole week. This afternoon he lost his temper with me and was ready to turn me out into the street. He said I would have to go home unless I agreed to what he wanted. I have tried to find other work. These past few days I have answered advertisements and been to agencies, but they had nothing to offer me. I think Charles must have known what I was doing, for he said:

' "Go home then, go back and tell them that you are a failure. You, the village belle, of whom they were to be so proud."

'I begged him to give me a real chance. I said I would scrub out the studios if only he would leave me alone.

' "There is only one thing you are fit for, my dear," he laughed.'

Mary's voice grew faint at the memory, and then she whispered:

'I think I went mad. I ran out of the flat. I don't know where I went or what I did. I walked about . . . it must have been for hours . . . . found myself by the river . . .'

'And then I came along and found you,' Michael interrupted. 'Well, all's well that ends well. I will find you something to do, I promise you that. You need not go home, and I will deal with your friend Mr. Charles Marsden.'

Mary looked at him as though she was not certain that she had heard aright.

'You will find me something to do,' she repeated— 'something decent?'

'Something decent,' Michael promised gravely.

At that moment the taxi stopped. Mary looked out of the window and then gave an exclamation.

'But where have you brought me?' she asked.

'Don't be frightened,' Michael answered. 'We are down in the heart of Dockland. You will understand why in a few minutes.'

He got out and paid the taxi and was well aware, as he turned towards the grey, gaunt building towering above him, that Mary was both apprehensive and afraid with new fears as to what was happening to her.

She looked up at his face as if for reassurance, and something in his smile seemed to give her courage.

'You are sure it is all right?' she asked tremulously.

'Quite sure,' Michael answered.

He led the way into a dark, narrow stone hall with iron stairs, which he started to climb, saying:

'I am afraid you have got a long walk. Feeling strong enough for it?'

'Of course,' Mary replied.

They passed several floors, and at the third, with a catch of her breath, she leant against the banister, saying:

'Where are you taking me to?'

'To the top floor,' Michael said. 'I am sorry there is not a lift, but this building is used for many things. The bottom floor is a warehouse, the second is a food store, and here on the third floor there is a nursery clinic. You will learn a great deal about that if you stay here for any time. And another two floors up is what I think is the nicest flat in London and it belongs to the nicest person in the world. Come and meet her.'

As if she was reassured by the calmness in his voice, Mary obeyed him. But she was looking very pale when finally Michael, drawing a latchkey from his pocket, opened the door on the top floor. He led her into a tiny hall painted in a warm shade of yellow; a big gilt mirror reflected a bowl of roses on an old oak refectory table. Michael threw his hat down on the table and called:

'Toogy!'

Instantly a door opened and a woman appeared. She

30

was small and her hair was grey, but somehow she gave the impression of terrific energy. Her voice was surprisingly young as she cried out:

'Michael darling! I was wondering what had happened to you.'

She walked across the hall and he bent down and kissed her. Then he turned to the girl beside him and said:

'Toogy, this is Mary Rankin. She has been rather unhappy, so I brought her along to you.'

'But of course,' Toogy answered, 'come along into the sitting-room, dear; or would you rather go and lie down?'

'I think she ought to take her shoes and stockings off,' Michael said, and without looking at all surprised at such an unusual request the grey-haired woman linked her arm in Mary's and drew her across the hall.

'Come to my bedroom,' she said, 'and I will lend you something.'

The two women disappeared and Michael went into the sitting-doom. It was a big long room with windows overlooking the river, and Michael, who thought it was the most beautiful view in the world, had often sat there as a boy watching the big ships laden with goods and merchandise going up to the Port of London.

He had seen there flags flying; he had seen sailors of all nationalities working upon them. They had fired his imagination until half the stories he had woven around those great vessels had become part of his own life, part of his character.

'How beautiful it is!' he thought as he had thought so often before, and then he turned from the open windows, stretching himself comfortably in one of Toogy's chintz-covered armchairs.

It was a very unpretentious, homely and comfortable room, and in sudden contrast Michael remembered the big ornate drawing-room at Melton House. He remembered, too, his Lordship's sanctuary on the top storey with its exotic profusion of flowers and a strange atmosphere of concentrated sunshine.

There was really, Michael thought, no comparison between the two. But then, how could Toogy be compared with anyone? And yet, in her own way, she was as great and as powerful as Lord Melton.

It must have been nearly half a century ago when Miss Trugrot, whose name was derived from some obscure Scandinavian ancestors, against her parents' wishes started work in Dockland. Well educated and delicately nurtured, she had wanted to work among the poorest of the poor—the flotsam and jetsam of the waterside.

The dock-hands in those days were the scum of the earth. They slept in the fo'c'sles of empty ships, worked with rotten plant, and when there were accidents they were left to perish in crippled misery or died at the dockside because there was no one to attend to them. Ragged and verminous, hungry and ill-paid, it was to them and their children that Miss Trugrot prepared to devote herself and the little money she had inherited.

At first she was laughed at and treated with suspicion, but soon the women got to know her and her intense sympathy and understanding made them love her. It was only a question of time before the name Trugrot became translated into Toogood and shortened to 'Toogy'.

Miss Toogy became a byword in Dockland. She settled there and lived amongst them. She started up her own welfare clinic and her own day nursery for the children long before such things were heard of in any other part of the country or any Government had given them so much as a passing thought.

She made no appeals for help. She collected what money she needed in her own way.

The police brought their troubles to her and the poor knew that they could rely on her. She had a unique position and she knew it. It was only sometimes that Michael,

32

watching her as now, knew that she was getting old, and was afraid not so much for her as for what would happen to her 'little kingdom' once she had left it.

He, personally, had known no other mother and no other home. His real mother, who had been Toogy's friend, had died shortly after he was born. He had been brought up as if he were Toogy's own child, and it had indeed been many years before he had realised that he was different from other boys.

He had been utterly happy in his childhood, though it had nearly broken his heart when Toogy sent him first to a well-known Preparatory School and then to one of the best Public Schools in England.

'Why,' he had asked her once when he was much older, 'why did you, who are so unconventional, choose the conventional for me?'

'I was brought up conventionally,' Toogy answered. 'If you are going to do the things in your life which I hope you will, Michael, you will find that the conventional by far the most convenient stepping-off place.'

He understood what she meant later on. For a time he had almost resented what he thought were her efforts to turn him into an ordinary Public School boy. And yet how wise she had been!

He knew that now, that the education he had received, the contacts he had made with other men, the insight he had had of his contemporaries' minds, were all part of a British Heritage which must be his if he were to represent, as he wanted to, the people of Britain.

He was thinking of Toogy as she came into the room. She came in briskly with her usual quick step, and yet it struck him as she crossed the room to sit down beside him that her face was almost transparent in its pallor and she looked unusually tired.

'What have you been doing?' he asked, and was aware of a sudden fear in his heart.

'It has been a long day,' Toogy answered. 'There was

an accident down at the wharf; two of the men were hurt and I had to go and see their wives. And then there were other things, but don't let's talk about that now. I want to ask you about Mary Rankin.'

'What is she doing?' Michael asked.

'I have put her to bed with a hot-water bottle,' Toogy answered. 'I could tell that she had been through some tremendous shock, either emotional or physical.'

'A little bit of both,' Michael said, and briefly he related the story as Mary had told him.

Toogy sighed.

'Poor child! It is such an ordinary commonplace story, yet I suppose such tragedies are happening day after day and we are not always there to save the victim.'

'I shall go and see Mr. Charles Marsden,' Michael said grimly.

'I shouldn't,' Toogy replied. 'You will only get annoyed and hit him and it won't do the slightest bit of good. I will arrange to have Mary's clothes fetched from there. It is better that the whole unsavoury episode should be forgotten.'

'And let the swine get away with it?' Michael asked.

'Your having a row with him won't stop him being a swine,' Toogy answered. 'People must be what they are. The only thing you will do is to make him more clever next time he is attracted, and he might try and make things unpleasant for Mary.

'He may allow nasty rumours to creep back to her home. I should leave him alone. If he doesn't know exactly what has happened to her, he will be apprehensive and will keep his mouth shut.'

'All right, Toogy, I leave it to you,' Michael said. 'I might have guessed you would not allow me to do what I wanted.'

'Have I ever stopped you from doing anything?' Toogy asked with a smile.

'That's just it! You don't say you are going to stop me,

but you make your way so much more reasonable that I just have to give in to you.'

Toogy laughed.

'And now, having talked about everyone else, let's talk about you. I have got news for you.'

Michael sat up and his eyes widened.

'West Winkley?' he asked.

Toogy nodded.

'The Chairman telephoned you this afternoon. It was lucky that I had just come in. He said he thought that you would like to know that the Selection Committee have decided to recommend you to the Executive. There's a meeting next week and he is writing.'

'Oh, Toogy! That's wonderful, isn't it?'

Michael's voice expressed sheer thankfulness. He got to his feet and walked across the room to the window.

'I don't know why,' he said, 'but I have always wanted to represent Melchester; and yet when I told you that the seat was vacant I had an idea that you were upset.'

'Did you?'

Toogy's voice was non-committal.

'Yes, you didn't say anything, but somehow—I may have been imagining things—I thought you were not awfully pleased, or else you didn't like Melchester or something.'

'Why did you want to go there particularly?' Toogy asked.

'I don't know. I can't explain. I hate most industrial cities, but Melchester has always attracted me. There is something big and powerful about it, something strong and resilient. I don't know why, but it always seemed to me to be one of the great pillars of this country. It is a city of men, a city of business and a city of money, yet with it all it is entirely British. I couldn't imagine Melchester in any other country in the world.'

'No, that's true,' Toogy said.

'Oh, Toogy, you are glad that they have accepted me?'

'Yes, I am glad,' Toogy said as if she came to a definite conclusion.

'Then that's settled. I couldn't have borne it if you weren't pleased.'

'Does my opinion matter so much?' Toogy asked.

Michael laughed at her.

'You know the answer to that one,' he said. 'Darling Toogy, I am so glad to be home again. When I was in the East I used to dream about standing here and looking out on the river. I used to think of you and I always had the feeling that you were thinking of me.'

'I was,' Toogy said quietly.

'It helped me on thousands of occasions.'

'I am glad about that.'

'And now at last I am home. I have been away for eight years, Toogy. It's a long time, isn't it? I am half afraid that I have got out of touch with things here.'

He told Toogy of Lord Melton's offer. For a moment she said nothing, and then crossing the room she linked her arm in his.

'I am glad you refused,' she said softly. 'You and I know that Britain and the British will never lose their grip.'

'I am sure of that,' Michael said.

'So am I,' Toogy agreed.

They were silent for a moment and then Michael said :

'I saw Cynthia Standish.'

'I am told she is very beautiful.'

'It is not the sort of beauty which I admire,' and his voice was suddenly harsh.

'You gave her David's things?'

'No, she wouldn't take them. It was funny, Toogy, but I don't think in all my life I have ever disliked—no, almost hated—anyone as much as I did Cynthia Standish this afternoon.'

Toogy looked surprised.

'Why so vehement?' she asked.

'I don't know,' Michael answered. 'She seemed to get under my skin. I had forgotten that women of that sort could have so much power and could care so little.'

'Are you sure you have got the right end of the story?' Toogy asked.

Michael didn't answer for a moment and then he shook himself as if to shake away some spell which lay over him.

'Oh, Toogy,' he said lightly, 'don't tell me that you are going to find exonerating circumstances or an unexpected approach to Cynthia Standish, because I won't believe it. She is bad, you wouldn't like her, and that is that.'

'The extraordinary thing is,' Toogy replied, 'that very few people are entirely bad; anyway, far fewer of them than Lord Melton's newspapers would have us believe.'

'If they listened to you,' Michael said, 'people would believe that half the world was inhabited by angels.'

'I am not certain that it isn't,' Toogy said.

Michael smiled and turned again towards the river, while Toogy went and sat in her low chair by the fireplace. She picked up her knitting and after a time said:

'What are you thinking about, Michael?'

He turned round with a start.

'It is awful to confess it, Toogy,' he said, 'but I was not thinking of Melchester and the wonderful things I would do at Westminster, I was thinking of Cynthia Standish and wondering why David loved her and how she could have been so unkind to him.'

'Is it unkind not to love someone who loves you?' Toogy asked.

'No,' Michael replied, 'but at the same time she must have encouraged him to get him to such a stage of dithering passion that he should behave as he did.'

37

'I wonder, Toogy said. 'Don't you think, Michael, it is a mistake to judge anyone on their actions to a third person?'

'Oh, Toogy, David was my friend.'

'Yes, I know. I, too, was fond of David, though I only saw him a few times, but at the same time I cannot believe that anyone can fight another person's battles for him.'

'You know that she behaved extremely badly to David?'

'I don't know. I didn't see the last letter she wrote to him, nor did you. We don't know what her reactions were to David. To us he was a very charming, lovable boy, but to her he may have been a very different person.'

Michael flung up his hands in a gesture.

'Toogy, you will drive me mad. You are too good-natured, too kind, too sweet; and yet, damn it all, you have fought and kicked and buffeted your way to get what you wanted.'

'. . . for the people I loved,' Toogy said.

'And I loved David,' Michael retorted sharply.

'You can't get Cynthia for him now.'

'No, that's true,' Michael said.

'Then don't waste your hate on her. Hating is poison; I have told you that since you were a little boy.'

'Yes, and I have always believed you,' Michael said. 'Yet when I think of her, so lovely for those who admire that type of beauty, so composed, surrounded with everything that money can buy and yet so hard, so brittle, so contemptuously cruel—then a woman like that can almost destroy my belief in the good which one finds in all human beings.'

Toogy went on knitting. For quite a long time she did not speak, and when at length she did she said:

'You have been away for a long time, Michael, and you have met very few women. Today you have met two, both in their own way opposite types; one strong, the other very weak.'

'Yes, I suppose that is true,' Michael agreed. 'Yes . . . I suppose . . . you would call Mary Rankin weak.'

He said the words stiffly, knowing that Toogy did not intend them as a compliment.

'Yes, very weak,' Toogy said.

It was at that moment that the door opened, moving very slowly as though the person outside was too frightened to make more than a tentative movement to open it. Softly Michael moved across the room and saw that Mary Rankin stood there.

She was wrapped in a pale blue dressing-gown which he recognised as one of Toogy's. She clutched it round her, her fair hair framing the almost deathly pallor of her face. She looked wildly round, saw Michael, and the panic which had been in her eyes was replaced by an expression of relief.

'Oh, you are here,' she exclaimed. 'I have been asleep, but I woke up suddenly and found myself alone. I was frightened—terribly frightened. I didn't know where I was.'

Her words fell over one another and tears welled into her eyes.

'It's all right,' Michael said reassuringly. 'Of course I am here, and here is Toogy, who put you to bed. We are looking after you and there is nobody and nothing which can hurt you.'

'Are you sure—quite sure?' Mary asked, looking round her as though some awful danger lurked in the corners of the room.

'Now listen,' Michael said gently, 'I am going to look after you, you can be sure of that. No one shall cause you any more unhappiness. I want you to go back to bed and have a good night. In the morning we will talk about what you can do. That's a promise!'

She stood irresolute for a moment and then suddenly,

as though she capitulated, her tension relaxed. A small flickering smile relieved the misery of her face.

'Thank you,' she said. '. . . I'm sorry.'

'Go back to bed,' Michael repeated. 'Will you find your own way?'

He looked uncertainly at Toogy as though she might offer to go with Mary, but to his surprise she made no movement.

'Yes, yes, I can find my own way,' Mary murmured. 'I don't want to be a nuisance. I am only so grateful.'

She slipped away, her footsteps almost inaudible as she crossed the hall, and then he heard the sound of the bedroom door shutting softly.

'Poor child!' he exclaimed.

Toogy looked up at him.

'What are you going to do about her?'

'I must find her a job, of course.'

'Do you think she is capable of doing one? It would really be much better for her if she went back to her mother.'

'But she can't do that. You do see. To be the heroine of the village, the school children hemming handkerchiefs . . .'

'Yes, I see,' Toogy said, 'and we have to be strong—very strong—to admit that we have made a mistake.'

Michael looked at her in surprise.

'Toogy, you are not being hard on the poor girl? Soft about Cynthia Standish and hard about this poor little unhappy creature! How very unlike you!'

'Is it?' Toogy asked. 'Oh well, Michael, she is your responsibility, not mine.'

'I will find something for her,' Michael said. 'But, Toogy, you are not walking out on me? You know I can't do anything without your help.'

Toogy looked up at him and there was laughter in her eyes.

'My dear Michael! You know the old saying: *Rescue someone from drowning and they are your responsibility for life.*'

'Heaven help me!' Michael exclaimed jokingly.

'That's just what I was thinking,' Toogy answered in all seriousness.

3

'I see your friend Michael Fielding won the by-election in Melchester,' Lord Melton said, looking up from the morning paper and speaking to Cynthia, who was re-arranging a big bowl of orchids on a gold console table. There was a moment's pause before she answered:

'He is no friend of mine.'

'No? Then I think you are making a mistake. He is a clever young man and will go far.'

'So would a bulldozer, but it doesn't follow that you want to be friendly with one.'

'Hardly a very subtle simile,' Lord Melton remarked, 'but I understand what you mean.'

Cynthia stared at the long spray of white orchids which she held in her hand. They were faintly flecked with red as if with drops of blood.

'Why do you think Michael Fielding will do so well?' she asked at length.

'Because he is the only young man I have met since the war who has faith in himself,' Lord Melton answered.

'I had no idea you admired him so much,' Cynthia said sarcastically.

There was a sudden sharp note in her voice as though she meant to be disagreeable.

'Did I say I admired him?'

'No, but obviously you do. It is unlike you to remember any young man, especially one who has refused to acquiesce in your wishes.'

Lord Melton raised his eyebrows.

'So vehement,' he said. 'I think if the truth were known, Cynthia, he made a very decided impression on you.'

'An unpleasant one, as I have told you before.'

'Maybe, but nevertheless an impression which exactly proves my point. How many young men whom one meets today are worth remembering, and even if they are, does one remember them? We are living in a tired, mediocre world, my child, although Michael Fielding tells me I am a fool to think so.'

'Oh, why do you listen to him, and anyway, why do you quote him?'

'Because I am interested,' Lord Melton said. 'Have you read the reports of the by-election in West Winkley the last three weeks? They were worth reading, Cynthia, and they would have given you something to think about, something better on which to exercise your brain than the meaningless meanderings of the Mayfair fops who take you out dancing.'

'Really, Daddy, this is so unlike you that I am astounded. In another moment I shall think you have got religion—or should we call it Fieldingitis?'

'So you have read the reports from West Winkley?' Lord Melton said.

To his surprise Cynthia looked embarrassed.

'I did see that some of the papers described the hysteria that this man was arousing as Fieldingitis.'

'And the papers that supported him described it as "unprecedented enthusiasm",' Lord Melton said. 'Well, never mind, the point is that Fielding goes to Westminster, and we will see what he does there.'

'I have told you before that I am not interested in him,' Cynthia said.

She put the orchids into the bowl without saying any more and went from the room.

Lord Melton's eyes followed her speculatively for a

moment and then as the door closed sharply behind her he returned to the perusal of his newspapers.

Cynthia went downstairs to her own suite of rooms. They were on the second floor, the big sitting-room facing south and a bedroom and bathroom opening out of it—all decorated in the extreme of fashion and regardless of expense.

She sat down at her writing-desk and, picking up a gold paper-knife jewelled with precious stones, turned it idly over and over in her hands. She was not conscious of what she was doing, but her brows were knitted together and there was a far-away expression in her eyes.

She was so absorbed in her own thoughts that she jumped when the door opened and she looked round to see her stepmother standing there.

Lavinia Melton was attractive in an exotic manner. Her father had been a Brazilian and her large, dark, liquid eyes were set in a smooth magnolia-white skin which was in almost startling contrast to the raven's-wing darkness of her hair. She had been a show-girl before Lord Melton married her.

She walked across the room now with the rhythmic, self-conscious ease of someone who is used to advertising the charms of her body.

'Good morning, Lavinia,' Cynthia said.

'Good morning,' Lavinia Melton replied. 'I wanted to know whether you are coming down to Cannes with us next week. There is not much room in the Villa, as you know, and there are various people I want to invite.'

There was no mistaking Lavinia's hint that Cynthia, should she decide to be amongst the party, was not really wanted, and Cynthia gave a little smile which was almost a grimace as she answered :

'Don't worry, Lavinia, I won't inconvenience you. I will make my own arrangements for the holiday.'

'Good,' Lavinia said with relief, 'but don't forget that most of the servants will be away on their holidays.'

'No, I won't forget,' Cynthia answered.

Lavinia looked round the room.

'How nice it is up here!' she said. 'Is that a Sickert over the mantelpiece?'

Cynthia followed the direction of her eyes.

'Yes, Daddy gave it to me for Christmas. Don't you remember?'

Lavinia's lips protruded a little, almost as though she pouted.

'It is very charming. I was just thinking how nice it would look in my sitting-room. Those shades of grey are just what I need to tone down the new crimson curtains.'

'Have it then by all means,' Cynthia said.

There was no impulsive generosity behind her words. She was too used to her stepmother's greed, which must acquire for herself everything she saw belonging to someone else.

'Can I really have it?' Lavinia asked quickly. 'How sweet of you, Cynthia! Thank you so much.'

'Yes, do take it,' Cynthia replied with something curiously like weariness in her voice.

She turned her head away and looked out of the window. Lavinia hesitated for a moment, looking first at the picture and then down at her long, blood-red pointed nails.

'You know, Cynthia,' she said at length, 'you ought to think seriously of getting married. No girl should stay on at home much after she is twenty-one.'

'I didn't think I was in your way in this great barrack of a house,' Cynthia said.

'Oh, you are not,' Lavinia said in a gushing tone, which was too sweet to be sincere. 'I didn't mean that. I was only thinking how much nicer for you it would be to have a home of your own, to be your own mistress.'

'I think I am that here,' Cynthia replied.

Lavinia looked at her, hesitated, and then spoke frankly:

45

'Your position here is . . . shall we put it bluntly? . . . somewhat uncomfortable. I don't want to chaperon a step-daughter nearly my own age, and you don't like my being your father's wife.'

Cynthia turned round and looked Lavinia straight in the eyes.

'Who said so?' she asked.

Lavinia shrugged her shoulders.

'It is not necessary to put the obvious into words.'

'All right then, if we are being so brutal,' Cynthia said, 'I don't think you are a very suitable wife for my father.'

'No?' Lavinia questioned, with raised eyebrows. 'Nevertheless, he has married me, dear Cynthia, and, frankly, I enjoy being Lady Melton.'

There was something so completely outrageous in her statement that Cynthia had to laugh.

'Oh, Lavinia,' she said, 'one can't be angry with you. And I am glad somebody enjoys living in this empty, soulless house.'

Lavinia put up a white hand glittering with a huge diamond ring and touched the brooch of diamonds and rubies which was pinned on her shoulder.

'It is very pleasant,' she said softly, 'to know security.'

Cynthia felt an impulse of sympathy towards this girl who had managed by some clever means of her own to persuade her father into matrimony. From all she had heard from various sources Lavinia's life, if eventful and adventurous, had indeed been insecure in the past. Certainly as Lady Melton she would never know want again either now or in the future.

Cynthia looked at her standing there. She had a vivid, colourful, almost poster-like attraction. But there was something a little too gaudy in her whole appearance and something vaguely vulgar in everything she said or did.

Across the room Cynthia could see the two of them reflected in an ancient gilt-edged mirror. She could see the peacock blue of Lavinia's dress, the white oval of her face under the darkness of her hair. There was the glitter and flash of her jewels as she moved and the long slim beauty of her legs in their transparent nylons.

Beside Lavinia she could see herself, and as she looked she knew without conceit where the advantage lay. There was something delicate and exquisite about her beauty which made Lavinia's seem tawdry.

Quite suddenly her sympathy was with her stepmother. She understood that Lavinia had enough perception to note the contrast that they were to each other and to want her out of the way. Cynthia got to her feet.

'I am not certain that marriage is a solution, Lavinia,' she said; 'but I shall be moving away from here very shortly.'

Lavinia smiled.

'I don't want to seem beastly, and after all it is your home.'

'It is nice of you to remember that. It has not been much of a home for a very long time, not since my mother died twelve years ago.'

'You were fond of her?'

'Very fond. Despite her persistent ill-health she was a wonderful person. She kept Daddy human. Try not to let him get too omnipotent, Lavinia.'

'Omnipotent? What do you mean by that?'

Cynthia sighed. She knew she could never explain, and even if she could Lavinia would never understand.

'Never mind,' she said. 'Just try to make him happy.'

'Why shouldn't he be?' Lavinia asked. 'He has got so much.'

'Has he?' Cynthia questioned; and she asked the same question of herself once again when Lavinia left the room with a last backward glance at the picture she had co-veted and which she intended having removed down-stairs immediately.

'Has Daddy so much?' Cynthia asked herself, and added: 'And what have I?'

She thought of the wealth and power with which their name was associated. She thought of the emptiness of the large, lofty rooms, the emptiness in their lives of all that really made life worth living. They had thousands of acquaintances, but few real friends. They had engagements to fill every hour of the day and yet not one appointment which would really matter if it were cancelled or they failed to turn up for it.

'Our lives are not unhappy,' Cynthia said out loud; 'they are merely empty. We have no sense of direction, no idea of where eventually our journey through life will end up.'

She shook her head quickly as if she would shake away a cloud of depression which threatened to settle on her.

'What do I want?' she asked. 'What do I want of life?'

As if in answer to the question she heard her father's voice saying again:

'He is a young man who has faith in himself.'

'What does that mean?' Cynthia asked herself, 'and how can I find faith in myself?'

The room in which she sat was suddenly suffocating. She jumped to her feet and going into her bedroom picked up a hat and coat which her maid had left ready for her on the chair. She put them on without looking at herself in the mirror and hurrying downstairs let herself out into the sunlit street.

She walked into the Park, moving quickly without an objective, conscious only of her own restlessness and the desire to escape the confining walls of Melton House. After she had walked some way she became aware that her feet, in thin, high-heeled sandals, were tired, so she sat down on a bench.

A newspaper had been left there, and without really

thinking what she was doing Cynthia picked it up and opened it. Michael's name stared at her.

'FIELDING IN FOR WEST WINKLEY.
TREMENDOUS MAJORITY FOR WAR HERO.'

Cynthia's fingers tightened on the paper. She read the paragraph through several times and then at the bottom she saw the words '*photographs on page* 6'. For a moment she hesitated as though she would deny her own curiosity; but slowly, almost reluctantly, she turned to page 6. The picture was captioned:

'*Wing Commander Fielding addresses a mass meeting on the Eve of the Poll.*'

The camera had caught Michael from an unusual angle. The light was full on his face and yet it outlined his head, giving him the appearance of almost being alight as he stood out from the dark mass of people around him. One could feel the vigour and vitality of him leaping from the pages of print.

He had been speaking when the photograph was taken, and from his look and the expression in his eyes Cynthia guessed that what he was saying had meant something tremendous to him personally.

She stared at the picture for a long time and then put the newspaper down on the seat. Here at last, she thought, was somebody real; somebody who knew how to live. And yet why should he only have the secret of it?

She threw back her head defiantly. She felt some new vigour and courage course through her as though even the thought of Michael Fielding had the power to galvanise her to action.

'I too can fight,' she thought.

She jumped to her feet, for she knew that she had come to a decision, and walked back swiftly to Melton House. As she came in through the front door Lavinia was just leaving. A long grey Rolls-Royce was waiting for her, and as Cynthia passed her in the hall a wave of perfume came from the thin, exotic figure of her step-mother. The two women smiled at each other, but it was merely a conventional gesture.

Cynthia went upstairs to her own sitting-room and picked up the telephone. She was just dialling 'Trunks' when the door opened and Toby Dawson looked in.

'Oh, you are back, Cynthia,' he said. 'They told me you had gone out. Your father wants you.'

'I have got a call to make,' Cynthia replied. 'Why don't "Trunks" answer? They always take such a time.'

'Let me do it for you,' Toby said. 'What number do you want?'

'Melchester 235.'

'Melchester?' Toby echoed in surprise.

Cynthia nodded.

'My godfather, Sir Norman Baltis, lives there. I am thinking of going to stay with him.'

'For any particular reason?' Toby asked.

'For many reasons,' Cynthia answered, 'and that's quite enough questions.'

Toby grinned. He had known Cynthia for many years and was one of the few people who dared to tease her.

'I bet you are going down to look at the conquering hero.'

'Michael Fielding?' Cynthia answered, not pretending to misunderstand him.

Toby nodded.

'I must admit he is jolly good-looking.'

'Tell me, Toby,' Cynthia said in a serious voice, 'if you were a woman and you wanted to have your revenge on somebody, what would you do?'

'Make him fall in love with me,' Toby replied promptly.

Cynthia looked startled.

'I hadn't thought of that.'

'Surely it's obvious,' Toby answered. 'Besides, if it is Fielding you are thinking of, it would do him good.

These idealists get far too much up in the clouds. They need to be brought down to earth a bit, and that, Cynthia dear, ought to be right up your street.'

Cynthia looked at him.

'You know, Toby, there is something heartless and heart-breaking about this house and about all of us. We allow no one any illusions, we allow no one even a shred of respect.'

'Good lord, Cynthia, what have I said now?'

'Nothing much, and anyway if I explained you wouldn't understand.'

'Try me!'

Cynthia shook her head.

'No, thank you, Toby; but don't tell Daddy I am going to Melchester.'

'Won't he ask where you are?'

'He is going to Cannes next week; and if the past is anything to judge by, neither he nor Lavinia will care a damn what happens to me as long as I am not inconveniencing them.'

She spoke with such bitterness that Toby looked at her in surprise.

'I say, Cynthia, you are not still sore about the old man marrying Lavinia, are you? It's a funny thing to say, but I think he was lonely, you know.'

'I dare say, but why Lavinia?'

Toby made an expressive gesture with his hands.

'Who else was there?'

'That's true enough,' Cynthia said. 'Every decent woman of marriageable age has shunned this house for years. Don't I know it? That's why I have never had any girl friends. Their mothers would not let them come here.'

'Good lord, I never thought of that,' Toby said. 'Do you mind?'

'No,' Cynthia replied. 'It is just one of the things I

51

have had to put up with. But I oughtn't to complain. Like Lavinia, I have got security.'

Toby walked across the doom and lit himself a cigarette.

'Stop ringing that number and talk to me. I have never thought of things quite like this.'

'I don't want to think of them just now. Besides, I want that number.'

There was a sudden click in her ear.

'At last! Is that "Trunks"? Will you give me Melchester 235, please?' She looked back at Toby. 'I am going to Melchester; at least it will give me a new interest in life.'

She remembered her words a week later as the train carried her through the ugly built-up suburbs of the city. Melchester people were traditionally hardhearted and hard-headed. They had to work and to work hard for their money, and to them money was not only something to be acquired, but also the very life-stream by which they lived.

Every city has an atmosphere of its own, and Melchester resembled closely the pounding power of a dynamo.

A car was waiting for Cynthia and it carried her safely through the busy main thoroughfare out into the less traffic-filled roads of the residential suburbs. Here in a big estate, which had once been situated in the heart of the country and which had now been gradually built around until it formed part of the city, was the home of Sir Norman Baltis.

The house itself was Regency, built with that beauty of proportion and elegance of conception which no modern architect can emulate. It stood on rising ground and its part was surrounded by a huge brick wall which still protected to a certain extent the wild birds from the intrusion of poachers and mischievous boys. ·

Sir Norman Baltis had bought Claverley soon after he

had made Melchester the centre of his aeroplane industry. He had factories in other parts of the country, but
he decided overnight, as it were, to centralise them in
one vast concern, to settle there himself, and not only
to own but to manage his own factories.

He was a self-made man, and proud of it. He had
started in life with no advantages save excellent health,
a steel-like determination and an insatiable ambition.
However much he achieved he always wanted more, and
he had succeeded beyond his wildest ambitions.

He was a strange man, as strange in his own way as
his friend, Robert Melton, which was perhaps the reason
why the two men, both struggling and striving for their
own ends and both eminently successful in their own
worlds, should become friends. There was a certain similarity, too, about their stories.

Both had been determined to reach the top, both had
fought savagely, and not always particularly honourably,
for what they wanted. Both had married gentle, well-
bred women and both had made failures of their mar-
riages.

Robert Melton's marriage had at least in the eyes of
the world been more successful than that of his friend
Sir Norman Baltis. Lady Melton had been a complete
invalid for the last eight years of her life, but while he
was still fond of his wife there was no doubt that Robert
Melton's affairs were the scandal and talk of Society.

Norman Baltis was left a widower three years after
his marriage, but in circumstances which gave people
the chance to whisper that they had been separated before she died. Unlike Robert Melton, Sir Norman after
his first unfortunate marriage not only had made no
attempt to marry again, but had literally forsworn
women from out of his life.

When he came to London, Norman Baltis invariably
called at Melton House and saw his friend Robert. Nobody could quite understand the friendship between the

two men, but their loyalty and devotion to each other were very real and they were always content in each other's company.

The sudden glimpse of the house with the sun shining on the windows, the exactly proportioned pillars standing above the white flight of stone steps, was just as magical as it had been when Cynthia was a child.

Sir Norman came out on to the steps to welcome her as the car drew up at the door, and behind him stood the small, grey and ineffectual figure of his sister, who kept house for him. Miss Helen, who was really rather a pathetic person if anyone had time for her, but she was so completely submerged by the strong personality of her brother.

'Well, here you are, Cynthia,' Sir Norman said obviously. 'To what do we owe the pleasure of this visit?'

'To my desire to see you of course, Uncle Norman,' Cynthia replied. She had always called him uncle as a child.

'I often see your father.'

'That's not the right answer,' Cynthia laughed, and kissed his cheek gently.

'Well, Cynthia dear, it is very nice to see you.' Miss Helen fluttered from the background.

'And it is nice to be back here again,' Cynthia replied as they went into the drawing-room with its Adam ceiling and long french windows opening out on to the stone terrace.

'What are you going to do now you are here?' Sir Norman asked gruffly.

Cynthia thought it was typical of him to try and get down to brass tacks as soon as she arrived.

'What do you suggest?' Cynthia parried. 'Are all the excitements in West Winkley over?'

'You mean the election, I suppose?'

'Of course. The newspapers have been full of you.'

'A lot of damned nonsense,' Sir Norman said. 'Too

54

much ballyhoo about the whole thing. Takes everybody's mind off their work and our production figures will be down this week just as they were last week. If I had my way, there would be a General Election once every ten years and no by-elections.'

'But I think we are very lucky to have such a nice Member as Wing Commander Fielding,' Miss Helen said suddenly. 'Such a nice-looking man and he speaks beautifully. I have been to hear him twice.'

'His speeches seem to have made a sensation,' Cynthia said.

'Oh yes, dear, you should have heard them clapping and cheering him. I have never seen people so excited. But I was not surprised. He seemed to rouse everybody . . . even me.'

'A lot of damned fools,' Sir Norman growled.

'Have you been to hear him, Uncle Norman?' Cynthia asked.

'No, I have something better to do with my time. As a matter of fact he is coming here this evening. That's the right attitude; make these Members of Parliament come and see us. Why should we go to them? We put them there and we pay them well.'

Cynthia laughed. Sir Norman Baltis's hatred of politicians and politics was an old story, deeply rooted in the fact that he had once, many years ago, offered himself as a candidate for a Melchester Division and been turned down by the Selection Committee.

'So Wing Commander Fielding is coming here?' she said quietly.

'Yes, dear, for supper,' Miss Helen answered. 'I wrote and asked him when Norman told me he had made an appointment to see him this evening.'

'Without my permission I would like to add,' Sir Norman said crossly.

Cynthia looked at Miss Helen in surprise. It was so

unlike her to take the initiative in anything that such an action must almost have been revolutionary.

'And he accepted?'

'He said he would love to come if nothing unexpected cropped up to keep him in London,' Miss Helen answered. 'Now, Norman, don't be rude to him. It is nice for Cynthia to have a young man to talk to her first evening here.'

'She has not come here to see young men,' Norman Baltis replied. 'If she wanted them, she could stay in London. Still, we may as well get to know the fellow. If I am not nice to these so-called "representatives of the people", they can make trouble in the works, and I won't have that.'

'I think Michael Fielding will be far too busy to make trouble, as you call it, Uncle,' Cynthia smiled.

'I don't know,' Sir Norman answered. 'I have been hearing things about this Fielding chap. He wants reforms and they tell me he is advocating all sorts of revolutionary innovations.'

'I read something of that sort,' Cynthia said.

'There are too many innovations already,' Sir Norman barked. 'Politicians should keep their ideas for Westminster and not worry us with their damn-fool ideals.'

'But surely that's what you elect them for,' Cynthia suggested, 'to see that their "damn-fool ideals" benefit the majority?'

There was an uncomfortable silence and then Miss Helen piped up:

'Well, personally I think Wing Commander Fielding is very attractive. He has "a way with him" as they say. You will like him, Cynthia. I know you will. And I am delighted that he is coming here this evening.'

'I, too, am delighted he is coming here,' Cynthia said slowly; and although Miss Helen did not notice it, there was something grim about her tone.

4

Michael opened the door of the small cottage which he had bought in Melchester and which Toogy, with her usual genius for home-making, had transformed into a comfortable place where he could live when visiting his constituency.

The rooms were low-ceilinged, and primrose yellow walls and gay chintz curtains had worked wonders and altered the appearance of the whole place. The bedrooms looked out not on the busy, noisy street, but on to a piece of common land at the back where in the early morning only the children's voices disturbed those who wished to sleep.

Michael put his hat down on the chair and opened the door into the sitting-room. It was the one large room in the house, for they had knocked down a wall and turned two rooms into one with windows facing both ways, north and south.

Toogy was sitting in an armchair with her inevitable knitting, and typing at a desk with her back to the door was Mary. It was all very peaceful, and Michael stood for a second taking in the scene with appreciation as Toogy looked up with a smile of greeting and rose to her feet.

'Welcome home, darling,' she said. 'How did it go?'

'Very well,' Michael answered, and added with a smile at Mary, who had also risen to her feet: 'Hello, Mary, have you been working hard?'

Mary nodded, her eyes shining. She was still pale, but she looked a very different person from the miserable waif he had rescued from the grey river.

'Tell us all about it,' Toogy pleaded impatiently.

Michael put his arm round her shoulders and, leading her across the room, forced her affectionately down into the great armchair she had just vacated.

'I felt like a new boy on my first day at school. I had exactly the same feeling of being lost and desolate and expecting something awful to happen. I nearly found myself crying out for you to come back to me, just as I did when you left me my first term.'

'Nonsense,' Toogy exclaimed. 'You are exaggerating.'

'Perhaps a little bit,' Michael admitted with a grin. 'But Parliament does have that effect on one.'

He walked across to the mantelpiece.

'I wish I could explain to you,' he said, 'what I felt today. Proud, yet humble; strong, but utterly impotent beside the overwhelming might of all that British justice and British democracy means and must go on meaning in a world of mumbo-jumbo.'

He paused for a moment and there was a far-away look in his eyes as if he saw vast horizons and longed to reach them.

'But were the Members nice to you?' Mary asked eagerly.

'Absolutely charming,' Michael answered, smiling a little at the femininity of the question. 'As a matter of fact my head is two or three inches bigger since I went to Westminster. I received congratulations and encouragement such as I never expected.'

'And you made your bow to the Speaker?' Mary asked.

'With much grace,' Michael answered jokingly, 'and there were quite an appreciable number of cheers as I took my seat. Oh, Toogy, I wish you had been there. I longed for you so much.'

'I know, darling, but there was so much to do here.'

'Yes, I know,' Michael said. 'Do you think we shall ever get it straight?'

'You will,' Toogy answered. 'I shall have to go home soon. I cannot think what is happening to all my babies while I am away.'

'They are perfectly all right,' Michael answered. 'I remembered to ring up Miss Smithers and she told me everything was under control and you were not to worry.'

'That's good,' Toogy said with relief.

'And I told her,' Michael went on, 'that you were going to stay here with me for a long time because I couldn't spare you.'

'What did she say to that?' Toogy asked.

'I am not going to tell you,' Michael replied. 'It will make you too conceited.'

He walked across the room and looked at what Mary was typing.

'Have you finished it?' he asked.

'It is just waiting for your signature,' she replied.

He looked at the heading on the letter.

' "Michael Fielding, M.P.",' he read out loud. 'Well, it's the first time that I have written to a newspaper with those letters after my name, but it certainly won't be the last.'

'Oh, Michael, it's a wonderful letter!' Mary said effusively.

'Do you think so?' Michael asked.

'Simply wonderful,' Mary repeated, 'but before we start talking about that, do go on telling us about the House of Commons. You have really told us nothing.'

'Very well,' Michael said good humouredly.

He sat down on the arm of Toogy's chair and launched off on the tale of all his adventures since he had left Melchester that morning; whom he had met, whom he had seen, and of his introduction to the House between his two sponsors. The two women listened breathlessly and when he had finished Toogy said very quietly:

'This is the beginning, darling. I feel sure you will make something worth while of it all.'

'If I do anything worth while,' Michael answered, 'it will be because of you and all that you have taught me, all that you have made me understand and see through your eyes.'

He bent down and kissed her forehead, and there was a moment's pause before either of them could speak. Mary broke the silence.

'Oh, Michael, you will promise to take me there one day, won't you? I will work my fingers to the bone if only you will take me to the House of Commons. I want to see you there and I want to hear you speak.'

'I am not going to be in a hurry to make my maiden speech,' he announced. 'It is always a mistake to be in too big a hurry. You have got to sense the atmosphere of the House and you have got to conduct yourself as befits a young and untried Member.'

'They won't be thinking of you as young and untried for long,' Mary cried. 'The local papers have reported your speech of last night word for word. And look at the headlines: "*A Crusader for Westminster.*" "*A Young Man With the Right Ideas and the Right Ideals.*" '

She held the newspaper out to him, but Michael jumped to his feet.

'Don't show them to me,' he said. 'I never believe anything I read in the newspapers. Tell me what you have been doing, Toogy.'

'I have been seeing an old friend of yours,' Toogy answered. 'I wonder if you remember him—Bill Evans.'

'Bill Evans!' Michael repeated. 'Of course I remember him. He was in my squadron in '43 and then he was invalided out of the R.A.F. Is he here?'

'Yes, he is here,' Toogy answered, 'living in Melchester in great poverty and great unhappiness.'

'Poor old Bill,' Michael said. 'I must see him. Where is he?'

'I found him quite by chance,' Toogy answered, 'and he is not certain that he really wants to see you. He is both ashamed of his circumstances and depressed by them.'

'But of course he must see me,' Michael said. 'What has happened?'

'He has experienced unceasing ill-health,' Toogy replied, 'which has left him depleted both financially and physically. He lives in a squalid, ghastly building which was once a workhouse but has now been let out in what they dare to call flatlets to no less than fifteen familes. There are forty people living there, Michael, and there is only one tap with running water and that is in the basement.'

'Good lord!' Michael exclaimed. 'Who is the landlord?'

'Sir Norman Baltis,' Toogy answered.

'Baltis? I am dining with him tonight! Isn't it tonight, Mary?'

'Yes,' Mary answered, looking at the engagement calendar by her side, 'at eight o'clock.'

'Good, I shall speak to him about it; but meantime I'll go and look at the place and meet Bill Evans.'

'You will find him shy and anxious to avoid you,' Toogy said. 'I happened to be calling on the woman on the same floor who wrote to you about a pension for her boy who was in the Navy. Do you remember the letter?'

'Yes, of course I do,' Michael said.

'Well, she had no ink to sign the papers which I took with me,' Toogy went on, 'so she ran in next door to get some, and as I noticed a young man sitting in the window I followed her into the room in order to speak to him. The first thing I saw on the mantelpiece was a photograph of you in uniform.'

'So after that you got talking,' Michael smiled.

'Yes, we got talking,' Toogy repeated, 'and I found out all about Bill. This is a very sad case, Michael, and I hope you can do something for him.'

'What can I do?' Michael asked.

'That will be for you to decide,' Toogy answered. 'He has lost confidence in himself. He feels useless and out of touch with everything and everybody.'

'It's ghastly, isn't it?' Michael said. 'There's a chap who did extremely well, and got the D.F.C. before he was nineteen. He was sent out East and would have been a success out there too if some beastly Eastern bug hadn't got hold of him. His health deteriorated and there was nothing we could do but send him home.'

'And so he feels a failure,' Toogy said quietly, 'trained for nothing; a hero too young and too quickly. Oh, Michael, there are so many cases similar to his and they break my heart.'

'I know,' Michael replied, 'and we have got to do something for them. We need young men like Bill; we need them just as much in peace as in war.'

There was a sudden fire and resolution in his voice. Then Michael said quietly:

'I will go and see Bill now. What did you say the address was?'

Toogy told him and without another word he left the room. As the door closed behind him, Mary gave a little sigh.

'He is wonderful, isn't he?' she said.

Toogy looked at her and answered drily:

'Don't you think you rather overwork that adjective, Mary?'

'Not where Michael is concerned,' Mary retorted; 'I do think he is wonderful. No one could be with him for long and not think the same thing.'

Toogy made no reply, but she counted the stitches on one of her needles, while Mary sat gazing out of the window, her face cupped in both her hands.

'Are you enjoying this work?' Toogy asked at last.

'What work?' Mary enquired, starting a little at the question as if her thoughts had been far away.

'The work you are doing for Michael.'

'You mean being his secretary?' Mary questioned.

'If that is what you like to call it,' Toogy answered.

Mary got up from the desk and, walking across the room, sat down on the hearth-rug in a little heap at Toogy's feet.

'Oh, Miss Toogy, I am so happy. It is heaven to work for him; it is heaven to do things for someone so clever, so . . .' She paused for words, and then added, almost defiantly, 'So wonderful.'

'And you think such employment will content you?' Toogy persisted.

There was a purpose and directness in her question which, however, entirely escaped Mary.

'But of course! To work for him . . . just to be with him.'

'This last month has been somewhat exceptional,' Toogy went on. 'A by-election is always an excitement, and the tiring, arduous part of it is forgotten among the cheers and thrills of Polling Day. Now, Mary, you have got to settle down to really hard work. Michael has got to have someone very efficient as his secretary. It will mean long hours and a very selfless existence for the person who is his private secretary.'

'But I don't mind long hours,' Mary said; 'as for being selfless . . . all I want is to devote myself to Michael . . . and his interests.'

'Entirely selflessly?' Toogy remarked drily.

'But of course,' Mary remarked with wide eyes.

Toogy looked at her, but she said nothing. It was difficult to know if she was pleased or displeased as she gathered up her knitting and got to her feet.

'Well, I think you will find your new job a hard one,' she said, 'but if you are prepared to tackle it . . .'

'Of course I am,' Mary said quickly. 'Besides, Michael has asked me to do it for him.'

There was just a hint in her voice that she dared Toogy to question Michael's decision, but it seemed as if Toogy had not heard her, for she went slowly across the room, and having passed through the door shut it quietly behind her. A moment later Mary heard her go upstairs to her bedroom.

Alone in the sitting-room, Mary raised herself on tiptoe to look at herself in the mirror on the mantelpiece. She patted her fair hair, which hung in heavy waves to her shoulders, and gave a little smile at her reflection in the mirror, then she went back to her desk.

There was a huge pile of papers waiting to be dealt with and for a moment she sighed as she looked at them. Then she looked through the window to where the evening sun was still shining.

'Come on, let's get it done,' she said out loud, and sat down again at the typewriter.

Twice she made a mistake in her typescript, for her thoughts were of Michael as he drove in his small car through the busy streets to see Bill Evans.

The former workhouse, which he found after some difficulty, was as unprepossessing as Toogy had described it. Gaunt and dreary, it stood a little way back from the road, surrounded by a dirty asphalt yard on which a large amount of refuse and odds and ends of building material had been left to accumulate.

Numberless window-panes had been broken and repaired with pieces of cardboard. The main door was off its hinges and the stone steps which led to the various floors of the building were not only in bad repair but also in a state of uncleanliness which proclaimed to the world at large that it was 'nobody's job' to wash them.

The shouts and screams of children playing and crying combined with the noise of at least three radio sets turned on to their fullest capacity made a volume of sound which was nearly as hideous as the building itself.

Michael strode up the stairs to the third floor and walked along a dark passage to a door which was numbered 16. He knocked and for a moment there was no reply, then he heard a woman's voice saying:

'See who the hell it is, Pa.'

In answer somebody swore forcibly that it was not his business to answer doors, and the woman answered back equally volubly. While they were still arguing, Michael knocked for the second time, and almost immediately the door was jerked open and he found himself confronting a thin, ugly-looking woman of middle age. Her hair was in tin curlers, her bare feet in dirty bedroom slippers.

'Good afternoon,' Michael said. 'Can I see Bill? He is your son, isn't he?'

'What do you want with him?' the woman asked truculently then suddenly her expression changed. 'Oh, it's Mr. Fielding, isn't it? I didn't recognise you for the moment. Pa and I came along to hear you speak the other night. Won't you come in, sir? Sorry you should see us like this, but we weren't expecting visitors.'

'That's all right,' Michael smiled, 'I just wanted to see Bill.'

He walked into the room as he spoke and saw Bill's face, white and strained, staring at him across the room.

'Hullo, Bill old boy. It's nice to see you.'

There was no welcome in Bill's expression or in the rather limp hand he held out after he had scrambled awkwardly to his feet, but Michael went on talking as if he did not notice his diffidence.

'I often wondered what had happened to you, Bill.

You never wrote to us after you left, or if you did we never got the letters. Do you remember how ghastly the mails were? We all got fed-up with them, didn't we? As for the parcels from home, they were always eaten by ants or pilfered before we got a chance to receive them.'

He sat down on the chair which Mrs. Evans brought up for him, and while she hurried round the dirty, littered room trying to straighten the untidiness of years, he went on talking to Bill until gradually he saw that the strained look was passing and there was a responsive light in the other man's eyes.

'Do you remember . . . ? Do you remember . . . ?'

The conversation was full of the past. The things they had done together, the dangers shared and the comradeship which was somehow not translatable into the terms of peace.

After a little while Mrs. Evans disappeared into the bedroom where her husband had vanished at the first sight of Michael, and Michael and Bill were alone together.

'It is good of you to come and see me,' Bill said at last; 'I don't see any of my old pals now.'

'Everybody has got scattered, I suppose,' Michael said. 'It was a bit of luck my turning up here and finding you again.'

Bill looked at him.

'What do you mean by that?'

'Well, I want you to help me. You will, won't you, Bill?'

'How could I help you? I'm no use to anyone.'

'Are you sure about that?' Michael asked. 'What do the doctors say about your health?'

'Oh, the doctors are just fools,' Bill answered; 'they say there is nothing wrong with me; but I feel rotten. There is nothing I can do; there is no work for chaps like myself. I suppose, living here, I could go into a factory;

but it is the one thing they have told me I'm not to do. I'm to stay out in the fresh air as much as possible. Fresh air! They might just as well tell me to live on champagne and oysters. What kind of job can I get in the fresh air? The only thing I am trained for is to fly an aeroplane, and there's enough fools who can do that.'

'You have been discharged as cured?' Michael asked.

'Cured!' Bill gave a snort. 'Yes, they call it cured. I am not to play rough games because of my heart, and I am not to stay in a bad atmosphere because of my lungs. I'm to have plenty of milk to drink, to be constantly in the open air and not allow myself to get depressed!'

He threw back his head and laughed, and it was not a pleasant sound.

'Charming, isn't it? And to keep myself from getting depressed I can always remember that I have the thanks of a grateful country. Gratitude! We don't want gratitude, we want work.'

'But of course!' Michael answered. 'That is exactly what you do want and what I am prepared to offer you.'

'You are prepared to offer me?' Bill said incredulously.

'Yes,' Michael answered. 'I want you to come along and see me tomorrow and we will talk over how you can help me. There's a lot to be done, Bill, and the only thing I hope you will realise is that I cannot offer you a very big salary.'

Bill was looking at him in a dazed manner.

'You will offer me work?' he said again. 'But, Michael . . .'

He stopped.

'You are doing this out of charity,' he ejaculated, and his tone was harsh.

Michael put his hands into his trousers pockets and tilted back his chair.

'My dear old boy,' he said, 'I am not a philanthropist;

I am a Member of Parliament with a great many ideas and very little money. There are a lot of things I want to do and a lot of things I intend to do because I believe them to be for the good of this country.

'I want men and women who will work with me and for me—and it will mean an act of sacrifice on their part, because they will get neither big wages nor in most cases much reward for their labours. But they will have the satisfaction of knowing that they are doing a decent job of work for their country, for this Britain of ours which only a few years ago we were prepared to die for. Are you going to help me, Bill?'

The question was a trumpet-call. Bill Evans straightened his thin shoulders and then held out his hand. As Michael took it he turned away to hide the tears which had suddenly come to his eyes.

'See you tomorrow, then,' Michael said, 'twelve o'clock.'

He got to his feet.

'I would like to say good-bye to your mother.'

'Mother!' Bill shouted awkwardly.

The door of the bedroom opened and Mrs. Evans, wearing a blue silk blouse and with her hair frizzed and curled, came into the room. She had put on stockings and shoes, and although the total effect of her best was unprepossessing, Michael realised that it was an effort on his behalf.

'I am so glad to have met you, Mrs. Evans. Bill is an old friend of mine and he is coming along to see me to-morrow.'

'I am glad about that, Mr. Fielding. Bill has had rotten luck. That's what he's had. I think the Government ought to have done more for him. They had no right to take away our young men ruin their health and then when they have got no further use for them, chuck them back at their families, who have to support them for the rest of their lives.'

68

'Oh, shut up, Mother!' Bill exclaimed.

'I am going to see what we can do about it,' Michael answered.

'That's real nice of you, Mr. Fielding,' Mrs. Evans said, and shouted over her shoulder: 'Here, Pa, come and say good-bye to Mr. Fielding. He's going to do something for our Bill.'

Mr. Evans came into the room. He had put on a coat and brushed his grey hair. He had once had a refined, intellectual face, but it was puffy now and sagging as if from debauchery, and Michael suddenly remembered hearing that Bill's father had at one time been a brilliant surgeon but had taken to drink. He had made a mistake over an operation which had proved fatal to the patient and he was struck off the Medical Register.

Only to look at him was to realise the tragedy of a man with brains and ability who had come so very much down in the world through his own weakness. His hand was shaking as Michael took it and he made no attempt to look him in the eyes, but his gaze shifted furtively from his son to the visitor and back again.

'It is kind of you if you can do anything for Bill,' he mumbled.

'I shall be only too pleased to do what I can,' Michael answered.

Mr. Evans looked at him.

'Nothing much wrong with the boy physically. It's mental, that's what his trouble is.'

His voice was thick, almost indistinct; yet Michael knew that he spoke with real knowledge, both from the paternal and from the medical point of view. But there was something nauseating in this wreck of a human being who had lost his self-respect and all hope for a future.

It was almost a relief to turn to the commonplace slovenliness of Mrs. Evans, and as he looked at her Michael recalled one night in India when four of them had sat round the fire until late and with the help of a bottle of whisky had grown confidential one with another. He could hear Bill's clear voice saying:

'My old man married his cook. She was the only person who would put up with him when he went to the devil.'

Yes, it all came back to him now, and he sighed for the depths to which they had sunk and the squalor to which they had grown accustomed. Once again he put out his hand to Bill.

'See you again tomorrow, old boy. I can't tell you how much I am looking forward to it.'

He saw the dawn of hope come into Bill's face, and then he turned away because it was so intensely pathetic.

He glanced at his watch. It was after half past seven and he realised that he had no time to spare. He had to go home, wash and tidy himself, and start off again for Claverley, which lay on the extreme edge of his constituency on the west side of the city of Melchester.

The traffic impeded his progress, and it was a quarter to eight before he reached the cottage. He had only time to run upstairs, change with lightning speed into a clean shirt, wash his hands and tear down again.

'You will be late, darling,' Toogy replied, as he called out his good-bye to her.

'I can't help it,' Michael replied. 'I saw Bill Evans. Thank God you found him.'

'Will you be able to do something for him?' Toogy asked.

'Of course I will!' Michael replied.

She smiled to herself at the confidence in his tone. It was so like Michael to be definite and to make up his mind quickly; to act impetuously, but always with decision. She stood for a moment looking out of the little window on the landing, watching him get into his car and drive away.

As Toogy watched Michael she prayed with all the

70

deep concentration of faith within her that, having chosen the right path, his instinct might always tell him what was right and good and never lead him astray.

Driving towards Claverley, Michael was thinking of the squalor he had seen and the building in which Bill Evans lived. He was remembering all the luxury and beauty which had always been ascribed to Claverley.

There were flowers in the great borders which stretched beneath the terraces of the house and there was a rose garden on one side of the ornamental lake. He thought of the dirty refuse-filled yard where the children played who lived in the old workhouse. He thought of the smell in the passages and the filth accumulated on the stone staircase.

Toogy would have recognised the steely glint in Michael's eyes and the tightening of his lips as she drove his car up to the white marble steps of Claverley. It was only a few minutes past eight o'clock as the butler ushered him into the drawing-room, but he saw Sir Norman waiting for him with a look of impatience, and he felt impelled to apologise.

'I am sorry to be late, Sir Norman. You must forgive me, but I had a pressing call to make.'

'We keep to our meal-times very punctiliously in this house,' Sir Norman said pompously, holding out his hand, 'but I am glad to see you, Fielding. I don't think you have been here before.'

'No, this is my first visit,' Michael answered.

'Have you met my sister?'

Sir Norman turned to where Miss Helen was standing behind him. He was used to drawing her forward from her obscurity, but this evening Miss Helen advanced eagerly.

'Yes, indeed, we met after your meeting at the City Hall,' she said, 'after that amazing speech, Wing Commander. I shall never forget it, never!'

'Thank you,' Michael said, 'and I'm so glad to meet you again.'

There was a moment's pause as Sir Norman drew a large watch from his waistcoat pocket.

'Five minutes past eight,' he said. 'Where is that girl? I won't be kept waiting for my meals.'

Even as he spoke the door opened and Cynthia came in. She had waited deliberately until after Michael's arrival; waited to make an entrance and to see the expression on his face when he saw her.

She came in very conscious of her beauty and the fact that her dinner-frock of flame-coloured chiffon enhanced it. The soft fullness of the skirt swirled round her feet and the low-cut neck revealed the whiteness of her skin. Her only ornament was a bunch of white roses at her waist.

She was smiling as she came across the room, but her eyes were fixed on Michael, so that she saw both his start of surprise and then the sudden hardening in his expression.

'You are late,' Sir Norman informed her.

'I am so sorry, Uncle Norman.'

'Do you know Wing Commander Fielding?'

'Yes, of course,' Cynthia said softly. 'We are old friends, or rather, should I say, old enemies?'

Michael inclined his head a little stiffly.

'Dinner is served,' the butler announced from the door.

'Come along, come along, let's go in,' Sir Norman said impatiently.

Cynthia linked her arm through Miss Helen's.

'Let us feed the brutes,' she said; 'they will be much better-tempered after they have had a meal.'

'But I am sure Wing Commander Fielding is never bad-tempered,' Miss Helen fluttered, looking up at Michael with eyes of intense admiration.

'You would be surprised,' Cynthia told her with a

glance at Michael which should have been provocative, only unfortunately he was not looking at her.

Dinner would have been stiff and difficult if it had not been for Cynthia. She talked sparklingly and amusingly, drawing out Sir Norman Baltis and making Miss Helen laugh until she wiped the tears from her eyes.

Only Michael remained stiff and a little aloof. Cynthia was clever enough to ignore his attitude and to make him feel that he was being uncouth when he tried once or twice to cross swords with her.

At last the meal came to an end and they retired to the drawing-room, where coffee was waiting on a big silver tray.

'I wonder if I might have a word with you, Sir Norman,' Michael said as he took a cup of coffee which Miss Helen had poured out.

'As many as you like,' said Sir Norman, who was now in a genial mood.

'I meant alone,' Michael said pointedly.

'Is there any need for that?' Sir Norman asked. 'Surely there is nothing that cannot be said in front of my sister and my god-child?'

'Just as you like, but it is rather a serious matter. It is about some property of yours, in particular a disused workhouse down Saunders Lane.'

'Ah, yes,' Sir Norman said, 'I know the place you mean. Dreadful neighbourhood and dreadful people.'

'I agree with you about the neighbourhood,' Michael said, 'but I wonder if the people can be blamed for an environment in which no self-respecting citizen should keep any living creature.'

There was something in his tone which made Sir Norman bristle.

'Now what exactly do you mean by that, Fielding?'

'I mean,' Michael replied, 'that while most of the property is, as far as I can judge, in pretty bad repair, the old workhouse in particular is a disgrace. Have you seen it recently? What is more, have you smelt it? Why there has been no epidemic among the children living there I cannot imagine, but I fancy that many of them have got little chance of survival.'

Sir Norman lay back in his chair and lit a cigar.

'I am afraid you are exaggerating, Fielding. Saunders Lane, I agree with you, is pretty unsavoury. In fact, the city authorities intend condemning it. They told me they would do this before the war, but with the housing shortage they have nowhere to put the people who live there and so they must remain there until new houses are available.'

'I appreciate the difficulties,' Michael said, 'but at the same time the buildings could be improved. Running water could be put on all floors; glass could be put in the windows, and a coat of paint would make a great deal of difference. Also the accumulation of refuse and dirt outside could be removed.'

'And who is to pay for all this?' Sir Norman asked.

'I imagine the responsibility lies with the landlord,' Michael replied bluntly.

Sir Norman laughed.

'My dear boy, do you think I am Rockefeller? As it happens, this piece of property belongs to me personally. A great deal of the land around here has been bought by the company, and no one shall say that Baltis Ltd. is not a model landlord in every way.

'Saunders Lane I acquired personally as part of a bad debt. I never wanted it, but it was thrust upon me. If anyone were fool enough to buy it from me I would sell it tomorrow. It's a nuisance and a liability.'

'Which doesn't make it any less a responsibility,' Michael answered.

'My dear young man,' Sir Norman replied, 'when you get as old as I am, you are not taken in by words. We all have our responsibilities, but it is usually an expression used by those who want you to do something which

74

you don't want to do. To put the Saunders Lane property in decent order would cost me thousands of pounds, and, quite frankly, I do not intend to spend it.'

'You prefer to allow the people who live there in squalor and misery to contract diseases and to bring up their children in filthy surroundings?'

'That is pretty plain speaking,' Sir Norman remarked.

'I mean it to be,' Michael replied.

'And my answer to you is just as plain,' Sir Norman said. 'It is—go to hell and mind your own business. This property is mine. I am an old man and I am not interested in it. Had I had a son . . .

For a moment almost despite himself his voice softened.

'. . . had I had a son,' he repeated, 'things might have been very different. But I have worked hard and now I intend to enjoy my old age. Reformers in Melchester have battered their heads against a brick wall and have gradually lost the wish to reform. Run along to Westminster and preach there to the masses about a new and finer world, but leave us in peace to work out our own salvation in our own way.'

Sir Norman ceased speaking and taking up his cup of coffee drank it down quickly. He was not angry. What was almost frightening, it seemed to Michael, was that he spoke entirely slowly and calculatingly.

'But, sir . . .' Michael began impatiently.

Sir Norman held up his hand.

'The conversation is finished, Fielding; if you wish to renew it, you must do so another time. I wish this to be a pleasant evening spent comfortably in the peace of my own house. Cynthia, my dear, will you play us something?'

'But of course, Uncle Norman.'

She got to her feet and moved gracefully to the big grand piano which stood in the alcove by the window.

She settled herself and arranged her full skirt over the piano stool.

Then she looked at Michael. A faint smile curved her lips and there was a hint of laughter in her eyes which made him realise, with a sudden sense of fury, that she was amused at his discomfiture and by the fact that he had lost the first round of his new battle.

5

Toogy took up her bag and gloves and, turning to glance at herself in the mirror in the little hall, adjusted the angle of her hat. She sighed as she did so, feeling unaccountably weary; but she told herself severely that at her age it must be expected.

They had all worked hard these past weeks, had meals at irregular hours and too little sleep, and now Nature was taking her toll.

Not for one moment had Toogy relaxed until she knew that Michael had been elected and that his majority had exceeded his supporters' most optimistic expectations. Then she heaved a sigh of relief and longed for her own fireside and the comforts of her own small flat overlooking the Thames.

The electric bell, which had been fixed up since they had taken the cottage, shrilled loudly. Toogy answered it. Standing on the step was an extremely pretty girl. She was dressed in a cool summer frock with a big shady straw hat. There was nothing ostentatious about her clothes, and yet the mere fact that she wore them gave them an elegance and a sophistication.

'Good morning. Could I speak to Wing Commander Fielding's secretary?'

She smiled as she spoke, Toogy noticed, and there was something assured and at ease about her which the older woman liked.

'I am afraid she is out,' Toogy answered. 'Can I help you?'

The girl hesitated.

'Are you . . . are you Mrs. Fielding?'

'Michael is my adopted son,' Toogy answered.

'Oh!'

The girl seemed surprised, and then she said:

'I am Cynthia Standish. I don't know whether you have ever heard of me.'

'Yes, Michael has spoken of you,' Toogy answered. 'Won't you come in?'

She was not surprised at Cynthia's unexpected call. She had too much experience and was too old to be surprised at anything; but as she led the way into the little sitting-room she wondered why she was here. Michael, oddly reticent for him, had not mentioned Cynthia's presence at Claverley the night before.

'Won't you sit down?' Toogy asked, indicating a chair.

Cynthia stood in the doorway looking around her.

'What a darling little room! Did you decorate it?'

'I did my best,' Toogy smiled. 'It all had to be done in a terrible hurry after we heard that Michael had been adopted for the Division.'

'It is charming,' Cynthia exclaimed; then crossing the room she said, 'Forgive me if I sound curious, but somehow your face is very familiar.'

'I don't think we ever met before,' Toogy said quietly.

'No? But I know you. I recognise you. Would it be awfully rude to ask your name?'

'Of course not!' Toogy answered, and told her.

Cynthia gave an exclamation.

'But of course! You are the wonderful person who works down in Dockland. I was reading an article about you only the other day. There were pictures illustrating it—of you, of the children's nurseries and the clinic you had started. It all comes back to me. I had no idea you had anything to do with Michael Fielding.'

'And yet he is one of my *good* works,' Toogy said quietly.

She stressed the adjective and Cynthia looked at her a little uncertainly, then a dimple appeared on either side of her mouth.

'Has he said anything about me?' she asked. 'Yes, he has! He hates me!'

Toogy frowned.

'That is a horrible word.'

'I am afraid it is true,' Cynthia answered. 'And I don't like him. I think he is very intolerant.'

'We always are when we are young,' Toogy said, stating a fact rather than making an excuse for Michael.

Cynthia frowned.

'Perhaps so, but Michael is very overbearing.'

'To those who disagree with him?'

'Exactly! And I disagree with him.'

Toogy smiled, then she said gently:

'I don't suppose you came here to tell me about that.'

Cynthia started a little guiltily as though she had been carried away by her thoughts.

'No, I came to get an address from Michael's secretary. I guessed he would be out this morning. As a matter of fact he said last night he was going round a glass factory.'

'What was the address you wanted?' Toogy asked.

'I wanted to know the whereabouts of Saunders Lane. There is a workhouse there which I particularly want to see.'

Toogy looked at her, and still without making any comment walked across the room to the desk where Mary had been writing before she went out. From the pile of papers she selected a small map which showed in some detail the streets and main buildings of the Division.

'If you will come over here,' she said over her shoulder.

Cynthia moved across the room to stand by her side.

'Saunders Lane is here,' Toogy said, pointing with a pencil. 'Go down Park Road, turn left and left again, and there is the Lane.'

'Thank you,' Cynthia said. 'May I take the map with me? I will return it.'

'Yes, do,' Toogy answered.

Cynthia folded it up and put it in her handbag.

'Thank you,' she said; and then once again the dimples at the corners of her mouth were prominent as she asked, 'Aren't you curious as to why I want to go there?'

Toogy shook her head.

'I don't think "curious" is the exact word. "Interested", perhaps, because anything which concerns Michael is of interest to me, and doubtless you or he will tell me the rhyme and reason for all this later on.'

Cynthia laughed out loud.

'If I didn't know so much about you I would say you were inhuman. Shall I say just this? I intended to teach Michael a sharp lesson, but now that I have met you I am not quite certain whether or not to go on with it.'

Toogy looked at Cynthia. She was very lovely standing there in the morning sunlight; there was something fearless and strong about her even though in physique she was small and delicately featured.

The thought came to Toogy suddenly that this was as she had once been many years ago. A young girl facing life with her head thrown back and a smile on her lips, no shadow of fear clouding her eyes. It was Toogy's principle seldom if ever to ask questions, but now she asked one, and it was unexpected:

'What do you do with yourself, Miss Standish?'

Cynthia answered impulsively.

'Nothing! That's just the trouble. I am always frightened that it will be a case of Satan finding mischief . . .

but, Miss Toogy, you who have done so many things in your life must try and understand how difficult it is for me.'

'Is it?'

'Yes, terribly. I am full of energy, I can do things, lots of things, and do them well; but the trouble is what are they and where are they? You see . . .' Cynthia hesitated and her voice sank on to a lower note. 'I have got two big obstacles in my way. The first is that I am well off and the second is that I am my father's daughter.'

'Are those . . . obstacles . . . unsurmountable?'

'No, not unsurmountable,' Cynthia replied, 'but definitely a hindrance. And there is a third, and that is something I am ashamed of.'

There was silence for a moment. Toogy did not speak. She knew with the sureness of long experience that this girl was about to confide in her. She knew the signs so well and she knew too that what she was about to hear was the truth, with no prevarication and no subterfuge about it.

'The third obstacle,' Cynthia said after a moment, 'is the fact that I don't know what I want. To achieve anything one has got to want something and want it pretty badly. I have thought and thought, but I still don't know what it is that I require of life. What do I want of myself and for myself? I just don't know.'

'Poor child!' Toogy spoke gently.

'You are sorry for me. Somehow I felt you would be. Most people would think I was mad, of course. They would look at my possessions, my background, at all the so-called fun I can have, and they would think that anybody who could ask for more must either be mentally deranged or greedy beyond expression. You understand, Miss Toogy. You know that all those things mean nothing unless one has something to work for, some goal towards which one can travel.'

Cynthia spoke pleadingly and with an intensity which

would have surprised many of her friends. Toogy put out her hand and laid it on her shoulder.

'I cannot help you, child,' she said; 'you can only help yourself, but I can tell you one thing. You are on the right road. "Ask and ye shall receive; knock and it shall be opened unto you." I have never known these two admonitions fail—never.'

'Thank you,' Cynthia said softly, and then with a quick change of mood she said: 'You must think I am crazy, coming in here like this, telling you so much and so quickly. But there is something about you, of course, which makes one want to talk. I expect you have been told that often enough?'

'Yes, I have,' Toogy admitted, 'but at the same time I am glad that you have talked to me.'

'May I come and see you again?' Cynthia asked.

Toogy nodded.

'Of course!'

'What will Michael have to say to that?'

'Why should he say anything? He is a very busy person, and besides, he knows where he is going and what he wants from life.'

Cynthia sighed and the smile faded from her lips.

'He is lucky, isn't he?' She held out her hand. 'Good-bye, Miss Toogy. I am not going to say thank you because you know how much you have helped me this morning. I only want to be certain that I can come again.'

'Whenever you like,' Toogy answered; and then added, 'Are you staying here in Melchester?'

Cynthia's eyes widened.

'Michael didn't tell you, then, that we met yesterday?'

'No, he didn't mention your name.'

'I am staying at Claverley with my godfather, Sir Norman Baltis. Michael came to dinner last night, but I don't think he enjoyed himself very much.'

'I am afraid he was angry with Sir Norman.'

'Angry is putting it mildly,' Cynthia said. 'His eyes

flashed and he looked like an avenging archangel. It was really very funny!'

'And it amused you enough to bring you here this morning?' Toogy asked.

'Exactly!' Cynthia answered. 'And thank you for telling me what I wanted to know. Can I give you a lift?'

She made a gesture with her hand and Toogy, glancing out of the window, saw that parked outside the door was a long, low car.

'It is Uncle Norman's very latest model,' Cynthia explained. 'He has presented it to me while I am staying with him. He thinks I might even prove an advertisement for it. Do let me drive you somewhere.'

'Very well, then,' Toogy replied. 'You can drop me at the bottom of Park Road. I can then show you where your turn is into Saunders Lane.'

They went out of the house together and Toogy got into the car. Cynthia drove her away.

Mary, who was coming up the road, saw them pass by. She recognised Toogy and was surprised to see her in the car, and even more surprised to see the girl who was driving it. She wondered who Cynthia was, noticing even in that flashing second not only the beauty of her face but the expensive simplicity of her clothes.

She opened the door of the little house with her latch-key and went into the sitting-room. She noticed at once that the papers on her desk had been moved and wondered what Toogy had been searching for. Surely this new and extremely pretty girl who had appeared from nowhere was not interested in them! Quite suddenly Mary felt a jealous fear grip her. Then she laughed.

'I am happy here, yes, happy,' she whispered to herself

She sat down at her typewriter, and no sooner had she begun than there was a knock at the door. It was a hesitant, rather feeble knock. Mary, having heard it, made no effort to get to her feet.

'Why can't they ring the bell?' she asked irritably. 'If there were any servants in this house they wouldn't hear a feeble knock like that.'

She had always rather resented the fact that Miss Toogy had decided that there was no room for a resident servant.

'The house is too small,' she had said decidedly. 'We shall be too cramped. I shall get someone to come in and clean during the day, and someone else to cook a meal for us in the evening. The rest of the time we will manage for ourselves. It will be much better that way.'

There was not much to do, it was true. The woman who came in the morning prepared the midday meal and the one who came in the evening did the washing-up. Nevertheless Mary thought that it was quite unreasonable to expect her when she was busy to answer the door or even to take in the bread, milk and groceries if they came late.

Mary typed another line and the knock came again. A moment later it was followed by a quick staccato peal of the electric bell.

'Found it at last,' Mary thought savagely. 'Well, as they are so stupid, they can wait a bit longer.'

She typed another line and then got to her feet. She moved along the passage, opened the door and was just in time to see a young man with a white face on the point of turning away. He started at the sight of her and said quickly:

'I thought there was no one at home.'

'Can I help you?' Mary asked sharply.

She looked him up and down and decided he was another suppliant, for his clothes were shabby and unpressed and his shoes were splitting at the seams.

'Mich—I mean Wing Commander Fielding told me to meet him here this morning,' the man said. 'My name is Evans . . . Bill Evans.'

'Well, the Wing Commander is not here at the moment,' Mary answered. 'What time did he say?'

'He just said this morning. Perhaps I had better . . . go away.'

He turned as if to leave, but Mary, aware that Michael would not have asked him here without a good reason, said:

'No, don't go. If he told you to meet him here, you had better come in and wait.'

'Thank you. . . . Are you sure that is all right?'

Bill Evans looked anxious. Mary, impatient to be back at her work, replied:

'Yes, yes, if he said so. Come in here. There's a chair.'

She led the way into the sitting-room, and indicated a hard, upright chair just inside the door. Bill sat down meekly upon it. He was very pale, as if the effort to get here had been too much for him, and as Mary turned her back on him he shut his eyes. The room seemed to be swimming dizzily round him. After several moments he opened them again and realised with relief that his giddiness had left him.

'You were a fool not to eat a bit more breakfast,' he told himself, adding: 'I have got out of the way of wanting food. If Michael really has a job for me I shall have to get strong somehow.'

There was something in the cool atmosphere of the low room which seemed to bring him relief. It was a long time, he thought, since he had been in such gracious surroundings. He was well aware of the contrast between it and the dirty, untidy place which he called home. He thought of his stepmother with her shiftless ways, and somehow for the first time he found himself making excuses for her.

'She could have done better,' he thought, 'if Dad and I had encouraged her. We have never done anything but complain. The old man drinks away what money he has and I bring nothing in. It is disheartening enough for any woman!'

Bill shook himself. What was this? A kind of confessional? He had no idea why, the first time he had got away from home, such thoughts had come to him, but there was something in this room which was reawakening all the old decencies within himself.

'I suppose in my own way I am as weak as the old man,' he told himself. 'I have not made any real effort since I got crocked up. Weakness, that's what it is! Now Michael was never weak.'

Even as he thought of him the door opened and Michael came in. He had a characteristic way of entering a room. There was never a second in which to anticipate him. Suddenly he was there, and because of his presence the tempo seemed to rise.

'Hullo, Bill, old boy!' he cried. 'I am sorry to be late. I got delayed going round the factory. You know what it is. There are so many things one wants to see and so many people to talk to.'

Bill got slowly to his feet. The hand he held out to Michael was surer and more definite in its grip than it had been the day before.

'I haven't been here long,' he said. 'It's good to see you.'

'Sit down, old boy. Not on that chair, it's more comfortable over there. I think we might have a drink. What about a glass of cider, or would you rather have beer?'

'Cider would be fine,' Bill said.

'That's what I would like myself,' Michael answered. 'Do you know if there is any in the kitchen, Mary?'

Mary got up from the writing-table.

'I will get it, Michael.'

She smiled at him, her eyes eloquent as she looked at him.

'Have you met Mary, Bill?' Michael asked.

'She . . . she let me in.'

'Mary, this is Bill Evans, a very old friend of mine. We were in the R.A.F. together. And, Bill, this is Mary Rankin. She has been helping me all through the Election. I don't know what I should have done without her. I want you two to get on well together, because you will be seeing a lot of each other.'

'Seeing a lot of each other?' Mary repeated the words almost incredulously.

'Yes,' Michael answered, not noticing her tone of voice. 'Bill is going to help you, Mary. I want him to do all the outside jobs. He has got to keep in the open air and he is also taking over the driving of my car. You are going to be my outside secretary, Bill, while Mary does the inside work. What do you think of that arrangement?'

There was no mistaking the light in Bill's eyes even while for a moment he was lost for words, and neither of the men noticed the ominous darkness of Mary's expression. Without saying anything, however, she flounced from the room to the kitchen and it was some moments before she returned. When she did, she brought a bottle of cider on a tray together with two glasses.

'What about you, Mary?' Michael asked. 'Have a glass with us. You have got to drink success to this new venture.'

'I am sorry, but I have got too much to do,' she replied with a frost in her voice which even Michael heard—and she went back to her place at the writing-table.

'Now, Bill,' Michael said, 'do you think you can manage this?'

Bill hesitated.

'Aren't you being rather foolhardy?'

'In what way?'

'Trusting me. Taking me on like this. I have done nothing to justify it, you know.'

'Nothing?' Michael asked. 'My dear Bill, we were together for over three years.'

'Was it all that long?'

'Yes.'

'But you have forgotten the years between; these past years . . .'

'I shouldn't trouble about them. I was not with you and you weren't with me. We start, you and I, Bill, where we left off.'

Bill took a gulp of cider. It was funny, he thought, how words like that could cause such a lump in one's throat that one could hardly swallow.

'There is only one condition I am going to make, Bill, before we start,' Michael went on, 'and I think you will agree to it like the sensible chap you always were.'

'What is that?' Bill asked.

'I want you to see my doctor. He has done marvellous things both for me and for many of my friends. I am not suggesting that there is anything wrong with you, but quite frankly I think you want a tonic. Working for me isn't going to be easy, and I have got the dickens of a lot to do in such a short space of time. Do you agree?'

There was a moment's pause while Bill made up his mind, instinctively making the greatest effort which had been required of him since he left the Service.

'I will do anything you wish,' he answered.

'Thank you,' Michael smiled. 'What I suggest now is that you stop and have some luncheon with us, then have a look at the car this afternoon. It is in Drake's garage just down the road. I didn't have it out this morning because they fetched me. You can get to know a bit about it, and perhaps you could drive it tomorrow.'

Bill put down his empty glass, and turning to Michael, said quietly, so that Mary at the other end of the room couldn't hear:

'Listen, Michael, I will do any damned thing you want as long as I have got the strength for it, but don't let's doll the whole thing up with roses and blue ribbon. I will come to you as chauffeur, and chauffeur I'll be. I will eat in the servants' hall, if there is one.'

Michael put his hand on Bill's shoulder.

'Bill, you idiot, if that was what I wanted I would have asked for it. You know well enough that I have no sentimentality where essential things are concerned. I want you as my friend and I want you to help me. The job I have offered you has not really a traditional title to it, but we will call you my outside secretary, although it is going to mean much more than that. Is that clear?'

'Thank you, Michael.'

There was a depth of gratitude in the simple words which told Michael all he needed to know. He looked at the clock over the mantelpiece.

'It is just after twelve o'clock,' he said. 'We have got a little time, so if you would like to come up to my bedroom we can go over some papers together. We shan't disturb Mary and there are one or two things I want to ask you about the Constituency. You know some of the places even better than I do.'

Michael led the way from the room, and as soon as they had gone Mary stopped working and straightened her back. It was true that Michael had a desk in his bedroom and many of his papers were kept there; but it was unlike him to take anyone up there, and she wondered if he had sensed her feelings of anger and distress and if that had driven him from the room.

She got to her feet quickly because she was angry and because for the moment she could not concentrate on what she was supposed to be doing. Her sudden movement caught the edge of a basket full of papers and they were scattered all over the floor.

Mary felt her anger well up inside her. She stamped her feet and suddenly she was in tears. The hot tears ran down her cheeks and fell on the carpet as she bent down to retrieve the fallen papers.

She was still sorting them out when the door-bell pealed again.

'I won't go,' she said, and then, catching sight of herself in a mirror on the other side of the room, added, 'I can't.'

She fled across the hall into the little cloak-room which led out of the dining-room and locked herself in. The bell pealed again and Michael came downstairs. He looked in the sitting-room and saw that Mary was not there. Then he opened the door. To his astonishment he found Cynthia on the doorstep.

'Oh!'

'Oh!'

They both ejaculated the monosyllable at the same moment. Cynthia recovered first.

'Good morning. I am so sorry to disturb you, but I have brought back a map which Miss Toogy lent me.'

'Lent you?' Michael questioned.

'Yes, I called early this morning.'

'But what for? I mean . . .'

Cynthia smiled up at him. She was by far the more composed of the two and yet there was a bright touch of colour in both her cheeks.

'I am afraid you didn't enjoy yourself very much last night.'

'I did not,' Michael replied grimly.

'And Claverley is such a beautiful house.'

Michael said nothing, but merely stood looking at her. Quite suddenly Cynthia's tone changed.

'Listen, Michael,' she said, 'you were right about Saunders Lane—quite right.'

'Thank you.'

There was a note of bitterness in his voice.

'Can I help you to get what you want?' Cynthia asked.

She spoke softly, but Michael was instantly on the defensive.

'Thank you, Miss Standish, but I think I can manage without your help and without your co-operation.'

She stood for a moment looking at him and then she said quietly:

'You are very obstinate, aren't you?'

Michael looked at her with active dislike.

'I think all this is rather unnecessary,' he said. 'It is unfortunate that we seem to cross each other's paths, but surely even that can be avoided with a little care.'

Cynthia sighed a little too obviously and exaggeratingly for it to be natural.

'You are still annoyed with me?'

Michael threw back his head.

' "Annoyed" is hardly the right word. My memory is a long one and I was very fond of David.'

'Very well then! Let battle commence!' Cynthia said. She held out the map. 'Don't forget to give this to Miss Toogy.'

'I will tell Miss Trugrot that you returned it,' Michael said.

Cynthia smiled mockingly as she got back into her car and drove away. Michael stood staring after her, feeling curiously shaken and perturbed by the whole encounter.

'What is she doing here?' he wondered, 'and why should she want to help me with Saunders Lane?'

He would deal with that in his own way. He had already that morning telephoned to the Chief Medical Officer of Health and the Sanitary Inspector and made appointments to see them. He was prepared to fight Sir Norman and fight him to the last ditch.

He was well aware that he making an important and influential enemy, but he was not afraid. No man had ever inspired him with fear, however much influence he might have behind him. Where women were concerned it was different. He knew so few of them. There was something about Cynthia . . .

He tried to shake the thought of her from him and slammed the front door. He was just turning to go upstairs when Mary came down the passage. He saw at once that there were traces of tears on her pale face and he followed her into the sitting-room.

'What is the matter, Mary?' he asked. 'Has something upset you?'

'Upset me?' she said in a broken voice. 'Of course it has!'

'But what? What do you mean?'

'This man, bringing him here. Pushing me out when I have worked so hard for you. . . . If you weren't satisfied, you might have told . . . me . . . so. . .'

'Mary, my dear, of course I am satisfied with all you have done for me. But there is a great deal more to be done in the future. You couldn't possibly do it all, and I want Bill to help us, not only for our sake but for his.'

'Oh, I know all that,' Mary exclaimed. 'But you are making a job for him at my expense, and I don't think it is fair.'

She spoke vehemently. Her hands were clenched together and her face was white and tense.

'But, Mary,' Michael expostulated—'Bill is a very old friend, and he won't interfere with you. I promise you that. You have your place, my dear, but honestly you will be glad of him once he gets into his stride. You will have to be kind to him at first and help him along. He has been inactive for so long and he has been ill. It is the will to succeed that he needs and that is where we can assist him.'

' "We"?' Mary spoke scornfully. 'I am not going to be allowed to do anything. All I am doing is having something that made me happy taken away. You are only interested in people when they are down and out. You and Miss Toogy! When I was the miserable waif and stray, you were kind enough to me; but now I am not interesting any longer. Now there is somebody new, and when he is on his feet there will be somebody else.'

She spoke almost hysterically, and Michael put out his hand to touch her arm.

'Listen, Mary, you are not to talk like that. There is always a place here for you. We have grown fond of you and it seems as though you belong here. At the beginning we helped you because you needed help; because, to use your own words, you were a waif and stray. But now you are Mary, and we would not part with you for anything in the world. Yet because we have helped you, surely that is all the more reason why you should work with us to try and help other people?'

'And let them push me out?'

Mary's eyes were swimming with tears.

'Mary, this isn't like you. You are being selfish. No one shall push you out; I promise you that. Bill is drowning even as you tried to drown, and we have got to save him. You and I and Toogy.'

'I hate him! I hate him!'

Mary was quivering all over. The tears were running unchecked down her cheeks.

'Don't, Mary,' Michael said.

He put his arm round her shoulders, for it seemed to him that at any moment she might collapse. Then suddenly and convulsively she flung up her arms and clasped them round his neck.

'Oh, Michael, Michael, I love you so!'

6

Bill walked down Saunders Lane with what for him was a jaunty air. It was the sixth day since he had started work with Michael and already his first feeling of strain and tension was passing. He was gaining confidence and was finding, too, that the terrible inertness and lassitude which had been his inescapable companions for years had almost left him.

He was sleeing better and eating well. Michael had been wise enough, knowing Bill's home environment, to insist that the midday meal was taken either at his house or wherever they might be together. Bill's new interest and enthusiasm had altered things at home, too.

At first Mrs. Evans had been both incredulous and pessimistic at the idea of Bill holding down a job.

'I shouldn't get all worked up,' she said; 'you'll find out your weakness quick enough when you try to do a man's work again. I've put up with you mooching about the place for nearly five years; I'm not going to get all excited now only to have you back again on my hands worse than you were before.'

She had grumbled and nagged just as she had always done, but somehow Bill acquired a new patience with which to deal with her.

Instead of snarling back, which invariably began a controversy, or remaining silent, which often infuriated his stepmother to the point of madness, he tried to speak quietly and to convey to her a little of that new sympathy for her which had been revealed to him that very first day in Michael's sitting-room.

'We've given you a rotten deal, Dad and I, Madre,' he said, reverting to the old name he had called her when she had first stood by his father in trouble, but which had never until then passed his lips since he had returned from the war.

She stared at him incredulously.

Bill smiled.

'It sounds funny,' he said, 'but I've just realised that I've got a lot to be ashamed of, that's all. Go on, say "like father—like son".'

She went on staring at him and then snapped:

'Now don't go abusing your father. There's many worse than him, I can tell you.'

Bill said nothing more that evening, but next day he asked her for an iron, and when he told her that he needed it to press his trousers, she gave it to him and then snatched it out of his hands.

'I'll press them for you,' she said. 'It's a woman's job anyway. You go and sit down. You'll be fit for nothing tomorrow if you don't rest now.'

Grumbling, she pressed his suit and even cleaned his shoes. After that the snarl had gone from her voice or else Bill had ceased to hear it.

As he entered the building that evening he was surprised to see various ladders lying about outside and to notice that someone had started to repair the broken balustrade of the main staircase.

He went up the stairs slowly, conscious that while he was still short of breath he was able to increase his speed quite considerably. He even attempted to whistle as he walked down the passage to No. 16. As a whistle it was a failure, but as an effort it was not so bad.

He opened the door. The room looked different somehow. For one startled second he thought he must be in the wrong flat, and then he realised that the whole place

95

had been tidied. The floor had been scrubbed, the windows cleaned, and the dingy faded rags which had been honoured by the name of curtains had been removed. The table, instead of being covered with an old newspaper, sported a cloth for the first time for years.

Bill stood looking around him. The door of the bedroom opened and Mrs. Evans came out.

'What on earth have you been doing, Madre?' he asked.

She smiled at him, a tight, wintry smile, but nevertheless a smile.

'I thought you would be surprised! I've been cleaning! Not before it was time,' she added hastily, as if she was afraid he might say it first.

Bill sat down on his usual chair at the window and was conscious that his legs ached as they always did in the evening. But it was not an unbearable weariness as if the world was sinking away from him.

'It looks splendid,' he commented.

'You wait,' Mrs. Evans answered. 'You have got some surprises coming to you, my boy.'

'Tell me about them.'

'The whole place is going to be done up.'

'Good lord! Who said so?'

'A young lady called here this afternoon. Pretty she was, and smart. I thought at first she must have made some mistake in coming to our door; then I was a bit suspicious. She might have been one of those Nosey-Parker snoopers, doing a census or something. But she wasn't. She comes in here and asks me what my favourite colours are. She had a man with her taking notes. We decided on primrose yellow walls and paintwork in a deeper tone. Now what do you think of that?'

'It sounds crazy to me,' Bill said. 'They can't have got busy already. Why, Michael only spoke to the City Surveyor and the Medical Officer of Health yesterday, and they said they would look into the matter. Michael

96

has arranged to bring them round sometime soon. I say, Madre, you don't suppose that old Baltis has got wind of it and is doing the place up before they arrive?'

'I wouldn't be surprised,' Mrs. Evans answered, 'the mean old skinflint, he's very likely frightened by your Michael.'

'Well, Michael certainly didn't get that impression,' Bill answered. 'It seems a bit strange, though, doesn't it, that someone should come in here today and talk about decorating the place?'

'And what's more,' Mrs. Evans said eagerly, 'we're going to have running water. A sink for every flat, and the young woman was talking about drying-rooms in the basement.'

'I don't understand it,' Bill repeated. 'It will cost a packet of money. Not that that would hurt Sir Norman.'

'There's somebody behind all this, you mark my words.'

'I wonder if I ought to telephone Michael and tell him what is going on.'

'Well, you can have your supper first,' Mrs. Evans said. 'I've got you a nice bit of pie and some pears which I bought off a barrow. The man swore they were ripe; not that I expect he is anything but a liar.'

Bill was not really hungry, for Michael had seen that he had a good tea; at the same time he would not disappoint Mrs. Evans. Everything around him was changing. Even the attitude of the people closest to him had altered and he had up to now felt they were as unchangeable as granite.

His father was the same, it was true, drinking away every penny he could obtain by fair means or foul, but Bill began to find excuses for him. Disillusionment was a hard thing to bear, and perhaps he had been disillusioned not only about his job but about his son as well.

He made every endeavour to interest the older man in the day's events, talking of Michael's activities and also discussing the various political books which he had found time to read when he was waiting in the car.

'How are you getting on with that lady secretary of his?' Mrs. Evans asked as she passed her stepson a cup of tea.

'Do you mean Miss Rankin?' Bill asked.

It was obvious the question was only an effort to gain time, for he flushed a little at the reference to Mary.

'Yes, her,' Mrs. Evans said.

Bill wished now that he had not been so ready with his confidences after his first day of work with Michael; but he had had to talk to somebody, and because his stepmother had been a willing listener he had told her that Mary seemed hostile towards him and that he was afraid she might undermine or at least damage Michael's belief in his ability to do his job.

'Yes, her,' Mrs. Evans repeated. 'I don't trust that girl.'

'Why, you have never seen her, Madre!'

'No, but I can paint a pretty good picture from what you have told me,' Mrs. Evans said. 'She's in love with your Michael. You can bet your bottom dollar on that.'

'Oh, I am sure she isn't,' Bill said, vaguely shocked at the idea of Mary's presuming to such a position in the scheme of things.

'Don't tell me,' Mrs. Evans said with a gesture. 'Besides, he is a fine-looking man and that's the truth. There's few enough of the manly sort about these days. Most of them look puny and undernourished and as though they would not know what to do with a girl if they had one in their arms.'

'I believe you are referring to me,' Bill said, but he laughed.

'Well, if the cap fits . . .' Mrs. Evans said, and she smiled too. 'You'll be all right in a little while.'

'I am not doing too badly,' Bill boasted. 'I only felt giddy once today and I have driven over sixty miles. We had to go up to the City Hall twice and then out to one of those factories near Winkley.'

'Well, that tonic the doctor has given you is doing you good. Go on, tell us more about that Mary Rankin. Did she say anything to you today?'

'Not much,' Bill answered. 'She doesn't ever speak to me if she can help it. One can't blame her; she thinks I am a bit beneath her.'

'There you go,' Mrs. Evans exclaimed, 'being humble. No woman cares for that sort of thing. It's just what I say about your Michael. He walks as though the world belonged to him. Put your chin up, and if that hussy cheeks you give her a good slap. That's what she wants.'

Bill laughed. He liked his stepmother when she was like this—frank, natural and good-humoured; but at the same time he could not help half admitting to himself that there might be something in what she said.

Mary had been consistently disagreeable to him ever since he had started to work for Michael. It was not so much what she said or did, but her whole manner seemed to him to ooze resentment and disdain. If there were parcels or letters to give him, she almost threw them at him; and if Michael left him a message, she usually wrote it on a piece of paper and handed it to him without comment.

Miss Toogy, on the other hand, was unfeignedly kind. She would talk to him; and where Michael stimulated his interest and his desire for activity, Miss Toogy soothed his frayed nerves and gave him a sense of peace within himself which he had never possessed before. Already he loved her, already he looked for her, hoping sometimes against hope that he would have the chance of a few words with her while he was waiting for Michael.

It was perhaps his descriptions of her, inadequately expressed and yet so wholeheartedly sincere, which had made Mrs. Evans conscious of her own shortcomings. Anyway, after listening to Bill talking of Miss Toogy she had started to clean up the place, to try and make the small, dingy rooms to which he returned at night more homelike than they had ever been before.

Tonight, however, she was almost too excited about the idea of the change in the buildings to listen to Bill. She described over and over again the appearance of the young lady who had visited her

'She was wearing a green dress,' she said. 'It must have cost a mint of money, too. It was simple and yet it had something about it. Oh, it's no use trying to describe it to a man, but I can recognise style when I see it even though I never was much of a dresser myself.'

'I am sure I ought to go and telephone Michael,' Bill said. 'Let me see, where is he tonight? He had to attend a meeting of the Association, I think; anyway, he said he would drive the car himself.'

'Sparing you, that's what he is,' Mrs. Evans said, but the words were spoken kindly and there was no sneer behind them.

'I know that,' Bill said humbly. 'Do you know, Madre, it's extraordinary to me how a man as busy as he is can find time to think of other people, and yet he always does, just as he remembers all the people he has met.'

'Oh, that's a gift,' Mrs. Evans said. 'They say the Royal Family are like that. They recognise a face which they haven't seen for years.'

'Can't say I was ever good at it myself,' Bill said. 'I wish I could recognise who this lady is of yours. You say she was pretty?'

'As pretty as any film star I've ever seen,' Mrs. Evans answered. 'And I bet she's a jolly sight too pretty for many people's peace of mind. Men must be after her like flies round a honey-pot.'

'Well, I've never seen anybody like that around here,' Bill said. 'Now there was a girl out in India . . .'

He started to reminisce, speaking for the first time

in years of when he was in the Service. Before this the memory of those carefree days hurt him and he had remained silent and sullen when questioned. Now he was afraid only for his own strength in case it might let him down and that he might lose Michael's interest.

It was getting late before he finished talking to Mrs. Evans and then he felt it was too late either to telephone Michael or to leave a message for him. After all, the news would keep until tomorrow and he was tired—very tired. He wanted to go to sleep.

He slept peacefully and awoke to eat a good breakfast and set off for work about nine o'clock. He had to collect the car from the garage as he had promised to pick up Michael at half past nine.

At present Michael insisted that the garage should clean the car and service it. Bill had expostulated at first, eager to take on anything that was required of him, whether it was possible for him to do it or not; but Michael had been firm.

'The garage has served me well, Bill. I wouldn't like to take the job away from them without any explanation. When we go back to London it will be a different matter; but until then you are just to drive the car and not to exhaust yourself working on it.'

'You are too good to me,' Bill said humbly, but Michael brushed away his gratitude impatiently.

'You would do the same for me. Besides, as I have said from the beginning, yours is not only a chauffeur's job, there is so much more in it than that. Now give me your advice about this. . . .'

As Bill got into the car at the garage, finding it polished and waiting for him, even the petrol tank filled, he thought as he had thought a thousand times before:

'I am lucky! Damned lucky!'

He drove up to the door of the little house. Toogy was arranging a bowl of flowers in the window of the sitting-room. She looked up and waved as the car stopped.

Bill got out and opened the front door with the latch-key Michael had given him. He went into the sitting-room. Toogy smiled across the room at him.

'Good morning, Bill. How are you feeling this morning?'

'Fighting fit, thank you.'

'You certainly look it! There is a glass of milk for you on the kitchen table.'

'Oh, I say, Miss Toogy, that's unnecessary.'

'Doctor's orders,' she said severely, 'and I put it ready for you myself.'

'I say, why do you do all this? I feel . . .' He stammered a little. 'Why are you so jolly decent to me?'

'Do you really want to know the truthful answer to that?' Toogy asked, standing back a little from the bowl of flowers and admiring her handiwork.

'Yes, tell me! Is it . . . because you and Michael have dedicated your lives to taking up lame dogs and putting them on their feet again?'

'Nothing of the sort,' Toogy answered, her voice clear and yet with a hint of laughter in it. 'You have spent far too long pitying yourself, Bill, my boy. The reason why we do things for you is because we like you. There, that's the truth. Put it in your pipe and smoke it.'

She was laughing at him, and to Bill it was the laughter of an angel. His face flushed and for a moment there was nothing he could say. Then with a muttered incoherent 'thank you' he bolted to the kitchen.

Toogy looked after him and there was a tender expression on her face. There was something very gratifying in seeing what had been a shambled wreck of a man gradually becoming resurrected into something fine and decent.

'And he is one of so many,' she whispered beneath her breath.

With a little sigh she took up the duster she had left on the table and went to the mantelpiece. She was going

102

carefully over a tiny ornament when Bill stood in the doorway again.

'Is Michael upstairs?' he asked. 'He told me to be here at nine-thirty.'

'Oh, goodness,' Miss Toogy said, 'I have forgotten to give you his message. He wants you to go straight to the City Hall and pick them up there. He had an unexpected appointment with the Chief Medical Officer of Health. Mary went with him. He asked me to tell you that he would like you to be there at a quarter to ten, so you had better hurry.'

'I can make it,' Bill said, and turned towards the door.

He changed his mind, however, and swung back again. He put his head in the sitting-room and said:

'I say, Miss Toogy, you're wizard, but you know that, don't you?'

Then he was gone again. Miss Toogy laughed. Bill lighthearted, being young again for the first time for many years, was something good to behold.

She heard the car drive away and a few minutes later, as she continued dusting, she heard another car drive up to the door. She looked up and then went to the front door.

Cynthia was standing there. She wore a red dress and hat and somehow there was something a little defiant about her as if she were bracing herself to do battle. When she saw Toogy her face softened.

'Oh, good morning, Miss Toogy. Is Michael here?' Toogy shook her head.

'No, I am afraid you have missed him.'

'Where has he gone to, do you know?'

'He has got a meeting at the City Hall.'

'And then?'

'I think he is going to inspect some property in Saunders Lane.'

'I guessed he was. That's just what I wanted to know. Thank you, Miss Toogy.'

Cynthia would have turned away, but Miss Toogy put out her hand and touched her arm.

'What are you up to?' she asked.

'How do you know I am up to anything?' Cynthia parried.

Miss Toogy smiled.

'My dear, I have brought up too many children in my life not to know when they are busy getting themselves into mischief.'

'Very well then, I am getting into mischief, but you will hear about it sooner or later from Michael.'

Cynthia was smiling, but there was something in the darkness of her eyes which made Toogy exclaim:

'You are not trying to hurt my Michael?'

Cynthia was silent for a moment and then she said:

'Would you be very angry with me if I did?'

'*If* you did,' Miss Toogy answered. 'But why should I be afraid? I must be getting old and anxious.'

Cynthia turned to her impulsively.

'I want to hurt Michael,' she said, 'but I would hate to hurt you. Can you understand that?'

'I don't think you really want to do the former,' Miss Toogy said slowly. 'But go along, dear, I am not going to interfere. There is only one thing I would like you to remember, and that is that if you try to hurt another person and you fail, you will invariably hurt yourself.'

'I am not going to let you frighten me,' Cynthia said.

She ran towards the car and waved her hand as she drove away. Toogy went back into the house.

'It must be wonderful to be young,' she thought, 'young, selfish and intent on one's own desires and interests.'

In her heart Michael held a very special place. She loved him so deeply, so tenderly—this man who had been as it were her own baby, given to her to bring up as her own son. But her love for him had never lessened her affection or interest in other people.

Once when Michael was a little boy he had been jealous of the interest she took in other children, and taking him in her arms she had tried to explain to him.

'I love you, Michael; but because I love you that doesn't stop me from loving other people. In fact, I love them more because I love you, and I love you more because I love them. Love grows when it is used. The more love you give out, the more there is to give. You must try and understand that, because it is one of the most important lessons we all learn in life.'

He had not understood at the time, but as he grew older he had realised the truth of what Toogy had tried to tell him. It is only the withered, narrow-minded people who dole out their love, giving it sparingly, hoarding it greedily as if like money there is so much and no more to be expended.

For big and fine people there is an unlimited supply of love. Like a vast ocean it is fed by a million streams running into it, and it will never run dry.

If Toogy gave love, she also inspired it. Cynthia, driving away from the house, thought of her with sudden warmth in her heart.

'How different things might be,' she thought, 'if I had someone in my life like Miss Toogy!'

She envied Michael and then was angry with him because she thought that he should be different with someone so wonderful to inspire and guide him. He should be more tolerant and understanding, even as Miss Toogy was.

'I hate him,' she said out loud, and repeated the words over and over again as she drove through the traffic as if she wished to convince herself that they were the truth.

She turned down Saunders Lane, drew up in front of the old workhouse and then changed her mind and drove round to the back so that no one approaching would see the empty car. There were workmen engaged in repairing the old iron balustrade on the stairs where it had become unsafe. Men were carrying paint-pots and ladders up to the top floor and others were erecting scaffolding outside the building.

Cynthia nodded to them cheerfully and then stood just inside the front door, a strange contrast in her vivid scarlet dress to the dirt and squalor around her. Several of the tenants coming downstairs stared at her curiously.

One or two of them, recognising her, said 'Good mornin' in embarrassed tones as if they were not quite sure of themselves or of her.

Cynthia had not been waiting long before she heard a car. She stepped back into the shadow of the building. She watched the car draw up outside and then she heard Michael's voice. There were two other men with him, elderly men, both carrying despatch cases. They got out of the car and Cynthia heard Michael say:

'There seems to be some workmen here. I wonder what they are doing.'

It was then that Cynthia stepped forward. She was fully conscious that her appearance in her flame-coloured dress would be startling and unexpected. She saw the surprised expression on Michael's face, saw his astonishment echoed by both the men who were with him. She spoke clearly as she advanced to meet them.

'Good morning, gentlemen; do you wish to inspect my property?'

7

Michael, following Cynthia round the building as she pointed out to the Medical Officer of Health and the Sanitary Inspector the improvements she intended doing, felt his anger mounting swiftly. It was not only that he minded being made a fool of—and Cynthia undoubtedly managed to do that—but it was also that for perhaps the first time in his life he realised his appalling ignorance in one subject—that of women.

He had experienced quite considerable shock when Mary flung herself into his arms and told him that she loved him. He had not really known how to deal with that situation; and the problem Mary presented was still with him, keeping him awake at night and being a constant irritation in the daytime.

Only a few minutes earlier, when, coming from the City Hall, they had dropped Mary at the corner of Saunders Lane. He suggested that she find her own way back to the house because he knew that there was a great deal of work to do, but her expression of disappointment, her pouting acquiescence and almost humiliating subservience had made him feel a brute.

It was a ridiculous situation. It was essential for him to have a secretary who worked for him efficiently and saved him work rather than created it. But Mary had become a difficulty which he could not dismiss easily, and for the moment he was quite unable to formulate even to himself what he could do about her.

And now there was Cynthia, gay and irrepressibly provocative, casting him little side-glances while she said something in a sweet voice but which nevertheless held a barbed sting in it for him personally.

He might have known, he told himself savagely, that when she returned the map the other evening and offered to help him over Saunders Lane she was up to mischief. But he had never in his wildest anticipations guessed that she would purchase the property from Sir Norman.

Although he told himself severely that he should be delighted that the conditions in the old workhouse were to be improved, he could only feel angry and irritated, yet in some grudging manner admiring, as he followed Cynthia from floor to floor.

She certainly had not let the grass grow under her feet once she had made up her mind what to do. The property had been transferred to her immediately and by some amazing methods of her own she had managed to get an emergency licence to have the alterations made and, what should have proved even more difficult, she had got a firm to undertake them at once.

'You are certainly a fast worker, Miss Standish,' the Medical Officer of Health remarked, and Cynthia, smiling at him, answered:

'I appreciate that compliment from you, because I have heard that you are like lightning yourself.'

Flattering, cajoling, getting them to agree to anything she suggested, she led her little party down the passages into the rooms which had already benefited from a coat of paint and into those which were awaiting decoration. At last the tour was completed and they went downstairs again.

'Well, Mr. Fielding, there doesn't seem much for us to do,' the Sanitary Inspector remarked jovially.

'No, I'm afraid I brought you out here on a wild-goose chase,' Michael answered, 'but Miss Standish had not informed me of her plans, otherwise I would have spared you the visit.'

'It has been a pleasure,' the Medical Officer remarked, and it was obvious that he meant it.

Bill was waiting to take them back to the City Hall. They shook hands with Cynthia and got into the car.

'Can we give you a lift, Wing Commander?' one of them asked.

Michael shook his head.

'I will walk back from here. I don't want to delay you more than is necessary.'

They drove off, and Michael turned to face Cynthia. They stood looking at each other. Behind them was the sound of hammers and in the courtyard men were shovelling the piles of refuse on to a lorry. Cynthia broke the tension between them, making a little gesture with her hands.

'I am sorry, Michael,' she said unexpectedly.

Her apology was such a surprise that Michael, who had been bracing himself for something different, felt as if the ground had been cut away from under his feet.

For a moment it looked as if he too would capitulate, then he stiffened himself against the appeal both in her eyes and on her lips.

'There is no reason for you to be sorry, Miss Standish,' he said formally. 'You are doing a good job here and I should in reality express my gratitude.'

'I offered to help you, if you remember.'

'Yes, I know you did.'

'And you refused.'

'I have not forgotten.'

'Well, then . . .'

Cynthia spread out her hands.

'Like you, I could not bear to do nothing.'

'I hope you will never regret it,' Michael said formally.

'Why should I?'

Michael hesitated a moment, then he spoke frankly.

'I cannot help feeling, Miss Standish, that you have done this not because you really cared about the suffering of the people who live here but because you wished to score off me. That is the truth, isn't it?'

'Shall I say my reasons were a little mixed? When I originally planned to do this, it was with the intention of scoring off you. Then I met Miss Toogy and I felt that you could not be so bad as you appeared . . . at least where I was concerned.'

'Thank you,' Michael said ironically.

'Now I'm not sure,' Cynthia went on, ignoring his interruption. 'You are not very noble in defeat, Michael Fielding.'

Michael looked at her with exasperation.

'I realised some time ago,' he said, 'that I knew very little about women; now it is undoubtedly something for which I should be sincerely grateful.'

Cynthia raised her eyebrows.

'You think so?' she asked. 'And yet, strange though it seems, you can't do without us. We are essential to all men, even to the smug, stuck-up, heroic Michael Fielding.'

For one moment she thought he was going to shake her. His face went quite white under his tan and his eyes blazed at her, then raising his hat almost automatically, he turned away.

'Good morning, Miss Standish.'

He strode out of the courtyard, and she watched him go with a smile on her lips. Only when he had gone out of sight did the smile fade to be replaced by another expression.

Michael, striding up the dusty, sunlit road, was furiously angry. He walked faster and faster as if his anger accelerated even his legs. There was no use pretending even to himself that he could take what Cynthia had done

110

to him dispassionately or treat it with the commendation which his brain told him logically was the correct and obvious course for him to adopt.

This slip of a girl had stolen every single bit of his thunder, and he was angry, so angry that it seemed to him there was the same roaring noise in his ears, the same tension in his muscles and the same determination in his heart as he had known in the skies when he had come swooping down upon his enemy.

What was there about this woman, he wondered, which made it impossible for him either to ignore her or to prevent her getting under his skin in such a way that she irritated him almost beyond forbearance?

She was so small, yet she assumed vast proportions when she defied him. She had an air of fragility and yet her strength matched his when it came to an exchange of words. He wanted to make her aware of his superiority, if only that of weight and muscle.

Suddenly Michael took off his hat and wiped his forehead. He was hot, but he knew that the sweat on his brow came from emotional disturbance rather than from the temperature of the day. He was nearing his own house now, and he slowed his pace, remembering as he drew near to it that Mary would be waiting.

He liked Mary and he was desperately sorry for her, but that was all. She was the first woman who had appealed to him for help. He had helped men, and he knew how to deal with a man who was afraid, a man who had let his nerves get the better of him, a man who had lost confidence in his ability to fly.

He could deal with those just as he could deal with the difficult types, the ones who were out to cause trouble and the ones who didn't care a tinker's cuss for anybody, especially those in authority.

Men were easy, Michael thought, but women . . . !

At first he had rather liked to feel that Mary was dependent on him. She looked to him both to protect her from herself and to guide and advise her as to the future. It had been pleasant to come back in the evening after a hard day's work and have Mary as well as Toogy waiting to hear what he had done, to listen almost breathlessly to everything he had to tell them.

After the hard years of war, when at times he had felt that his posts of responsibility were positions of great loneliness, it was pleasant to be flattered a little and to know that one mattered so tremendously to at least two women in the world.

But he had never meant the situation to get out of hand and he was in fact modest enough to have no idea that Mary was falling desperately in love with him until the moment when he felt her arms round his neck and looked down into her tear-filled but adoring eyes.

'Oh, Michael, Michael, I love you,' she had said, and he had felt both dismayed and afraid.

Very gently he had unclasped her hands and made an effort to smile down at her.

'You are upsetting yourself,' he said in what he hoped was a soothing tone of voice.

She had linked her fingers in his and held on tightly to him.

'But I do love you, Michael,' she insisted. 'Why should I go on hiding it from you? You must realise that I love you.'

Michael glanced almost involuntarily towards the open door. He wondered if Bill upstairs in his bedroom could hear what was going on. But Mary was past worrying about anything save herself and her own feelings.

Quite suddenly she released her hold of him and covered her face with her hands.

'Why didn't you let me die?' she cried. 'You saved me from the river to throw me into an even greater hell. I love you . . . and if you turn me away now I . . . I shall kill myself because . . . there is nothing else left for me!'

'Please, Mary, be sensible,' Michael begged, feeling

awkward, embarrassed and **at a** loss to know what to do.

He wished above all else that he could escape from the room, could leave Mary alone and forget this ever happened. Too late he saw the pit which he had dug for himself and he wondered now almost desperately how he was to get out of it.

Mary sobbed bitterly, crying with the same abandonment as she had done on that first night when he met her.

'Sit down,' Michael said gently. 'Let me get you something. Oh, Mary, do stop!'

He guided her to the writing-table, and then at last she took her hands from her eyes. She appeared utterly exhausted and the tears were wet on her cheeks. She looked at him desperately, her lips trembling as her hands went out to him again.

'Oh, Michael, I cannot help it. I can't really. Try and understand.'

'I am sorry—really sorry for you.'

Her eyes searched his face.

'I love you,' she repeated. 'You can't prevent me doing that.'

'But you mustn't,' Michael said. 'It's all rather silly. Really, Mary, I think you are imagining it. I have managed to rescue you and you have thought yourself into being fond of me. It happened to so many of our fellows in the war when they were wounded. They fell in love with the girl who nursed them back to health. Well, I have tried to nurse you back to health and you imagine yourself in love with me, but you are not, you know.'

'I am!'

Her voice was low and passionate, and he realised his attempt at speaking sanely and sensibly had fallen on deaf ears.

'I love you so desperately with everything that is in me. I think of you every moment and dream of you every night. Oh, Michael!'

She was still holding on to his hands. Michael tried to turn away, but still she held him.

'I can't listen to this,' Michael said frantically, and then she released him, only to begin to cry again.

Putting her arms down on the writing-desk and laying her head on them, she sobbed with utter abandonment. Michael looked at her helplessly. He didn't know what to do. Then to his relief he saw through the window Toogy coming up the road.

'Here is Toogy,' he said joyfully. 'Let us talk to her, Mary; I am sure she will be able to help you.'

To his astonishment, Mary jumped to her feet as if pulled by a string.

'Don't you say a word to Miss Toogy,' she said quickly. 'Promise me you won't? Not a word!'

'Why not?' Michael asked.

'Because it is my business—my very own,' she answered, and as there came the sound of Miss Toogy turning her key in the front door, Mary shot across the hall and running upstairs to her own bedroom slammed the door just as Toogy came into the sitting-room.

'Hullo, Michael dear.'

She smiled at him and then, as if she sensed that something was wrong, enquired:

'Anything the matter?'

'No . . . nothing,' Michael answered.

Toogy glanced towards the writing-desk.

'Where is Mary? Is she out?'

'No . . . I think she went upstairs for something.'

He made an effort to pull himself together.

'Bill Evans is here, Toogy. He is up in my bedroom. I am just telling him what I want him to do.'

'Oh, good, that is splendid!'

She had already heard Michael's plans for Bill.

'I have suggested that he stays here for luncheon.'

'I am glad you have told me. I will see that there is

114

something solid. If you ask me, what Bill wants is feeding up and something to occupy his mind.'

'He is going to get both,' Michael answered.

He walked across the room and put his arm round Toogy's shoulders.

'You always know what is best for us, don't you?'

'It depends on whom you mean by "us",' Toogy said quietly, looking up at him.

He held on to her for a moment as if he needed reassurance.

'Perhaps I only meant myself,' he answered. 'I have always been jealous of all the other people whom you have helped.'

Toogy reached up her hand and touched his cheek.

'Silly boy! But I like to hear you say it. I am afraid we are all stupid enough to be jealous when we love somebody very much.'

'Even you?' Michael asked.

Toogy laughed.

'Why should I be different from anyone else? I remember feeling very jealous the first time you came back from school and told me how pretty your teacher was. I remember her name to this very day. It was Miss Willow.'

Michael threw back his head.

'Toogy! I must have been seven at the time. I remember Miss Willow too. She had red hair. I really think she was my first love.'

'The first of many?' Toogy asked.

Michael bent his head and kissed her cheek.

'You know how precious few there have been,' he said, 'and never anyone that I could even begin to love as I love you.'

'Dear Michael!' Toogy gave a little sigh. 'One day you will find the right person. I would like to see you happily married and settled before . . .'

She stopped.

'Before what?' Michael asked.

'Never mind.'

She would have moved away from him, but his hold tightened round her shoulders.

'You are not thinking of . . . I mean you are not feeling ill . . . or anything?'

'No, but we have got to face the fact that I am not getting any younger.'

'Don't let us think of it.' There was a sudden panic in Michael's voice. 'If I had to do without you now I think I should go to pieces. You mean everything to me—you always have!'

Toogy drew herself away from him.

'Listen, Michael, you must never say things like that. It is only weak people who are dependent on others. I have always believed that one of the reasons why we are sent into this world is to learn to walk alone. To each one of us comes the moment when we have got to rely on our own strength.'

Toogy spoke very seriously, and Michael suddenly reached out his hand, took hers and raised it to his lips.

'You are right, darling, as you always are.'

'I knew you would agree with me,' Toogy said. 'Michael, remember what I have said—that it is the strong people who count in this world. The others are often only ballast.'

He knew there was an inner meaning in her words. He knew that she was warning him against Mary and he could not meet her eyes. Now would have been the moment to ask her help, to explain to Toogy the difficulties in which he found himself, but somehow the words would not come.

'Damn all women!' he muttered under his breath.

Here he was, a grown man who had never been afraid of a dangerous and unscrupulous enemy during the war, running away from one woman and dreading every encounter with another.

116

In fancy he saw himself a pinpoint figure on a board with Cynthia, in her red dress and with a smile on her lips, at one end and Mary, with tear-filled eyes and outstretched arms, at the other. Between them he was in a jam—and he knew it!

He let himself into the house and was conscious of quick relief as he saw Toogy waiting for him in the sitting-room.

'Well, how did it go off?' she asked, and, seeing Michael's face, knew the answer without his telling her. But she waited for details, wise, as Mary was not, to know that he would tell her in his own good time.

Mary jumped out of her writing-chair and came across the room.

'Oh, Michael, I have been thinking of you. I have been praying that they will do the right thing. Have they promised to see that Sir Norman puts the place in order? They seemed such nice men. I felt sure that they would.'

Michael opened the cigarette-box and lit a cigarette before he answered her, and then in a tone of cold detachment he answered:

'Actually the visit was unnecessary. Miss Standish has already bought the building and is in the process of doing it up.'

Toogy went on knitting. She did not even raise her head at the announcement. Mary let out a cry of astonishment.

'Miss Standish!' she said. 'You mean Lord Melton's daughter? The one who was here the other day? You remember, Miss Toogy, you told me who it was who gave you a lift? Why has she bought it? Why? Surely it was a great surprise?'

'A great surprise,' Michael said drily.

'Oh, Michael, why didn't she tell you? Did she tell you, Miss Toogy?'

117

Mary's vocal astonishment was more than Michael could bear.

'Must you ask so many questions?' he demanded savagely, and walked out of the room.

Mary looked at Miss Toogy helplessly, her eyes full of tears.

'What have I said? Why is he so cross?'

Toogy looked up.

'I should leave him alone. Michael hates being fussed.'

'But I wasn't fussing him. I only wanted to know. Surely he could have told us?'

'If he wants to tell us anything, he will do so,' Miss Toogy said quietly. 'In the meantime I should go back to your work.'

Mary made a gesture of impatience.

'Oh, why must he be so strange, and why should this girl buy the old workhouse? I . . . I don't understand.'

'Does it matter very much if you do or don't?' Miss Toogy asked. 'I should leave Michael to tell you about it in his own good time.'

'Oh, you are all so peculiar,' Mary said petulantly, 'or else it is because I am kept out of things. Nobody tells me anything! I am only here to do the dull work.'

Toogy made no reply. She only looked at her, and there was something in her glance which made Mary turn away and go back to her desk in the window.

Toogy picked up her knitting and quietly went from the room, shutting the door behind her. Mary drew her handkerchief from her handbag and mopped her eyes. She was powdering her nose when the door opened and Bill Evans came in. He looked at Mary apologetically.

'Am I too early?' he asked. 'I thought it was nearly time for luncheon.'

Mary turned towards him.

'I say, what happened? Tell me quickly before the others come back.'

'Happened? What do you mean?' Bill asked.

'At the old workhouse, of course. I hear Miss Standish has bought it.'

'Oh yes, I believe she has,' Bill answered. 'The gentlemen I took there were talking about it on the way back to the City Hall.'

'And was she there?'

'Yes, when we arrived she was.'

'Oh, go on, tell me,' Mary said impatiently.

It was the first time she had really had a conversation with Bill and been pleasant to him. But he did not resent her sudden change of front nor her curiosity.

'She is awfully pretty, or so she appeared to me. I saw her when we arrived and when we left.'

'What was she wearing?' Mary asked.

'Red. I didn't know she had bought the place, of course, but I did know she was seeing about new decorations in the building.'

'You knew that?' Mary exclaimed.

'Yes,' Bill answered. 'She called on my stepmother yesterday and they chose the colours for our rooms. I meant to tell Michael about it, but I didn't get a chance. You were with him this morning and . . .'

Mary turned on him furiously.

'You fool! Fancy not telling Michael! Can't you see this has been a shock for him? Being told by her? That's why he is so cross now.'

'Cross?' Bill looked worried. 'Oh, I say! How awful!'

'Awful!' Mary echoed. 'It strikes me that you have let yourself play a pretty low-down trick on him.'

'Oh, I didn't mean to,' Bill expostulated. 'I had no idea . . . at least, I did think perhaps I ought to telephone him, and I would have come out last night, only I was tired. . . .'

Mary snorted.

'So, thinking of yourself, you went to bed and never even mentioned it this morning.'

'I didn't realise it was anything so urgent,' Bill said; 'I must tell Michael I'm sorry.'

Mary looked at him scornfully and left the room. She shut the door behind her and went in search of Michael.

She hoped to find him alone, but she could hear from the sound of voices that he was in Miss Toogy's bedroom. She knocked at the door and opened it gently.

'Excuse me,' she said primly, 'but I thought you ought to know that Bill is here and he knew last night that Miss Standish had bought the old workhouse. He did think of telephoning you, but he says he was too lazy or too tired. As a matter of fact she had promised to do all sorts of things to their flat, so I suppose he was afraid of offending you. I thought you ought to know.'

There was a silence. Toogy, who was sitting in a chair by the window, said nothing and Michael, who was leaning against the mantelpiece, looked not at Mary but at Toogy.

Mary waited a moment and then she said very, very softly:

'I know it is not for me to make suggestions, but I do feel we ought to be a little careful of what we say in front of Mr. Evans if he is a friend of Miss Standish.'

'A friend of Miss Standish!' Michael repeated, and then quickly, before he could say any more, Toogy intervened.

'Thank you, Mary,' she said, 'and if you have got nothing else to do I wonder if you would just see everything is ready for luncheon. I told Mrs. Gubbins to leave the pie in the oven. Michael and I will be down in a few minutes.'

Mary was dismissed and she knew it, but as she walked downstairs she was smiling. This, she felt, would definitely prove to Michael once and for all that old friends were more reliable than new ones. Bill Evans had slipped up badly.

She took the pie out of the oven, put it on a dish and carried it into the dining-room. She went back for the plates and the vegetables, which were all ready in Pyrex dishes. There was a little mirror over the dresser in the kitchen, and she glanced at herself, noticing with satisfaction that her recent tears had not made her eyes puffy but had merely given her a soft look which should appeal to anyone unless he was particularly hard-hearted.

'I love you . . . Michael,' she whispered into the mirror, noting the way her lips curved over his name.

As she raised her hand to her hair she was aware that one of her fingers was dirty. She went to the cloakroom to wash, and when she came out Miss Toogy, Michael and Bill were already in the dining-room.

Mary entered a little self-consciously. She had precipitated what she hoped was a sensation. She disliked Bill Evans and she had no intention, as she formulated to herself, 'of letting him get away with anything'.

To her surprise, Bill and Michael were talking happily together. Explanations must have been made and accepted while she was washing her hands. Anyway, there was no sound of restraint, and Bill's air of apology and worry had vanished.

'Come and sit down, Mary,' Toogy said. 'You must be hungry after your morning's work.'

Mary slipped into her place, giving Michael a shy smile as she did so, then looked across the table at Bill with an air of surprise. Neither of the men seemed to notice her, and after a moment it was Miss Toogy who recalled her attention as she asked her to help herself to some vegetables.

'By the way, Toogy,' Michael said, 'you haven't forgotten I am going to London tomorrow?'

'No, I haven't forgotten,' Toogy answered, 'and I have made arrangements with Mrs. Gubbins's sister to come and stay here. She is a very nice woman—a war

121

widow—and she is only too glad to look after the house when we are away. She will be able to take down your telephone messages accurately because she was in an office for some time during the war.'

'That is splendid,' Michael said. 'Really you are amazing, Toogy, the way you always find the right person at the right moment, and I am glad to say that I heard this morning from the agent that they have accepted my offer of that service flat off Smith Square. It is the ideal home-from-home for an M.P., it even has a Division bell which rings in the hall.'

'I am so glad you have got it,' Toogy said.

'It is a bit of luck,' Michael answered, 'and Bill is coming up with me. There is an extra bedroom he can use and we can park the car almost round the corner. In fact it all sounds too good to be true and I expect there must be a snag somewhere.'

'But if you are going to London, what about me?' Mary asked, and her question was a cry.

'You are coming, of course,' Michael answered, 'and Toogy very sweetly says that you can live with her. There is a room in my flat which I am turning into an office, and you will find it all quite convenient, although it will take you quite a time to get to us in the morning by bus.'

Mary was none too pleased at the arrangement, but there was nothing she could do. It seemed to her grossly unfair that Bill should stay in Michael's flat while she should live with Miss Toogy and have the long trek to to work in the morning and home in the evening.

All the same, she comforted herself, Michael would be going to Miss Toogy's often and she would get a lift in the car.

She would not have minded the arrangement so much if Bill had not been getting preferential treatment. She looked across the table at him and hated him; not personally—he was too negative for that—but because he

122

seemed to her to be yet another obstacle between her and Michael.

She wondered what she could do to put Michael against Bill. It was unfortunate that he should come into their lives just when she was making herself indispensable and finding many opportunities of being alone with Michael when Miss Toogy wasn't about.

'Won't you have a little more, Mary?' Toogy interrupted Mary's train of thought, and she started almost guiltily.

'No, thank you, Miss Toogy. Shall I fetch the pudding?'

'That would be kind of you,' Miss Toogy answered.

Bill jumped to his feet.

'I say, let me do it.'

'I can manage perfectly,' Mary answered tartly, but he followed her into the kitchen.

She took the jelly and stewed fruit off the dresser and Bill picked up the plates.

'I say,' he whispered, 'it was all right. Michael was not a bit angry. You did frighten me!'

'I think you behaved very badly,' Mary answered.

'I didn't mean to,' Bill said. 'You know I wouldn't do anything in the world to hurt Michael, don't you?'

'It's all very well for him to excuse carelessness, but I don't. I feel very responsible for his happiness.'

Bill looked at her for a moment, but to her surprise he did not look abashed. Instead he smiled.

'I say,' he said, 'I like to hear you talk like that. You are the sort of girl Michael ought to have as a secretary. Someone who will look after him a little bit. He is always so busy doing things for other people that he never has time to do anything for himself.'

Despite herself Mary was mollified by the admiring tone of Bill's voice.

'You be careful another time,' she admonished.

'You bet!' Bill answered, and turned towards the door. 'Come on, I'm hungry!'

For all her intention to be severe Mary melted before his good humour.

'I'm coming,' she answered, and smiled back at him.

8

The two women stood for a few minutes in the Lobby of the House of Commons holding their green tickets in their hands and looking about them with interested faces.

There was the usual hurly-burly of people passing to and fro. Members came from the luncheon-room, secretaries hurried by with piles of letters or waited their turn for telephone-boxes. A Member would come out from the Chamber, speak to two or three of his Constituents who had been waiting for him, and then either direct them to the Gallery or carry them off on an inspection of the House.

A policeman on duty, seeing the two ladies waiting, went forward.

'Can I help you, madam?'

'We have got our tickets for the Gallery,' one of the women answered, 'but we do want to know if Mr. Michael Fielding is in the House.'

The policeman smiled.

'I think I saw him go into the Chamber about ten minutes ago.'

The two women looked excited.

'Oh, then we shall see him,' they said. 'Thank you, officer, thank you very much.'

The policeman looked after them as they bustled away. He was getting used to enquiries about Michael Fielding. For a new Member he was causing something of a sensation, and the policeman and the staff of the House of

Commons are always the first to know when anything untoward is happening.

The policeman went back to his post at the swing door which led directly into the Outer Lobby, and as he reached it Michael came through it.

'Good afternoon, Mr. Fielding,' the policeman exclaimed. 'There were some ladies enquiring for you just now. I thought I saw you go into the Chamber.'

'You are quite right, I did go in,' Michael said, 'but I remembered that there was someone I wanted to see and that I told him to meet me outside. Do you know who the ladies were? Were they Constituents of mine?'

The policeman shook his head.

'I don't think they were, sir. Anyway, they will be satisfied if they can see you from the gallery.'

Michael laughed.

'Well, that ought to be easy,' he said; 'I want to try and speak this afternoon.'

'Good luck, sir!'

Michael thanked the policeman with a smile and turned away. It was extraordinary, he thought humbly as he went, how kind everyone was to him. It seemed to him that they had all gone out of their way to assist him in every possible manner and even in so short a time he had many friends on both sides of the House.

His maiden speech had been acclaimed by the newspapers as a *'remarkable effort on the part of a newcomer'*. The more sensational of them had proclaimed that *'here was something remarkable—a man with ideals and ideas—a crusader come to Westminster'*.

'In a dull and bored House,' the *Daily Tempest* wrote, *'among a company of tired and apathetic men, Michael Fielding was something of a phenomenon, a young man with fire and courage, a young man curiously unafraid.'*

'What impression did you make on them?' Toogy

126

had asked when he told her he had made his maiden speech.

'I am not quite certain,' Michael answered. 'I would not pretend for one moment that I aroused them, but at least they listened to me.'

'That is something,' Toogy admitted.

Actually Michael had received more than polite attention; he had been the recipient of many congratulations when his speech was over and even one or two of the elder Ministers had patted him on the back and said 'good boy'.

But he realised full well that he was only a small drop of water in a mighty ocean and there was a great deal for him to do and a huge amount of work to be got through before he could command the respect of the House.

Meanwhile, his popularity outside Westminster, enhanced by stories of him in the public Press, was mounting. The Press, bored with politics in the past year or so, was thrilled to have someone new to write about and someone whose speeches, whether made in the House or in his own Constituency, were always good enough for headlines.

Toogy herself had been increasingly busy since she returned from Melchester. Miss Smithers had run the clinic and the day nursery extremely well in her absence, but these were but a small part of Toogy's work. It was as a friend and adviser that she mattered tremendously to the people with whom she had cast in her lot in Dockland, and when she was away there was no one to take her place because they trusted no one but her.

She got back to find innumerable messages, little notes pathetically scrawled on dirty bits of paper, children waiting at the door, old people sending appealing cries for her to visit them, one and all demanding her attention and her time.

'I had better not go away again,' she said to Agnes,

the lame girl who answered the door for her and took the messages over the telephone.

Agnes was one of the waifs and strays whom Toogy had adopted as her own particular responsibility. She was eight when Toogy had rescued her from a home of such misery and privation that they thought it unlikely that the child would live.

Her stepfather had broken her leg by throwing her downstairs after repeated beatings that had left scars on her back which would never entirely vanish. Her mother drank and found the child a continual nuisance.

Toogy had sent Agnes to hospital and when she was well enough to be discharged had brought her into her own house. They had set her leg, but it was so badly broken that it would always be shorter than the other and she found it difficult to walk without a crutch.

Agnes did not grow into the sweet, sunny-tempered character which she would have become had she been the creation of a novelist. Instead she was a queer, twisted little creature both physically and mentally. She loved Toogy, but she would rather have died than have said so. She showed her fondness by expressing her thoughts with an almost cynical frankness.

There was no doubt that Toogy had a real affection for her, and Michael, though he found her disconcerting and at times irritating, was amused by her sharp tongue and defensive air of always being on her guard. No one quite knew of what Agnes was thinking.

She had a thin, pointed face, dark eyebrows and her hair was perpetually untidy. She was a Cockney from the soles of her feet to the top of her head, and there was a wealth of courage and humour in her unplumbed Cockney heart.

Michael often told Toogy that he thought Agnes was like a mongrel dog, snarling and barking at everybody who came to the flat. Toogy would always laugh and her reply was inevitably the same.

'Agnes does her best to protect me,' she said. 'I like to know she is there.'

It was Agnes who opened the door to Michael that evening when he returned from the House of Commons. It was eleven o'clock, and though he had telephoned Toogy that he would be coming round to see her he had not expected to find Agnes still up.

'Why aren't you in bed?' he asked, half seriously and half jovially.

'I wanted to see you, of course,' Agnes answered impertinently. 'Would you like to give me yer autograph?'

Michael looked down at her.

'What do you mean by that?'

'We hear you've been and set the Thames on fire.'

'Who said so? What have you heard?'

'Oh, quite a mouthful,' Agnes answered. 'Two of Miss Toogy's friends have telephoned. They were there! All thrilled and excited they were! Mind yer 'ead doesn't get too big for yer 'at, Mr. Michael.'

She hobbled away towards the kitchen quarters and Michael, laughing, went into the sitting-room. To his relief Toogy was alone. Mary must have gone to bed. She was sitting in her usual armchair and held out her arms to him. He went across to her and dropped down on his knees beside her.

'Well, I've done it.'

'So I've heard,' Toogy said.

'I've burnt my boats! I attacked both the Prime Minister and our foreign policy.'

'Tell me all about it,' Toogy said quietly.

'It was no use,' Michael said, 'I couldn't stand it any longer. Our whole approach to the problem has been one of shilly-shallying and the Prime Minister's explanation of the Government's attitude was just expedience at its worst. The usual thing, "Let us not be in a hurry because something better may turn up."'

'I suddenly saw red. I tried to speak in the afternoon but didn't manage to catch the Speaker's eye; then when he called my name I tore up my notes. I spoke from my heart, Toogy. For a parliamentary performance it was lamentable, but as an honest-to-God expression of what one Britisher thought it wasn't too bad.'

'And then?' Toogy questioned.

'I was cheered by the Opposition, of course,' Michael went on. 'My own Party sat stunned. A good deal more might have been said if the House had not risen. When it did, I came straight away. I didn't want to be drawn into discussions tonight while feelings were still running high.'

'You are not sorry for what you said?' Toogy asked.

Michael shook his head.

'It is what I have believed always. It is what you and I have faith in. How could I be sorry?'

'Then that is all that matters. You must have some food, dear. I know Agnes is getting it ready now.'

Even as she spoke the door opened and Agnes came in. She was not carrying a tray but pushing a little trolley and on it was some cold meat, a salad and a fresh cream cheese.

'Thank you, Agnes,' Michael said gravely. 'I have only just this moment realised how hungry I am.'

'Got some beer for you in the fridge,' Agnes said. 'Drink it slowly or you'll give yerself indigestion.'

She hobbled from the room and Michael looked across at Toogy with a smile.

'She never alters, does she? How old is she now?'

'She will be twenty-one this year, but I still feel I am much younger than she is.'

'I can quite believe it. She always makes me feel that I have been irresponsible or naughty. Well, on this occasion I have!'

'Nonsense!' Toogy said, 'Don't think the wrong thoughts. You have done what you believed was the

130

right and only thing for you to do as an honest and decent representative of the people. Don't start being apologetic.'

'I'm not,' Michael replied, 'but I know what you mean. It is easy to get into the way of deprecating oneself.'

'People take you at your own valuation in nine cases out of ten,' Toogy said.

'All the same,' Michael answered, 'to be honest I am a little frightened. One small voice among such a mountain of pomposity!'

'Don't think about it until the morning,' Toogy advised. 'Are you going to stay here tonight?'

'May I?'

'You know I would like to have you.'

'Then I shall stay,' Michael said, helping himself to salad. 'It is a funny thing, Toogy, but when anything happens I always want to come straight home to you. I suppose most men feel like that about their mothers.'

'I wonder if they do?' Toogy questioned. 'But I am well aware, Michael dear, of the compliment.'

'A compliment?' Michael answered. 'That is a ridiculous word between you and me. It is just that in moments of stress and trial it is only your family that counts, people with whom you can be utterly frank, people who will stand beside you whether you are a success or a failure.'

Toogy said nothing and Michael ate for a moment in silence. The door opened and Agnes came in with the beer. She put it down on the trolley and said:

'Anything else you want?'

'Nothing, thank you,' Michael said, 'and it was nice of you to stay up, Agnes.'

'I'd rather get things ready myself than have you snooping round the kitchen.'

'Whatever the intention,' Michael said, 'I am grateful all the same.'

131

'I'm going to bed now,' Agnes answered. 'If you feel energetic, you can put the trolley back in the kitchen, if not, leave it where it is and I'll collect it in the morning.'

She turned towards the door. When she reached it, she paused for a moment leaning on her crutch, her thin pointed face seeming somehow impish in the shadows.

'By the way, I didn't tell Her Ladyship that you'd rung up or she'd have been fluttering around all full of curiosity.'

She went out of the room and shut the door with a bang.

Michael looked across the room at Toogy.

'Her Ladyship?' he questioned.

Toogy smiled.

'I regret to say that is Agnes's way of referring to Mary. She doesn't like the girl and makes no bones about it. I have told her to be more respectful, but Agnes, as you know, is a law unto herself.'

Michael chuckled.

'Agnes has always been the same. I think really she is jealous of anyone who is here, whether it is Mary or me or anyone else who comes too near to you.'

'My watchdog!' Toogy smiled.

'Exactly,' Michael answered, 'and I think that is the reason why, though I may be wrong, she really dislikes poor Mary.'

'Not half as much as Mary dislikes Agnes. I'm afraid Mary, being brought up without brothers and sisters, has never been teased. Agnes shatters her dignity and she can't bear her in consequence.'

Michael poured himself out some beer.

'Toogy, I am lonely in my flat. I miss living here, I miss Agnes's sharp tongue, the constant stream of strange visitors, and above all I miss you.'

'I was afraid you would,' Toogy said sensibly, 'but at the same time it is too far out for you when you have so much to do.'

'Yes, I know,' Michael said. 'But I don't like living alone, and that's a fact.'

'There is always an easy solution to that.'

'And that is?'

'That you should get married, of course. Haven't you ever thought about it?'

'Thought about it! Yes, of course I have,' Michael answered. 'If you had lived in the wilds for as many years as I have with men who talked of nothing else, you would begin to understand what an important part women play in the average man's life. The difficulty is, Toogy, to find someone like you—someone I could love and someone I could respect.'

'Thank you, darling; but at the same time I am a very old woman. I was not like this when I was in my twenties and perhaps you would not have loved me then.'

'I should always have loved you,' Michael said affectionately. 'Oh, Toogy, where can I find her—my young Toogy?'

'These things happen,' Toogy said quietly. 'You will fall in love one day, Michael, and she won't be a bit the type of person you are looking for. Things happen like that.'

I suppose they do,' Michael answered; 'at least so everybody tells me. But, Toogy, I am distressingly hard to please. I am wedded to my career. It is only when I go back to the flat, when it's dark and Bill has gone to bed in his small room, that I sit in my armchair and think it would be nice to have a woman to talk to, someone who would be as interested as you are, someone who would be perhaps a little proud of me and a little encouraging too.'

'One day you will find someone like that,' Toogy said prophetically. 'But, Michael, when you do marry, look for somebody strong, somebody who will give as well as take. There are strong women, you know, who can still manage to be feminine.'

133

'Like you,' Michael said.

'If you please,' Toogy answered. 'I was certainly strong in my determination and in my ambition. I had no one to cling to and so I learned to stand on my own feet. Women who cling and whine are not the type to produce fine sons or to support one in the wilderness.'

Michael laughed.

'So you think I shall go there?'

'There are moments in all our lives when we find ourselves in the wilderness,' Toogy replied.

She got to her feet.

'If you have finished, go to bed, dear boy. I have a feeling that you will want a clear head with which to face tomorrow.'

Toogy was right, for the following day brought forth a bewildering and chaotic collection of impressions. The newspapers made headlines of Michael's speech, but in many of the older and more staid ones there was a note of surprise as well as of commendation.

'*Young M.P. Burns his Boats.*'

'*Sensation in the House of Commons.*'

'*Attack on the Prime Minister.*'

'*Who is St. George and Who is the Dragon?*'

Nearly every paper spoke of Michael as if he had thrown a bombshell into the Chamber; and it was only when he got down to the House after luncheon, having spent the morning receiving telegrams, letters and telephone messages from all over the country that he realised how seriously his speech was being taken.

There was a small crowd waiting to get into the House and when they saw him they broke into a somewhat discordant cheer. Michael looked at them first in astonishment, then in embarrassment, and hurried away. As he crossed the road, one of the women yelled after him:

'That's right, Mikey! That's the stuff to give them. Don't you weaken, my boy!'

134

In his own house telegrams and messages were still arriving. Mary was sitting at her desk and there was a long list of messages in front of her. She jumped up as he entered the sitting-room.

'Oh, here you are, Michael. I am glad you have come back. There are one or two rather ugent telephone calls.'

She handed him the list and Michael glanced down it. One of the first names he saw was that of Major Whitlock, Chairman of the West Winkley Executive Committee.

'What did Whitlock want?' he asked.

'He wanted to speak to you, but I said you were out. He asked if you would telephone him as soon as you came in. He will be at his office. I have put the number there.'

'I will speak to him,' Michael said.

He would have turned away, but Mary stopped him.

'You sound upset, Michael. Oh, my dear, I do hope it is going to be all right.'

'Of course it is,' Michael answered. 'You are not afraid, are you? This is only the start, Mary. You mustn't be faint-hearted at the very beginning.'

Mary sighed.

'I'm not,' she said, 'but the papers are all so puzzling. Most of them seem to think that you are doing yourself harm.'

Michael smiled.

'Strange though it may seem, I was not thinking of myself nor of my career.'

'No, of course,' Mary answered, 'but don't you think it's a mistake to upset people? Suppose the Prime Minister does know better than you?'

Michael laughed.

'But he doesn't, Mary, that is just the point.'

'Oh, Michael, how can you be sure?'

Michael opened his lips as if he would answer her and then he changed his mind.

135

'Don't worry your head about me,' he said. 'I will do all the worrying.'

Mary looked at him uncertainly and then she clasped her hands together.

'You see,' she said softly, 'I do want you to be a success, a real success. I want you to be Prime Minister.'

'And you think the way to do it,' Michael asked, 'is to follow painstakingly in the footsteps of those who have gone before me?'

'I didn't say that,' Mary answered, 'but I don't like to read the newspapers when they are . . . are . . . sort of . . . against you. And there are a lot of these letters which are not kind. They seem to think you are upsetting things, starting a revolution of your own.'

'Everyone who has any ideas in England is branded as a revolutionary,' Michael answered. 'Don't worry, Mary.'

'But I do,' Mary replied. And here's a collection of telegrams. I thought you might like to read them.'

She put them down on his desk and hesitated a moment as though she hoped Michael would say something to her; but when he seemed absorbed in reading the telegrams she went and left him alone.

Michael looked through them.

'Well done, that's the spirit. A Constituent.'
'Wizard show, sir. 3 R.A.F. from Burma.'
'You are making a mistake, shut up. Disgusted.'

There was another half-dozen in the same vein, then Michael came to one which surprised him.

'Good luck and we are with you. The tenants of Saunders Lane workhouse.'

Michael stared at it, a little touched and yet at the same time perturbed.

'Whose thought was this?' he wondered, and insistently Cynthia's lovely oval face was before him. He could see the look in her eyes when she was being provoking, the curve of her lips, the beauty of her small straight nose.

'Damn her!' he exclaimed suddenly. 'Why can't I forget her very existence?'

9

Cynthia read quickly through the evening paper as if she were searching for something. She turned the pages over, scanning each paragraph, and then, not finding what she sought, threw it down with a sigh.

For over a week now there had been controversy and comment over Michael's speech in the House of Commons. It was, of course, almost unprecedented that the speech of a back-bencher should incite so much comment, but there was no doubt at all that Michael had voiced inside the House the feelings of many who were outside and therefore usually unheard.

Nevertheless there was a storm brewing, for Michael and Cynthia had heard a good deal about it. Sir Norman was violently anti-Michael. He had, it appeared, been convinced on that very night when Michael came to dinner that this young man was up to no good.

'I will break him if it is the last thing I do,' he said aggressively. 'I don't usually trouble myself about politics, but this young upstart has got to be stopped. I am not without influence in Melchester and I shall use that influence to get rid of a young jackanapes who will have the whole country ruined if he goes on this way.'

Cynthia went from Claverley to Saunders Lane and there she learned that Michael had loyal supporters who might not have influence but whose votes were just as valuable, when it came to the Polling Booth, as Sir Norman's.

'We've put him in and we'll keep him there,' they told her. 'It's about time someone up and spoke to those old dodder-heads in Westminster. They talk about representing us. A fat lot of representation we got until "our Michael" came along!'

Cynthia got into the way of spending a good part of the day at the old workhouse. The first thing she had done was to christen it, for it had never had a name and had been known as 'the old workhouse' ever since it had ceased to be used as a public institution. Now it proclaimed itself as 'Saunders Court' in white and gold letters over its new bright green front door.

The place would never be a very prepossessing building. Its Victorian builders had seen to that. But paint and window-panes and the clearing of the courtyard had worked wonders. And what was far more wonderful was the effect in the interior.

The alteration was not only in bright, clean walls and fresh, sweet-smelling passages, but in the whole appearance of the people who lived there.

Cynthia got to know her tenants and was soon a welcome visitor in practically every room in the building. Some of them at first were inclined to be suspicious. But Cynthia exerted her charm and her tact, which had served her in good stead in the social world, and soon they accepted her and began to like her not only for what she could give them but for herself.

When things were really getting going, she returned to London. She would not admit even to herself exactly why she wanted to leave Claverley at such a moment; but it was shortly after Michael's sensational speech and somehow she had a longing to be in the thick of it, to hear what other people besides Sir Norman had to say.

Her father and Lavinia were back from the South of France; but Cynthia was surprised to see that Lord Melton was looking drawn and tired as if his holiday had not only done him no good but had also sapped some of his famous energy.

The house was full day and night, for Lavinia had apparently acquired a feverish desire to entertain, and as there was very little of the London season left she offered hospitality to all who would accept it. There were luncheon parties, dinner parties and, it seemed to Cynthia, an almost continuous cocktail party taking place in the house.

Her father withdrew to his rooms on the top storey, but even he was drawn into the general *mêlée* and she hardly got an opportunity to see him alone. She was shy of mentioning Michael's name to him and yet she wondered what he thought of the sensation achieved by the young man who had so confidently contradicted him and refused his offer.

One day Cynthia sat quietly in a corner of the room watching her father and not listening to the quick, almost staccato conversation in which he was interrogating two visitors, who, she guessed, were journalists.

He looked tired and she fancied that the hair at his temples was greyer. He had lived so fast and so furiously for so long, she told herself, that sooner or later he would have to ease up.

'I wonder why I am worrying about him?' Cynthia questioned.

She found the answer for herself, knowing that the past weeks had altered her outlook where all human beings were concerned. For the first time in her life she had begun to consider people individually, to seek them out, to try to understand them, to find within herself a sympathy with their problems and their difficulties.

The education she had received through the purchase of Saunders Court had given her a new interest in her father. Perhaps she had never really looked at him before. Perhaps for a long time he had been tired and dispirited and she had not noticed or cared.

The newspaper men had finished their conversation and were moving from the room. Lord Melton picked up a telephone, spoke into it, put it down again and turned to look at Cynthia.

'Hullo, my dear, did you want me?'

She got up and walked across the room. She was conscious as she did so that the fragrance of the flowers was almost overpowering. There was something very unreal about this room. It had been a dull day and for once there was no sunshine coming in at the windows. Yet the profusion of light gave an almost luminous effect and she had an impression of moving in a fantastic world divorced from all reality.

She realised suddenly that she was standing beside her father, that she had been there a few moments and had not spoken. He was looking up at her enquiringly, one dark eyebrow cocked a little higher than the other.

'Well?'

As a monosyllable it expressed a great deal.

'I was thinking of you,' Cynthia replied, and it was not what she had meant to say.

'I am honoured,' Lord Melton said. 'But why?'

'When I was watching you just now,' Cynthia answered, 'I fancied you were looking tired and that you were finding things more difficult than you used to.'

He looked at her intently with his dark eyes which saw so much and expressed so little; then he shrugged his shoulders.

'I am getting old, my dear. It happens to all of us, you know.'

'I never thought it would to you.'

Lord Melton smiled.

'You are very serious about it, Cynthia. If you will forgive my saying so, this interest is unlike you.'

Cynthia considered this statement for a moment. Then she sat down in a low chair, put her arms round her knees and linked her fingers together.

141

'You say it is unlike me,' she said quietly. 'I wonder just how much you know about me, and for that matter how much you care.'

Again Lord Melton raised his eyebrows, but he made no answer, and after a moment Cynthia said quickly:

'But we were talking about you. You say you are getting older. I would like to ask you rather an impertinent question; may I?'

'You may certainly ask it,' Lord Melton answered, 'but I don't promise to give you an answer.'

'It is quite a simple one really. Are you happy?'

It seemed to her that her father sank back a little further into his cushioned armchair. Then he made a gesture with his thin expressive hands and asked in a voice purposely light:

'What is happiness?'

'If one is happy there is no need to explain it,' Cynthia replied.

'That is true enough! Very well then, I am not happy.'

It was a frankness from him she had not expected. But she accepted it gravely, nodding her head, before she remarked:

'Neither am I.'

'That is what you came to tell me,' Lord Melton said quickly.

There was the familiar touch of a man who always probes the reactions of others, and Cynthia, recognising it, smiled at him.

'As a matter of fact, I didn't. I came up here to talk to you. You have been honest: I will be honest too. I wanted to know what you are thinking now of Michael Fielding.'

'So he still interests you?'

'Yes,' Cynthia admitted frankly. 'He still interests me.'

'What does Norman think of him?' Lord Melton asked.

Cynthia, however, was not to be drawn.

'I am quite certain he has told you that himself,' she answered. 'He has been much too vehement on the subject not to mention it to you. Daddy, be honest with me for once; what do you think?'

'I rather resent the expression "for once",' Lord Melton said. 'Strange though it may seem, in a long life and over a wide and varied experience I have invariably, unless it was to my disadvantage, told the truth. As a general rule people have been far too frightened of me to have known it was the truth until it was too late for them to do anything about it.'

'Tell me the truth now,' Cynthia prompted.

'Well, if you want my candid opinion, Michael Fielding may, if he continues, save Great Britain.'

'He was right then,' Cynthia said softly, as though she was speaking to herself.

'Of course he was right,' Lord Melton said. There was a moment's silence and then he added: 'What does the fellow mean to you?'

'Nothing,' Cynthia answered, 'and incidentally . . . he hates me.'

'That is a pity,' Lord Melton said. 'He is worth all the jackanapes who come to this house.'

Cynthia got to her feet suddenly.

'Yes . . . of course he is.'

She stood looking out of the window at the Green Park. The children were playing underneath the trees, and without turning round she asked:

'Why don't you do something, Daddy . . . to help?'

'I will give you a truthful answer to that,' Lord Melton said. 'It is because, Cynthia, my dear, I am too old. Twenty years ago I should have known what to do, twenty years ago I should have been at Fielding's side; today I too am indecisive. I don't see my way clearly. It is a legend that I am at the wheel of all my interests—that the control lies entirely in my hands. It is not true.'

143

He spoke quietly, without bitterness, and there was none of his usual cynicism in his voice. Cynthia turned to him.

'Oh, Daddy, and I always thought you were omnipotent—a god in your sphere.'

'And now you find I am only an old man,' Lord Melton said. He picked up a telephone receiver.

'Send Dawson to me,' he said. 'Oh, he is downstairs: well, it doesn't matter.'

He put the receiver down again.

'Do you want Toby?' Cynthia asked. 'I'll find him if you like. I am going down now.'

Lord Melton made no reply; and she went from the room, suddenly aware that she was very tired.

'It is no use,' she told herself as she went down in the lift. 'This house defeats me. It is too big, too empty, and the people in it are made of shadows, not of flesh and blood.'

She reached the first floor, got out and went into the big drawing-room. Tables were laden with drinks and big silver dishes held an assortment of dainty food ready for a cocktail party. There was no one there. Cynthia looked at her watch. It was ten minutes to six. She walked up the wide staircase to the next floor. She expected that Toby would be in her stepmother's boudoir, doubtless, she thought bitterly, planning another party for the morrow.

The sitting-room was empty, but the door to the bedroom was half open, and Cynthia's footsteps crossing the room over the thick carpet made no sound. She stopped in the doorway.

The two people in the inner room who had been locked in each other's arms looked up. Very slowly Lavinia Melton raised her dark head from Toby's shoulder.

'What do you want?' she asked, and managed to make the question both insolent and a challenge.

'My father wants you, Toby,' Cynthia said quietly.

Crimson in the face, Toby Dawson started to stammer.

'I . . . I'm sorry, Cynthia.'

'Please don't make your apologies to me,' Cynthia said acidly. 'You should keep them for my father.'

Lavinia made a gesture.

'Go on, Toby. Get out.'

He almost bolted from the room, an embarrassed and undignified figure. The two women were left facing each other. Lavinia, apparently unperturbed, looked at her reflection in the long gold mirror on the dressing-table and smoothed her hair.

'You are not very tactful, Cynthia dear.'

'I didn't know there was any need for it,' Cynthia answered calmly, and added: 'Must you flirt with my father's secretaries? I should have thought there were plenty of men without choosing Toby Dawson.'

Lavinia smiled somewhat unpleasantly.

'It would be more polite to say that he chose me.'

'I think that is unlikely. Toby is rather a fool; nevertheless he is a gentleman. He is not the type of man to make love to his employer's wife unless he were invited to do so.'

A flicker of annoyance showed itself in Lavinia's dark eyes.

'Really, Cynthia, you might be trying to make yourself disagreeable. Surely, if you will forgive me for saying so, it is none of your business?'

'I am just wondering if it is or isn't,' Cynthia answered. 'After all, you have married my father and you do bear the name which was once my mother's.'

Lavinia turned round sharply to face her.

'Get out of here and shut up! I am not going to be preached at by you or any girl. You are jealous because I am a success. With all the money you have got behind you you ought to have got a man long ago, not even taking into account all the opportunities you have had.'

'Perhaps I am rather particular,' Cynthia said. 'All the same, Lavinia, I do suggest that you try and keep up a little dignity in this house. There is not much of it, I will admit; but where one can forgive a man for behaving badly, there is something horribly shaming when it is a woman.'

'I have told you to be quiet,' Lavinia said, 'and get out of here. If you don't like this house, then don't live in it.'

'I have already decided that I am not going to do that,' Cynthia said.

'You are leaving?'

'Yes, I am leaving,' Cynthia answered.

There was a smile of pleasure on Lavinia's face before she added, 'Well, if you are really going, we might as well part pleasantly.' She hesitated for a moment, looking down at her long finger-nails. 'Are you going to mention what you have just seen to your father?'

'No,' Cynthia replied, 'I am not. Not for your sake, Lavinia, nor for my father's. He is unhappy already and I don't suppose it would make him any unhappier. I shall keep silent for Toby's sake. He is not a bad boy and I don't want to ruin his career. Leave him alone. He is too good for someone like you.'

Lavinia gave a splutter of rage, but Cynthia did not even wait to hear her reply. She moved swiftly across the room and shut the sitting-room door behind her. She walked up the stairs to her own bedroom and as she went up she felt slightly sick.

'I must get away,' she told herself, 'and at once.'

She stood for a moment irresolute in the centre of the room and then taking up the telephone directory she looked up a name. It was not listed, and after searching for some time she threw down the book petulantly and went into her bedroom. She rang the bell for the maid and told her to begin packing.

'What will you be wanting, Miss?'

146

'I am taking everything I possess,' Cynthia answered, and when the maid looked at her in astonishment, added, 'I am going away and I shan't be coming back.'

'Oh, Miss, I am sorry to hear that.'

Cynthia's expression softened.

'It is nice of you to say so. I am afraid there are not many people who will miss me in this house.'

'Oh, you mustn't say that, Miss. We're all very fond of you, I'm sure.'

'Thank you,' Cynthia answered, but somehow she felt empty and unsatisfied as if the words were a mere formality and there was nothing sincere behind them.

'I was a fool to stay here so long,' she told herself.

She went to the wardrobe, and taking out one or two simple suits and plain woollen frocks, put them on the bed.

'Put these into a suitcase,' she told the maid. 'I will take those and my dressing-case now. Get the other things packed and I will send for them.'

'Yes, Miss.'

The maid went from the room, and Cynthia imagined that while she sent a footman for the suitcase she would also take the opportunity of informing the rest of the servants of the new development.

'It will give them something to talk about,' she thought savagely.

She was well aware that most of the servants disliked Lavinia. They treated her with almost ironic civility, and while her father was always well served she had the idea that Lavinia was somewhat despised in the domestic scheme of things.

'Oh, what does it matter?' Cynthia asked herself.

She would soon be able to forget this house and the times when she had been miserable and afraid, curious and shocked. She remembered the series of attractive women, most of them of doubtful reputation, whom her father had brought home through the years.

She recalled how some of them would try to make her look foolish, while others would treat her with disdain, except when her father was present.

'What a darling child!' they would exclaim then, hoping to please him. 'She is exactly like you; you must be so proud of her.'

Cynthia had hated them instinctively. She had known they were cheap, even as she had known that many of her own friends in later life were cheap and unworthy, yet somehow she had been unable to escape, to find a way out.

She had not fully realised how notorious her father was until she had admirers of her own. It had been a tremendous shock to her the first time she had realised that men thought that because she lived in her father's house she would be easy to make love to, ready for a flirtation with anyone who suggested it.

She had been disgusted and dismayed the first time a man had insulted her by his intentions, not realising how innocent and how unsophisticated she was.

'Come on,' he had said reproachfully. 'You're not going to tell me that you're afraid of being kissed? And you your father's daughter! You're just playing with me. I bet you have a pretty good time on the quiet one way and another.'

She had fled from him in horror, for until that moment she had believed that he had been genuinely attracted by her and she had been young enough then to be in love with love. He proved to be one of many, and Cynthia began to dread that moment when alone with a man he would reach out too quickly and take her in his arms, looking incredulously surprised when she would not let him touch her.

Again and again she learned that what she had thought was friendship and the tender beginnings of real love was only desire in its crudest and rawest form.

'I should have gone away long ago,' she told herself now.

She knew it was some inner fatalism rather than just weakness which had prevented her from striking out for herself and taking the plunge. Lavinia was only the last straw. There were so many other things which should have decided her long before Lavinia had tripped into a Register Office with Lord Melton at her side.

The maid came back with the suitcase. While she packed, Cynthia sat down at her dressing-table and took from it the things she would need for her dressing-case: face creams, powder, combs and setting lotion.

She slipped them into their appointed places, pushing aside with a fastidious hand the great bottle of French scent which Lavinia had brought back for her from Monte Carlo. For a moment she contemplated chucking it into the waste-paper basket, then on an impulse she turned to the maid beside her.

'Would this be any use to you?'

The girl's eyes widened.

'Oh . . . are you quite sure you can spare it, Miss?'

'Yes, of course.'

'Well, thanks ever so. I likes a bit of perfume myself and so does my young man.'

She giggled a little and looked coy.

'Are you engaged?' Cynthia asked gently.

The girl nodded.

'I have been walking out with the same fellow for five years. We are going to be married in September.'

'I am glad,' Cynthia said. 'I hope you will be very happy.'

'Oh, we shall. He is ever so nice and steady. I'm lucky to have him.'

'I expect he is lucky to have you, too,' Cynthia answered.

The girl smiled at her.

'Thanks, Miss. I expect you will find somebody yourself some day. We have often wondered downstairs why you didn't get married; but then, Miss, they weren't good enough for you.'

She spoke impulsively and Cynthia realised that she meant it in all genuineness. She held out her hand.

'I want to wish you luck and perhaps you will wish me the same; I need it.'

'Oh, Miss, I do, and thanks . . . thanks ever so for the perfume. It'll make me feel all glamorous.'

'I'm glad,' Cynthia said. 'But what matters really is that you have someone who loves you and whom you love.'

'That's what I always says myself. Oh, Miss, I do hope you'll be happy.'

Cynthia turned away.

Ten minutes later she went downstairs and left for good the house where she had lived for so many years. She said good-bye to nobody with the exception of the housemaid who had packed for her. She told the footman to get her a taxi. He lifted in the suitcases and waited for her to give him the address. Instead she leant forward and spoke to the taxi-driver herself.

'I want to go to 253 Wharfside Road,' she said. 'Do you know where it is?'

'Do I know where it is?' the taxi-driver asked. 'Blimey, it's Miss Toogy's! If it hadn't been for her my boy would have died when he was three years old.'

'Will you take me there?' Cynthia asked.

'You betcha!' the taxi-driver replied.

10

Toogy was tired as she turned homewards. She had spent a long day visiting the people she loved and who loved and trusted her.

She had been into homes which disgusted her by their filth, lack of ventilation and sanitation; yet she had found in them a cheerfulness and a humanity which was often lacking in more prosperous neighbourhoods.

She had given unsparingly, her sympathy and her understanding; and her reward for the long day's work lay in the knowledge that she had done good, that she had in many cases brought not only comfort but fresh courage into the lives of many of those with whom she had talked.

'I am getting old,' she told herself now as she turned the corner and saw stretching before her a long narrow street running along behind the warehouses.

She sighed as she walked, wondering how long she would be able to continue her work, and wondering, too, with something akin to dismay, what would happen when she could no longer carry on.

It was a long pull up the stone stairs to her flat at the top. She often wondered what would happen when she was too old to go up them. Once she had dreamt of putting in a lift, but the building was too old to stand alteration even if she could afford the tremendous price which one would cost.

She reached her own door and drew out her latch-key. On entering the quietness of her own hall she felt a sense of peace. It was an atmosphere which she had herself created and yet she had never failed to appreciate it.

Toogy crossed the hall and opened the door of her bedroom. It was a small room furnished austerely, but it contained many treasures which she loved to have around her.

There were photographs of Michael when he was a boy, a few souvenirs of her childhood, a crucifix which had been brought to her from Rome, and many other gifts—most of them uncostly but nevertheless valuable because they had been given her by those she loved.

Toogy was sitting in front of her dressing-table changing her shoes when Agnes came to the door. Toogy heard the pitter-pat of her crutch and, looking up at her, smiled.

'I am back, Agnes!'

'So I see. There's someone here to see you.'

'Oh no,' Toogy said, speaking almost involuntarily, as every tired nerve in her body rebelled.

'That's exactly what I told her,' Agnes said. 'I knew you wouldn't want to see anyone, but budge she would not; might as well try and move the Rock of Gibraltar.'

'Who is it, Agnes?' Toogy asked.

'I don't know. She's never been here before.' Agnes paused a moment and then she added, 'I thought maybe you'd want to see her.'

Toogy, buttoning on her old-fashioned strapped shoes, digested Agnes's remark. She knew quite well that had Agnes really wished to keep someone from seeing her, not even a regiment of soldiers would have got in through the front door.

Agnes, when she wished, could be as hard as nails and utterly indifferent to anyone's sufferings. But for some reason Agnes wished her to see this person. Slowly Toogy got to her feet.

'Very well, Agnes,' she said, 'I will see her now.'

'There are some messages for you, too,' Agnes said grudgingly, 'but nothing important.'

'Nothing from Mr. Michael?'

Agnes shook her head.

'No. Would you like me to telephone his flat to see if he's coming down here?'

'No, of course not!' Toogy answered. 'There is no reason why I should expect him, but I just had the feeling that he might come this evening.'

'If you feel like that, I expect he'll turn up,' Agnes said; then she looked at Miss Toogy sharply. 'Here, you do look tired. I will tell the woman in the sitting-room that you can't see her. She can come another day.'

'No, Agnes, it is all right. What I would love is a cup of tea, if you can manage it for me.'

'I'll send her away,' Agnes persisted, but Toogy knew in some curious way that she was not anxious to do so.

In spite of her tiredness, Toogy was curious enough to see who had managed to get past Agnes's vigilance.

'Nonsense,' she said, straightening her weary shoulders. 'I shall be all right after a cup of tea.'

She walked across the hall to the sitting-room and opened the door. Cynthia, who had been sitting in an armchair turning over the pages of a magazine, jumped to her feet.

'Oh, Miss Toogy,' she said, 'I had to come and see you.'

'That is nice of you,' Toogy said quietly, moving to her usual chair on the other side of the fireplace.

'It isn't exactly a friendly call,' Cynthia said. 'I have come because I am desperate, because I want you to help me.'

She spoke humbly and her tone and her expression were very different from the last time that Toogy had seen her, when her head was held high and there was an air of defiance about her, a smile of mischief curving her lips. She knew now that the girl was unhappy, and stretching out her hand she indicated invitingly a small chair beside her own.

'Come and sit down,' she said, 'and tell me all about it.'

'The awful thing is,' Cynthia answered, 'that there is not very much to tell. It is just a story of emptiness, of years wasted and of time thrown away. I have done nothing, Miss Toogy, nothing worth while, and suddenly I have woken up to the fact that I am getting older and growing as worthless and as empty-headed as the people with whom I live.'

Cynthia paused for a moment, linking her fingers together in her lap, and then she added in a low voice:

'My father is a brilliant man, of course, but he is not happy. I have a feeling he has let so many opportunities slip past him that now he is afraid to change his sense of direction. My home is a very lonely place, Miss Toogy. I think I have known that ever since I was a little girl, but always I felt ashamed of criticising it when I had so much. But now I realise how very little I have had of the things that matter.'

She gave a deep sigh, then she put out her hand and touched Toogy on the knee.

'Please help me.'

'In what way?'

'I want to do something worth doing. I want to learn about people, to understand them even as you do. I want to feel I have a place in the scheme of things, so that I should matter to just a few people if I lived or died.'

'What has made you feel like this?' Toogy asked.

'I don't know,' Cynthia replied, 'perhaps it is since I met you . . . and Michael. I felt restless before that, but it has all culminated in a climax since I went down to Melchester and since I bought the Saunders Lane workhouse. The condition of the people there horrified me; but it was much more than that.

'It was not a case of being shocked. I suppose one has always known that there were such places and such squalor. It was getting to know the people themselves, seeing them as human beings, knowing them individually, talking to them. And, strangely, I feel I have helped them—some of them, at any rate.'

'I am sure you have,' Toogy smiled.

'But not properly . . . not like you help and advise people. I was shy of them and that made them shy of me. I didn't know exactly what to say; I wanted to help and I didn't want to sound patronising; I wanted to pay for things and yet leave them independent. Oh, it is all so difficult to put into words, and yet I believe you understand.'

'Of course I do,' Toogy said quietly.

The door opened and Agnes came in, pushing before her a little trolley with the tea-things on it.

'Thank you, Agnes,' Toogy said. 'That is what I have been wanting.'

'It'll do you good,' Agnes replied, 'but not half as much good as a real rest would do you.'

She glanced at Cynthia from under her eyelashes as she spoke, but there was no venom in her glance such as she so often vented on hapless callers who took up Miss Toogy's time.

Also Toogy noticed that there were two cups on the tray, which had a significance of its own, for if Agnes did not like the caller she would lay only one cup and when asked for another would fetch it grudgingly, accentuating her limp so that the visitor would be embarrassingly conscious of the extra trouble that was being given.

She turned to leave the room, but when she reached the door she glanced back at Cynthia. There was something in her expression which even Miss Toogy could not fathom. Then she went out, closing the door softly

155

behind her. Toogy poured out the tea in silence until, passing the cup to Cynthia, she said:

'Let us go on talking; there is more you want to tell me, isn't there?'

'It all sounds so banal and so utterly trivial compared with some of the problems which must be presented to you every day,' Cynthia sighed; 'but the truth is that my stepmother doesn't like me and doesn't want me at home. She has been making life pretty unbearable for some time and this afternoon something happened which decided me that it was time I left once and for all. So I have come away. What I am going to do or where I am going I have no idea. I thought perhaps you could advise me.'

Even as she said the words Cynthia realised that they were audacious in their simplicity. She had come to this woman she hardly knew with her problems, certain in her heart of hearts that Miss Toogy would solve them. Toogy finished her cup of tea and helped herself to a slice of bread-and-butter; then after a moment she spoke:

'I am going to make you an offer,' she said. 'It is an offer I have never made to anyone else in my life; but I am going to tell you quite frankly that I am not making it because you have come to me for advice, but because I believe that you are the right person, in fact the only person I have ever met, to whom I have wished to make such an offer.'

Cynthia held her breath for a moment, and her eyes were very wide as they were fixed on Toogy's face.

'I am going to ask you to come here and work with me,' Toogy said. 'It will be hard work, Cynthia; all the harder because I am getting old and I do not find things as easy as I used to; but I would like to have you with me and I believe that you could in your own way carry on much of the work which sooner or later I shall have to relinquish.'

There was a moment's silence, a moment so tense that

it seemed as if time itself stood still. Then at last Cynthia spoke.

'Miss Toogy!' she exclaimed, and hesitated a moment as if she searched vainly for some expression of her feelings. Then she moved and was on her knees beside Toogy's chair.

'Do you mean that?' she asked.

Toogy laid her hand for a moment against Cynthia's soft cheek.

'It is not going to be easy for you, my child.'

'But I wouldn't expect it to be,' Cynthia answered. 'What matters is that it will be something worth doing, something which I shall be proud to do.'

Her voice quivered and Toogy knew without being told that in the past there had been so many things of which she had been ashamed.

She looked at Cynthia and thought the girl was even more beautiful than she had thought when she first saw her. Her eyes were shining now and there was the same expression in them as there must have been in those of the knights when they dedicated themselves to a Crusade.

'I won't fail you,' Cynthia said softly.

Both women knew that in those four simple words she took an oath. Toogy liked the strength of the words. There was nothing bumptious in them, merely a statement of someone who had confidence in her own ability to do what was best and what was right.

'I am sure you won't,' Toogy answered.

Cynthia got to her feet. She walked away from Toogy across the room and stood looking out of the window, at the wide grey river as Michael had done so often to draw from it both strength and resolution. When she turned back into the room, it seemed to Toogy there was a new peace about her, a sense of relaxation which had not been there before.

'When can I start?' Cynthia asked.

Toogy smiled.

'Now, at once, if you have brought your things. I can only offer you a very tiny room. I have two guest-rooms and Mary is sleeping in one of them. The third is mine and out of it is a dressing-room which belongs to Michael. No one else may use it, for it is always kept ready for him so that he can come here whenever he wishes.'

'Michael.' Cynthia repeated the word slowly. 'Somehow I had forgotten about him. He won't like this, you know.'

'He has his own life,' Toogy said, 'just as I have mine.'

'But he hates me!'

Toogy frowned.

'I dislike that word. You have a difference of opinion.'

'It is deeper than that,' Cynthia said: 'much, much deeper.'

'I'm not worried,' Toogy smiled.

'Then nothing else matters,' Cynthia replied.

She gave a deep sigh and suddenly stretched her hands above her head.

'Oh, I am happy, happier than I have ever been for many years. I feel as if you have lifted a great burden from my shoulders. I feel reborn . . . resurrected if you like. I want to start to work now, at once!'

'You can't be in too much of a hurry,' Toogy warned. 'You have got to remember, Cynthia, that we are dealing with human beings. It is not like turning a screw in a factory, driving a car or tapping on a typewriter. You have got to approach people quietly and tactfully so that they believe that they have approached you. You have got to make them trust you and most of all you have to be lovable so that they come to love you.'

Cynthia put her hands to her face.

'Don't, you are frightening me.'

'So soon?' Toogy said teasingly.

Cynthia threw back her head.

'Not really, because I know that if you didn't believe in me you wouldn't have taken me on. That's what matters more than anything, your faith in me.' She paused for a moment and then said quickly, 'You are not doing this out of kindness?'

Toogy laughed.

'Why should I be kind to the rich and beautiful Miss Standish?'

'You might be,' Cynthia answered, 'because only you would understand that wealth and beauty mean very little if one is sick at heart.'

'That's true enough,' Toogy said seriously, 'and I promise you that I have made my offer for a very different reason. I'll tell you what it is—ever since I first saw you there has been something about you which reminds me of myself.'

'You couldn't have said anything more flattering,' Cynthia answered. She hesitated for a moment and then she asked, 'Shall I take this trolley back to the kitchen?'

Toogy smiled. She realised in that moment that Cynthia had taken her place in the household. It was a gesture and yet at the same time it was the kind of gesture she appreciated.

'Yes, do. It would be a help to Agnes. It won't be difficult for you to find the kitchen, the flat is so small.'

'Shall I offer to wash them up?'

'I shouldn't,' Toogy answered. 'Agnes would be likely to snap your head off. She hates interference and is jealous of anyone else doing anything in her department.'

'I'm glad you warned me,' Cynthia said quietly.

She pulled the trolley across the room, opened the door and drew the trolley through it. When she was alone, Toogy shut her eyes for a moment. She must have dozed for a little while, for when she opened them again the room seemed darker and Michael was silhouetted against the window.

'Michael!'

159

It was a cry of welcome. He walked across to her.

'I am sorry to waken you, darling. You were asleep when I came in.'

'Only forty winks,' Toogy apologised. 'I have had a long day. Have you been here long?'

'No, I have just arrived this very second.'

'Did Agnes let you in?'

'No, she doesn't know I am here. There is someone in the kitchen with her. I heard them laughing as I came across the hall.'

'You don't want any tea?'

'Good gracious no, it is too late! All I wanted, Toogy darling, was to see you. I am worried!'

Toogy sat up in her chair.

'Worried? Tell me all about it and switch on the light.'

'No, I don't want the light. I like it as it is. It's thundery outside, that's why it is so dark, but it's restful in here. Let us talk as we are.'

'Of course.'

Toogy leant back in her chair, waiting for him to begin, deliberately receptive, as she always was when somebody wished to talk to her. Michael hesitated for a moment and then he got up and walked about the room.

'There is nothing we can do about it, Toogy,' he said, 'but somehow I had to tell you. You know I always feel better when I have told you my troubles.'

'Which are?' Toogy prompted.

'It's the Constituency,' Michael said. 'There is trouble brewing there, Toogy, and I don't quite know what to do about it. I had a long conversation with Thomas this morning—you remember he helped in the Election—and he told me pretty frankly who was for me and who was against me. They are calling a meeting of the Executive Committee and I think that means they will ask the Association to pass a vote of "No Confidence" in me.'

'Oh, Michael, surely they won't do that.'

'I am afraid so. Whitlock, the Chairman, is of course

a good man, but Thomas says he is entirely ruled by Sir Norman Baltis.'

'Norman Baltis,' Toogy repeated the words softly.

'Yes, he is bitterly and violently against me. It isn't surprising, of course. I suppose really it was stupid of me to antagonise him at the very beginning of our acquaintance, but I don't see what else I could have done.

'He is determined to make things as difficult for me as he possibly can, and you know as well as I do that he can make things very difficult. He is a man of great importance, the biggest employer of labour in the whole of Melchester and a man of considerable standing in the community.'

'What did you think of him?' Toogy asked.

'Personally?' Michael asked. 'Well, funnily enough, I liked him. He is honest and he is on the whole, I imagine, a very decent chap. But at the same time he was pig-headed over Saunders Lane and I was unfortunate enough to come up against his blind spot before we even had a chance to get acquainted on any other subjects. There is nothing I can do now.'

'But we must not forget the people—it is they who have elected you.'

'Yes, of course, and for the moment no one can turn me out,' Michael said, 'although the Association might choose to run a candidate against me at the next Election. But that is not the real worry.'

'Then what is?' Toogy asked.

'I will tell you,' Michael answered. 'The debate on Foreign Affairs comes up next week. I am going to speak again and I am going to speak very strongly this time. I have been promised, in confidence, the support of a large number of the younger Members of both Parties, but—and here is the difficulty, Toogy—many of them are a little nervous.

'It is understandable. If things go on as they are going, we may easily bring about the fall of the Government.

161

If we do, it will mean a General Election. Some of the men who support me are not particularly secure in their seats. They are frightened of what their Constituents may do and at this particular moment there is every likelihood of their being scared away. They will feel—and it is understandable—that it is better for them to "play safe".'

'And the future of Britain?'

'You understand? I knew you would! That is why I am worried. That is why I don't know quite what to do. Shall I go down to West Winkley and see Sir Norman? Shall I talk to him? Shall I tell him what is at stake? Is he the type of fellow who would react, or would it make him push home his advantage all the more bitterly?

'The newspapers are watching me and they are watching West Winkley too. If I make a false move now, I may ruin everything. If I fall, it doesn't matter very much; but I believe that at this moment I am carrying on my shoulders something far more important than the structure of my own small life.'

Michael stopped walking about the room and sat down.

'I'm worried, Toogy,' he said, and dropped his head in his hands.

Toogy was silent for a moment and then at last she said:

'Will you do nothing for twenty-four hours?'

Michael looked up at her in surprise.

'Twenty-four hours?' he repeated. 'What do you mean?'

'What I say,' Toogy repeated. 'I want you to do nothing for twenty-four hours. When is the Debate?'

'Next Wednesday.'

'That gives me a little time then. As I say, do nothing until I tell you.'

'But I don't understand.'

She smiled at him.

'Can't you trust me?'

'Toogy dear, of course I can and do, but even you can't work miracles where this is concerned.'

'I don't know,' Toogy answered, 'but you asked me for my advice; please take it.'

'Of course I will! Have I ever been so foolish as to ignore your advice? All the same . . .'

'I am not going to argue,' Toogy said. 'I have a feeling, darling, that it will all come right. All you have got to do is to believe in yourself and in the righteousness of your cause.'

'I believe in the cause all right,' Michael said. 'It is the only possible attitude for us as a nation to adopt. We have got to be strong, Toogy; it is the weak people in the world who cause such havoc and bring destruction in their train.'

'I have always believed that, too,' Toogy answered. 'At the same time the strong have great responsibilities.'

'Which England has never shirked until now.' Slowly Michael clenched his fists. 'Toogy, we have got to win through. This is a battle of strength against weakness. We can do anything if all that is young and virile rises up against everything that is old and dead. The young men are behind me, and this is the one chance they have had since the war ended.'

Michael was speaking forcibly now, speaking with that fire of faith which burnt so fiercely within him that everyone who listened to him was instantly aware of it.

Toogy put out her hands and touched his.

'Don't be afraid, my dear, you will convince them.'

Michael took her hand in his and raised it to his lips.

'You never fail me,' he said.

His head was bent, so he did not hear the door open.

'Agnes says supper will be ready in five minutes, Miss Toogy,' Cynthia said.

Only as she finished her sentence did she see Michael, and at the same moment he saw her and gave an incoherent exclamation. Cynthia recovered her presence of mind first.

'Good evening,' she said, and smiled.

To Michael her smile was only an impertinence, but Toogy noticed the appeal in her eyes as if she were asking him to be kind.

'What are you doing here?' he asked, and his tone was harsh.

'I'm . . . I'm staying; Miss Toogy will tell you about it.'

Cynthia turned tail and fled. The door closed behind her and Michael turned to Toogy with such an astonished expression on his face that it was comical and she laughed out loud.

'What is she doing here?'

'What she said.'

'Staying here?'

'Yes.'

'Have you gone mad?'

'Not that I am aware of.'

'Then why?' Michael pushed his hand over his hair. 'Toogy, you must give me some explanation. What is Cynthia Standish doing in my home and why does she say she is staying?'

'Because she is. Sit down, Michael.'

'I am going to do nothing of the sort. This is more than I can understand. That woman, of all people, forcing herself upon you.'

'She is doing nothing of the sort. Do you imagine, Michael, that I would allow anyone to force themselves upon me?'

'I don't know. It is easy to obtain your sympathy, and I imagine that is what she has done.'

'So you think she has a lot for me to be sympathetic about?'

'No. . . . Well, I don't know. . . . I don't know anything about her.'

'Exactly, you know little or nothing about Cynthia Standish. I know a great deal. I have asked her to come here, Michael, because I believe in her, because I believe she is the one person who can help me.'

'Help you?' Michael's voice was incredulous.

'Yes; I repeat I believe she is the one person who can help me.'

'But, Toogy, you must have gone crazy. This girl can't help you. What does she know about your work and what does she care, for that matter? You know the way she treated David. Can you imagine a girl like that would have any understanding with the people here, the people whom you understand, the people who love you? . . .'

'Yes, I believe she can both understand and sympathise with them.'

Michael threw his arms up in the air.

'I give up! I don't understand!'

'No, darling, you don't. And does it matter very much? You are busy with your life, I am busy with mine.'

'Toogy, how can you say such a thing to me? You know we have always been so close together. You have been like my mother; in fact you have been my mother.'

'No, darling, you had your own mother. You don't remember her, but she was a very sweet and very lovable woman.'

'I don't remember her, therefore you have been my mother,' Michael said obstinately, 'and although you know that I dislike this woman, you have taken her into my home.'

'To help me,' Toogy added.

'There are other people who could help you.'

'Are there?'

'Good lord, there must be!'

'Cynthia is inexperienced, Michael, but she has two things which I require—courage and strength. These are good foundations on which to build anything. Experience will come with age and sympathy with knowledge. Courage and strength are what are required first. I find them in very few young women.'

'But you have never told me you wanted anyone to help you,' Michael persisted. 'If you had told me, I dare say I could have found someone.'

'Someone like Mary perhaps?'

Toogy was laughing at him and Michael made a gesture of despair.

'You are tying me up in knots and you know it. You know I don't mean somebody like Mary.'

'You mean somebody like Cynthia?'

'Oh, my goodness!' Michael was laughing now despite himself. 'You are incorrigible. I don't know what to say.'

'Therefore I shouldn't say it.'

The door opened abruptly.

'Supper's ready,' Agnes said sharply, 'and you're to come at once because I've made an omelette and I don't want it spoilt. Her Ladyship is back and she's dolling herself up because she heard her Lord and Master was here.'

She made what was almost a grimace at Michael.

'Agnes, you are not to talk like that,' Toogy said, but she spoke feebly, for she knew quite well that Agnes would say what she pleased however much one tried to prevent her.

'Well, I am not going to doll myself up,' Michael said. 'I am coming in just as I am.'

'And quite right too,' Agnes answered. 'All these women!'

There was scorn in her voice as she walked across the hall to the little slip of a room they called the dining-room which led out of the kitchen. Toogy entered first, followed by Michael.

Cynthia was waiting for them. She was standing and something in her attitude struck at Toogy's heart. She

166

was like a child on her first day at school. Apprehensive and unsure of herself, and Toogy knew without looking that Cynthia's eyes were on Michael.

'Come along, dear,' Toogy said. 'You had better sit on my right. Michael always has his own chair at the top of the table and Mary can sit opposite.'

Without a word Cynthia slipped into her place. There was a moment's embarrassed silence as Agnes put the omelette through the hatch and Michael rose to get it.

'The plates are hot,' Agnes admonished sharply.

Michael picked them up gingerly and put them on the table. As he did so Mary came into the room.

'I am so sorry to be late, Miss Toogy,' she said, and then she saw Cynthia.

She hesitated ominously and Toogy effected the introductions.

'Cynthia, I don't think you have met Mary Rankin, who is working for Michael. Mary, this is Miss Cynthia Standish.'

'How do you do?'

The two women touched each other's hands across the table and both sat down quickly as if pulled by a string.

'You bought Saunders Lane workhouse, didn't you?' Mary said conversationally.

'Yes,' Cynthia replied.

She glanced at Michael, who was feeling embarrassed at the topic being introduced.

'And a very good job you have made of it,' Toogy said. 'As a matter of fact I had a letter from one of the tenants there yesterday. She was thrilled that Michael was able to get her son a pension, but even more thrilled at the alterations that had been made to her home. You have made a great many people very happy, Cynthia. I hope they will remain so.'

'It must have cost you a lot of money,' Mary said sourly.

'I haven't had the bill yet, but whatever it costs I feel it was worth while,' Cynthia replied.

'It's easy to be able to talk like that if you can afford such things,' Mary remarked

There was an unexpected spot of colour in her cheeks and it was quite obvious that she was very much surprised at finding Cynthia here for dinner. Toogy looked at her and something in the calm and honest eyes of the older woman made Mary drop her own and attend to her food.

It was not an easy meal, but somehow no one could remain awkward nor could animosities flourish for long when Toogy was present. In a little while they were all talking about some neutral subject, calmly and without the intrusion of personalities.

When supper was finished, Michael looked at his watch.

'I must get back to the House,' he said. 'They are expecting a Division about 9.30 and I have got to vote.'

He crossed the room and kissed Toogy affectionately; then he turned to the two girls.

'Good night, Mary, I will see you tomorrow. Good night, Miss Standish.'

'Good night, Michael.'

She used his Christian name deliberately, and he realised that she was asking him to be friendly, asking him to forget the gulf which lay between them. He was aware at that moment of her loveliness, of her small face upturned to his, of the darkness of her eyes, and the softness of her curved mouth; then quickly he turned away.

'Good night,' he said, and he could not bring himself to call her by her name.

As soon as he had gone Toogy also said good night.

'I am going to bed,' she said. 'I am very tired.'

She went into her own room and shut the door, but she did not at once begin to undress. Instead she picked up a photograph of Michael from her dressing-table and sat looking at it. He had been only a few months old when it was taken—a fat, sturdy-looking baby sitting on a cushion, his toys spread around him.

He had looked up at the camera as the photograph was taken and there was a look of eagerness about his face, which held just a reflection of that vivid alertness which was to be so characteristic of him as he grew older.

For a long time Toogy sat looking at the photograph; then she put it down. There was a telephone beside her bed and she picked up the receiver. She dialled 'Trunks', and when the operator answered she gave the number:

'Melchester 235.'

11

Toogy, watching for the first glimpse of Claverley between the trees, found herself anticipating with very
mixed feelings the interview which lay before her.

It was difficult to know whether she was pleased or
sorry at the thought of seeing Norman again. Her emotions concerning him had undergone so many changes
during the years; and yet even now, when she was old
and when only Michael's interests mattered, Norman
Baltis still had the power to disturb her very much as he
had done the first time she met him.

How well she could remember that morning half a
century ago when her brother at breakfast had said:

'I hear there's a chap in the village who has invented
a new kind of bicycle.'

'How exciting!' Susan Trugrot exclaimed. 'What's
his name?'

'Baltis, I believe. He is a nephew of old Millard who
keeps the "Green Man". They say he is a clever boy.'

'Oh, but we must go and see the bicycle.'

Bicycles had just become the rage and Susan was considered particularly daring because she was one of the
first girls in the neighbourhood to possess one.

'We will ride down there this morning,' her brother
promised. 'We had better not tell Mother about it. She
was giving me a long lecture only last night and telling
me that I mustn't encourage you in your fast ideas.'

Susan laughed. Life was very good at eighteen. There

was so much to do and there were so many exciting things to savour and enjoy.

She got up from the table and looked across the smooth, green lawns where the three gardeners were at work. Many generations had contributed towards the beauty of the lawns with their background of great trees:

'How pretty it is!' she said suddenly.

Her brother laughed.

'Good gracious, Susan, one would think you had never seen the place before.'

'Can't one admire something one knows well?' Susan asked.

'I believe it is permissible,' he replied; 'and incidentally you are getting very pretty yourself. And I feel entitled to say so even though I do know you so well.'

'Thank you,' she answered, giving him a little mocking bow before she ran upstairs to get her things.

They rode down to the village, the lodge-keeper curtsying to them as she opened the big iron gates at the end of the drive, the labourers touching their forelocks as they passed by.

The village, nestling under the shadow of the Cotswold Hills, was a cluster of black and white thatched cottages with the square-built, grey Norman church in its midst. The 'Green Man' was the only public house; and when they had reined up outside it the old ostler, who had known them since they were children, hurried out to hold their horses.

'We have come to see Millard's nephew,' her brother said.

'You'll find him round at the back, sir. He is working on some iron contraption. Unnatural, I calls it, when one can have a decent animal to ride.'

Laughing at the disgust in the old man's voice, Susan followed her brother into a big shed at the back of the public house. Norman Baltis was at work. He was a well-built young man about the same age as herself. He had flaming red hair and the first thing Susan noticed about him was how blue his eyes were.

It was his eyes which held her attention. She had never before met anyone whose eyes were so alive, so vividly expressive. Susan had been brought up to think that young men not of her own class and social standing were not to be considered as creatures of flesh and blood. But she was conscious of Norman Baltis's manhood from the first second of their meeting.

He greeted them politely, but without enthusiasm, and she had sensed that he was annoyed at being interrupted in his work.

'Well, Baltis,' her brother said. 'I hear you are making a new bicycle. My sister and I have come to see it.'

'It's not ready yet—sir.'

'Well, let us have a look at what you have done.'

Almost reluctantly Norman Baltis had shown them his bicycle. It was not very much to look at, but as he showed it to them there was a note of enthusiasm and excitement in his voice which was infectious.

'See the way the wheels run, and the handlebars are lower. You can get a greater speed this way.'

Susan did not look at the machine; instead she watched the boy who was demonstrating what he had made. He was so unlike anyone she had ever met in her life before. There was a drive and a determination about him. But there was something else, too; something which she had never found in anyone she had spoken to before; she could only describe it as a kind of unbridled aliveness.

She was used to languid young men. It was fashionable at that period for gentlemen to drawl, to take everything that was done for them as a matter of course and to be affectedly unenthusiastic about their pleasures. Norman was different in that he obviously believed in his bicycle and—what was more impressive—he believed in himself!

172

'When you have finished it, what are you going to do with it?' Susan's brother asked.

'I'm going to show it to a man I know in Coventry. He was over here about a fortnight ago and I told him what I was trying to do. He said he would be interested.'

'And after that?'

Norman smiled.

'Go ahead and make another and better one.'

There had been nothing sensational in the conversation, yet Susan was to remember every word of it all her life.

'Well, I would like to see the machine when you have finished it,' her brother said.

'I will send word up to the Hall, sir.'

'You might bring it up yourself.'

There was a hint of rebuke in the suggestion.

'Certainly, if I have the time.'

It was the answer of a man who was not there to be put upon and who had his own ideas of subservience.

'Come along, Susan.'

Toogy's brother slipped his arm through hers, but she hung back.

'Good-bye,' she said to Norman Baltis. 'Thank you for showing us your invention.'

'It has been a pleasure.'

He looked at her now, as if it were for the first time, and suddenly she saw an expression in his eyes which she understood only too well. It was admiration. She had known it often enough from other men, but somehow this time it was different.

She felt herself to blush and yet she had not dropped her eyes before his. Something passed between them—a moment of magnetism, a moment when all distinction of birth and upbringing were forgotten. They were boy and girl—no, man and woman—face to face, and they recognised each other as such. Their spirits touched and bridged the gulf between them.

173

'Susan!'

Her brother's voice, sharp and peremptory, broke in upon them. Quickly she turned away. Her heart was beating rapidly and she had known instinctively and surely that Norman's was beating too.

She went home and tried to forget him; but that moment in the shed at the back of the 'Green Man' had been a deciding factor in her life. A week later she refused to marry one of the most eligible young men in the neighbourhood. Her parents were astonished.

'Susan, he is so suitable!'

'That is why I don't want to marry him.'

'What do you mean, dear?'

There was both astonishment and concern in the question.

'I should be stifled. I could not live his sort of conventional life, year after year.'

'But it is our life . . . and the life you have always lived.'

'Yes, I know; that is why I know I should be unhappy.'

'But, Susan, what alternative is there?'

'There must be one and I'm going to find it!'

'But . . . what do you want to do?'

'To work!'

If she had suggested going on the stage or into a circus they could not have been more astounded. Then they thought it was only a passing whim and that Susan would change her mind.

They took her to London; they took her round the world; but Susan did not change her mind. The day she was twenty-one she went to work in Dockland.

Her parents behaved as if she were going into a convent or a lunatic asylum, but she was obdurate. She had known what she wanted; and the first knowledge of it had come to her that day when Norman Baltis looked deep into her eyes and she had seen there not only admiration for herself, but the strivings and struggles of a young man who was living his life fully, doing what he wanted to do, and who was free from the narrow conventions of upper-class Society.

Toogy had not seen Norman again for more than twenty years. She heard of him occasionally, and read in the newspapers of the man who was making his name first in the motor-car world and then as a pioneer in the manufacture of aircraft. It was immediately after the First World War that he came back into her life.

Toogy had been a nurse all through the war and had only recently returned to her own place in Dockland. She was busy putting her affairs in order when one day she received a letter from her cousin, Elizabeth Claver.

She had met her only two or three times and remembered very little about her save that she was extremely pretty and that someone had said that she wrote poetry. The letter was urgent and to Toogy, reading between the lines, it was almost one of desperation.

'Please see me, Cousin Susan' [Elizabeth wrote], *'I want your advice and your help. Please let me know— and as quickly as you can—when I can come to London and talk to you.'*

Toogy had written by return asking the girl to luncheon in two days' time. She came, and Toogy saw that her memory had not played her false. Elizabeth was very pretty, but she had something more than prettiness in her face—a look almost of spirituality; and when they talked Toogy realised that this was no mere facial illusion.

Elizabeth Claver at twenty-seven was a very unusual person. She was extremely intelligent, well read, and artistic in her outlook. Sensitive to the point of clairvoyance, she had a strong streak of mysticism in her.

'You must help me, Cousin Susan,' she said, bending

175

forward in her chair and clasping her hands. 'Only you can tell me what to do, because you made your own decision when you were young. You went your own way despite everything anyone could say to you.'

'And you want to do the same?' Toogy asked.

Elizabeth nodded.

'But I don't want to work like you. I want to be revolutionary for another reason.'

'Yes?'

'I have fallen in love,' Elizabeth said, 'and the family are horrified. They have forbidden me ever to see him again. They have told me that if I marry him I can leave home and never come back.'

She paused a moment and then laughed—a quiet, rather attractive sound.

'As a matter of fact, it won't be a question of leaving home. You see, the man I want to marry has just bought Claverley.'

'Oh, I remember hearing that it had been sold. I am so sorry.'

'Yes, it is sad, for it has belonged to the Clavers for nearly three hundred years, but we can't afford to live there any more. It was a struggle before the war and now we are reduced to a gardener and two servants. The house, too, is going to rack and ruin for want of repairs. When somebody came along and offered Daddy a fantastic price for it, he felt he had to accept. And after all, as my brother Teddy was killed in the war, there is no Claver to inherit.'

Elizabeth paused a moment and then she said:

'That is how I met him . . . the man I love. He came to buy the house, Father hating him, of course, even before he saw him, so I was told to show him round. I acted as guide and we talked. Oh, Cousin Susan, I realised then that he was quite different from anyone I had ever known before.'

'You fell in love with each other?'

'Yes, at first sight.'

'But why are the family so disapproving?'

Elizabeth made an expressive gesture with her hands.

'Oh, I'm not really surprised. To begin with, he is twenty years older than I am; secondly he is a man of the people. Knowing my family, you will realise that that, of course, damns him more than anything else. If he had been a dipsomaniac, a lunatic, or over eighty with one foot in the grave, they wouldn't have minded so much. What annoys them is having to say, "He is not one of us." '

'And he is buying Claverley?'

'He has bought it. We are supposed to be out in a month's time. But I intend to stay on there.'

'You are quite, quite sure you are doing the right thing in wanting to marry this man?'

'Quite, quite sure! I love Norman and he loves me.'

Toogy was startled.

'What is his name? You haven't told me.'

'Norman Baltis. He is the head of the Baltis Motor Company in Melchester.'

Norman had married Elizabeth and Toogy had gone to their wedding. Seeing him again after all those years she had thought that much of the determination and aliveness which she had sensed in him when they first met was still there.

But at forty-seven Norman was a very different person from the enthusiastic young boy he had been at eighteen. He had lived a hard life. He had had to fight, and like many fighters he had ceased to know when to stop fighting.

He loved Elizabeth, but he was furious and humiliated that her family would not accept him. He was very rich and he had begun to believe in the power of his own money.

That the Clavers had cut Elizabeth out of their lives

because she had married, as they thought, a man beneath her hurt him far more than he cared to admit even to himself, so that he was like an animal who snarled at everyone including Elizabeth.

He made her desperately unhappy, and actually, as Toogy had feared from the first, they were completely unsuited to each other. They lived together for three years and then Elizabeth ran away.

Toogy saw them on several occasions during those three years and she had been desperately sorry for them both. For Elizabeth because she was in love with Norman and because she was too spiritual for the tough world in which she had chosen to live. Love could not span the enormous difference between herself and her husband.

Love could not bridge the utter dissimilarity of their characters when both were set in their ways and when both found it hard to reach a common viewpoint on anything, however trivial.

As for Norman, Toogy had to be sorry for him, too. Had he loved someone earlier in his life, he might have been a very different person. But he had had no time for women. Ambition had driven him on and on.

If Elizabeth was unhappy, Norman was equally so, but he could escape into his factories and could forget love in a business world where his reputation grew year by year and he became richer and richer.

When the end came and Elizabeth could stand her unhappiness no more, she had come to Toogy in an agony of despair:

'I have lost everything—my family, the people I love and who love me, my husband, and I think even my soul.'

It had been a cry so tragic in its intensity that Toogy had no words to answer it. She could only put her arms round Elizabeth and hold her close. She had never seen Norman since Elizabeth had run away from him.

'Poor Norman!' Toogy said the words aloud as the

car in which she was travelling turned in at the gates of Claverley.

There were the two small stone lodges on either side of the beautiful Regency gate surmounted by stone leopards. In the Park, the great trees casting purple shadows on the green grass; and there ahead was Claverley—white and fairylike in its exquisite beauty.

The car drew up at the front door. Toogy got out slowly and a little stiffly. It was twenty-five years since she came there last. Then she had been able to jump out with youthful elasticity and run up the steps in her eagerness to see Elizabeth.

'Dear Elizabeth!' It seemed strange to come to Claverley and know that she would not be waiting for her, to know that she would not come across the hall with her hands outstretched or run in from the garden with her arms full of flowers, her smile of welcome more lovely than any blossom that ever bloomed.

The butler showed Toogy into the long drawing-room. This had been Elizabeth's favourite room. How well she remembered it! It looked a little stiff now and she thought that no other woman would ever have the knack that Elizabeth had of making a place beautiful because of her presence in it.

'I will tell Sir Norman you are here,' the butler said, and shut the door behind him.

Toogy walked across to the fireplace at the far end of the room. Suddenly she felt apprehensive and afraid. Had she been wise to come? Had her own decision to break the silence of many years been a wise one? Almost she had the impulse to turn and go away, but even as she hesitated the door opened and Sir Norman Baltis came in, white-haired, lined and very thin.

Toogy's first impression was one of dismay. He was an old man! He seemed smaller somehow and less imposing, and then she realised that he was nervous and a little uncertain of himself.

He came forward slowly and there was a slight air of defiance about him. How well she knew the way he had of protruding his lower lip and of narrowing his eyes. It made him appear formidable to those who met him for the first time.

But Toogy remembered that he only did this when he was shy, and her apprehensions and her anxiety disappeared. She went to meet him, her hands outstretched.

'It is very kind of you to see me, Norman.'

'I'm glad to see you, Susan.'

He took her hand and she noticed that his grip was as firm as it had ever been.

'He is still a strong man,' she thought, and was glad that age had not yet taken its full toll of someone who had always been almost overpoweringly forceful.

'Sit down,' he suggested. 'Here on the sofa; and you had better sit on my left side, I am slightly deaf in my right ear.'

Toogy felt her heart cry out; Norman admitting his infirmities! Somehow there was something infinitely pathetic about it.

'I am sorry, Norman.'

'It's nothing,' he said gruffly. 'We are getting old, Susan, that's all. It is no use pretending.'

'I never did,' Toogy answered. 'Nor did you, Norman. You were always honest and frank whatever your faults.'

'Faults! I haven't got any!' he growled, and then he smiled. 'Susan, it's good to see you.'

'Thank you, Norman. It has been a long time.'

'Too long! I was a fool! I'm sorry.'

Again Toogy's heart turned over in her breast. Norman apologising! Norman, the strong man who never said he was in the wrong, who had fought his way to his objective whatever the cost. She felt the tears in her eyes, and suddenly she was utterly ashamed of herself.

She should have come here long ago. She should have broken her silence before this. She had been cruel as

180

only a woman can be cruel. Impulsively Toogy put out her hand and touched his.

'I am sorry, too,' she said. 'I should have come to see you a long time ago.'

He stirred a little in his seat as though even now the unhappiness of his short married life had the power to wound him.

'I'm sorry about Elizabeth. She was too good for me, that was the trouble.'

'She was too good for all of us,' Toogy said.

'After she died I should have come and seen you,' Norman said gruffly, 'but . . . damn it, I am not going to make any explanations. You know them all, Susan.'

'Yes, I know.'

Of course, she knew! She knew that he had been still smarting over Elizabeth's decision to leave him. It was one thing to quarrel with one's wife, but another to have her walk out of the house without a word of explanation, to go away and refuse to see him. Elizabeth had made Toogy write to tell Norman that she never intended to return to him.

'He has defeated me,' she said, 'not once, but a thousand times, and I cannot allow my body and my mind to be a battlefield any longer.'

Toogy had understood what she meant, but she doubted whether Norman would. She knew now that never in a hundred years could he have understood the gentle strength of the woman he had married.

There was a short silence. Toogy, looking back over the past, saw how easily the wounds had been given and received, how hard it was to say how they might have been avoided. Perhaps Norman was seeing or thinking the same thing. Again he stirred uneasily and then remarked in his gruff voice:

'Well, that's all over! Why have you come here now?'

It was so characteristic of him, Toogy thought, to come

to the point. He almost challenged her arrival even though she knew that he was glad to see her.

'I have come to tell you something, Norman,' Toogy said quietly. 'It concerns someone that I love very deeply.'

'Yes?'

'You know who it is, of course.'

'I have an idea, naturally,' Sir Norman replied. 'I understand that you are interested in this Fielding man.'

'Interested is hardly the right word, Norman. He is my adopted son. I brought him up and he has been to me exactly as if he had in fact been my own son. I only wish I had been privileged enough to bear him.'

'Well, he is making a fool of himself now, at any rate.'

'Do you think so?'

'Of course he is! Even you must see that, Susan. The young jackanapes! Telling us how to run our affairs abroad. He is getting repercussions in industry, and that is something I do know about.'

'Are you quite sure they are not the right sort of repercussions?'

'Now look here, Susan, I am not going to talk politics with you. If you are fond of this fellow—and of course you are if you have brought him up—you had better tell him to change his tune. If not, he will be made to do so, and pretty quickly too.'

'This all sounds very unlike you, Norman,' Toogy said softly.

'Unlike me? What do you mean?'

'When I knew you first you were a revolutionary. You were bringing forward new ideas that surprised all the people who were conventional, all the people who thought—and there were a great many in those days— that what was good enough for their fathers was good enough for them. I believe you had a great deal of opposition when you first started your car works.'

'Opposition!' Norman snarled. 'Of course I did! But

I was strong enough for them and I stood up against them. And still I have not done so badly.'

'I know you haven't, Norman; but why did you stand up against them, and why did you succeed? Can you tell me that?'

He looked at her from under his bushy eyebrows.

'What are you getting at?' he asked suspiciously.

'Well, if you won't answer that question I will do it for you. You believed in yourself; you believed that what you had to offer was the best for those who wanted a motor-car. You were progressive! You were a pioneer! You were not afraid! You did well and you succeeded because of those things. Well, Michael is just the same.'

'The case is not at all similar,' Sir Norman shouted.

'It is very similar, as a matter of fact,' Toogy answered. 'Michael believes that he has a plan, at present in its infancy, which is essential to Britain and, as such, essential to the world. He believes in it, Norman, just the same as you believed in your inventions. Because he believes in it there is no question of his ceasing to speak or for that fact of his failing.'

'But he will fail!'

'Are you so sure of that? Many people were sure that you would!'

'I have told you, Susan, there is no similarity between the two.'

Sir Norman got to his feet and walked across to the mantelpiece.

'I don't want to argue, Susan. I'm glad to see you, and I want us to be friends, but young Michael Fielding is wrong.'

'No, Norman, he isn't! You are old; I am old! We are finding it difficult to accept new ideas, and we are forgetting the fire of faith which drove us forward when we were young.'

'Stuff and nonsense,' Sir Norman said. 'We may be getting old, Susan, but we have got experience. That's what counts—experience and knowledge. I tell you that Fielding is on the wrong lines. We are having a meeting tonight. I am going to tell the Association what I think and I shall tell them plainly and bluntly. Politicians must not be allowed to interfere in business. West Winkley cannot afford to be represented by a man whose ideas do not coincide with ours.'

'With yours is what you mean.'

'All right, with mine. I am not ashamed of my opinions.'

'No? I am sure you are not, but at the same time it is all a pity . . . a terrible pity.'

Toogy spoke softly. Norman looked at her again.

'It is no use your coming here and trying to change my point of view. You are clever—I am not denying you that—and you have managed to get your own way where other people have failed, but not with me; no, not with me.'

'No . . . Norman?'

'Why do you say it so doubtfully?'

'I was just thinking of something.'

'Well, why don't you tell me?'

'I'm not quite certain how you will take it. It is going to be a shock to you.'

'A shock? What do you mean?'

'Come and sit down,' Toogy said softly.

Sir Norman would have spoken, but something in her voice made him cross over to the sofa and sit down.

'Listen to me,' Toogy began. 'When Elizabeth left you, she came to me.'

'Yes, I know she did.'

'She came to me for two reasons. First of all because she was too proud to go back to her family and admit that they were right—that her marriage to you had been a failure; and secondly, because she had a secret, and she knew I was the one person to keep it.'

'A secret? What was it?'

'That is what I am going to tell you. It was a secret, Norman, of such importance that I would never on my own responsibility have kept it from you. Elizabeth made me promise to keep this secret, made me swear by all that I held sacred that I would tell no one except in the direst necessity for at least twenty-one years. I have kept my promise, Norman, for twenty-six years.'

'Well, what of it?'

Sir Norman's tone was not only gruff, but there was an air of bewilderment about it, and perhaps, too, of apprehension. Toogy took a deep breath.

'When Elizabeth came to me, desperately unhappy, certain that whatever happened she would never return to you, she was going to have a baby.'

Toogy spoke the momentous words quietly, then she felt Norman stiffen beside her. There was a long silence; then at last, in a voice so weak, so faint, that it seemed to come from far away, he said:

'Did ... she ... have ... it?'

Toogy nodded.

'Yes, Norman, the baby was born seven months after she came to me. She had the best doctors and the best nurses; I saw to that. It was no one's fault that having the child should kill Elizabeth. Before she died she gave the child into my keeping, and she made me give her my solemn promise that I would reveal to no one whose child it was for at least twenty-one years. I was to bring him up; he was to be like my own son. I was to give him all the love and affection that would have been his had his mother lived.'

There was a silence in the room so tense, so poignant, that it seemed as if the old man on the sofa had turned to stone. At last he spoke and his voice was hoarse and broken.

'It was a boy,' he said, 'and he ... is ...'

'He was christened Michael Fielding,' Toogy said quietly.

185

12

Michael left the House with his own words echoing in his ears. He had finished his speech with the peroration:

'It is the closed mind we must battle against. And above all we must avoid the quack recipes that advertise shortcuts and quick results, false standards for men or nations, and the belief that we can find salvation and success through the efforts of others.'

He had spoken strongly and with utter sincerity straight from his heart. As he walked through the dark streets to his flat, he felt very humble; and yet the fire of his purpose was still burning fiercely within him.

As always when something unusual and important had occurred in his life, he wanted to see Toogy. He wanted to be with her. He wanted her attention so that he could pour out the fullness of his heart.

His car was standing outside the front door of the flats. He had told Bill to leave it there, being, when he went to the House, uncertain whether on his return home he would merely put it away in the garage or drive to Toogy's. He knew, now that he had in reality always meant to do the latter. His fears and doubts had come only from an inherent modesty and not from any fear of failure.

He went towards the car, and then as he did so some instinct made him take out his latch-key and open the front door. Why, he was not sure. He just had an urge to go upstairs to his flat and find out if there were any messages for him.

He passed from the small lobby into his sitting-room, where the high windows looked over the quiet square. Michael went into the room quickly, meaning to cross to the big mahogany desk to see what messages awaited him there.

Then something made him look towards the sofa drawn up near the fireplace and he saw to his astonishment that Mary lay there asleep. Her head was against the cushion and she had turned it in slumber; her feet were resting on a stool.

Michael stood looking down at her. She looked very pale and very young. There was something pathetic about her, he felt, something which reminded him vividly of her appearance that first night when he had rescued her from the river.

She was sleeping quietly so that her breathing hardly stirred the thin silk of her dress. One hand was flung out, a little open, the fingers wide and defenceless.

'Poor Mary!' He almost said the words aloud. He was sorry for her even while she irritated him by her adoration and by her intensity, of which he was uncomfortably aware whenever he encountered her.

He had been so busy the last few days that it had been easy to forget her, to let the problem which she presented to him sink out of sight. Nevertheless, he knew there was no escape. Something sooner or later had to be done about Mary. What, he didn't quite know.

He sighed and suddenly she awoke, moving a little restlessly and then opening her eyes wide to look up at him.

'Michael!' The way she said his name was almost a cry, and then she sat upright. 'I am sorry, I have been asleep.'

'You must have been tired,' Michael said, 'and you ought to have been home a long time ago.'

'How could I go home when I was so anxious?' Mary said. 'I wanted to hear what had happened. You wouldn't let me come to the House, so I waited here, and I suppose I fell asleep because you were so long.'

Michael looked at the clock on the mantelpiece.

'It's after twelve o'clock,' he said. 'Toogy will be wondering what has happened to you.'

Mary got to her feet, smoothing her hair as she did so. The colour had come into her cheeks and her eyes were shining so that she looked almost pretty.

'What happened, Michael?'

'I think it was a success,' Michael said quietly.

Toogy would have known that perversely he did not wish to speak of what had happened. He wanted to wait, wanted to tell it all in his own time. Not now, not with questions being forced upon him.

'But tell me, what did they say?' Mary asked.

'They were very kind to me,' Michael answered evasively, moving over to his desk.

'No letters?' he enquired.

'No! And, Michael, tell me ...'

He turned round and interrupted her.

'Listen, Mary, I am tired. I want to have a drink and then I am going to drive you home. We will talk as we go.'

She smiled at him happily.

'That will be lovely. What would you like to drink?'

'A whisky-and-soda, but a very mild one. I'll get it for myself.'

'No, let me,' Mary answered, going across the room to where the decanter and syphons were laid out on a tray just inside the door.

Michael stood watching her, unreasonably irritated, he told himself, that she should be so eager to do things for him. These little attentions were at times almost more than he could bear.

188

'How unkind I am!' he chided himself, yet he could not help it.

He never had been fussed over. Toogy had been too wise, with her knowledge of men and particularly of him, ever to be obtrusive in her attentions. The few other women he had known in his life had always made him wait on them. Mary's desire to please and the eager way in which she tried to help him was always an embarrassment when it was not an active irritation.

'Thank you,' he said when Mary brought him the tumbler.

'Is that how you like it?' she asked.

'It's quite all right, thank you.'

'I can easily put in some more soda if I haven't given you enough.'

'It's all right, Mary.'

'You're sure?'

'Quite sure!'

He would have turned back to his desk, but Mary was beside him, her hand on his arm.

'Oh, Michael, I am so thrilled about tonight. I was so sure you would succeed.'

'There is a great deal to be done yet.'

'I am sure of that, but you will do it wonderfully, as you always do.'

'Thank you, Mary.'

He turned away from the look in her eyes, but her hand was still on his arm.

'Michael!'

Michael suddenly drained his glass in one draught.

'Come on,' he said, and his voice was quite rough. 'It's time you were in bed. There is a lot of work to be done tomorrow and we both need our sleep.'

'Are you coming back here?' she asked.

'I don't know,' Michael said from the doorway. 'Put your coat on and hurry up.'

He opened the front door and ran downstairs. He got

into the car and started the engine. It was a moment or two before Mary came out. A street light shone on her fair hair, a thin coat covered her silk dress.

Michael fancied he saw a faint smile on her lips as she got into the car. Somehow it annoyed him, so he drove at high speed, turning down on to the Embankment and making no effort at conversation. Mary, however, did not seem to mind.

She moved a little closer to him, her hand lying listlessly in her lap as though tempting him to take it. Michael drove quicker, breaking all police regulations and yet surprisingly not being stopped by the few policemen they saw at this late hour. They had nearly reached Wharfside Road when Mary spoke.

'I am very happy tonight, Michael.'

'Good!'

Michael's reply was made in a hard and incurious tone.

'Are you happy?' she asked.

'I don't know,' Michael replied, feeling he must reply to the question and hating himself and Mary because he could not give her the answer she wanted. 'I suppose so. I am afraid I don't keep thinking about my feelings.'

'Oh, Michael, I wish you would.'

Her answer was very soft, but at that moment they drew up outside Toogy's building.

'Jump out,' Michael said, 'and I will put the car round the corner.'

There was an arrangement by which he could put the car into the warehouse yard. He ran it in and then walked slowly back. He was thankful to see that Mary had not waited for him, but had gone up the stone stairs. He followed her up them. Just as he reached the flat door she turned and smiled at him, the key in her hand. There was an invitation in her eyes, but once again he ignored it.

'Are you going to open the door?' he asked. 'Or am I?'

She inserted the key and turned it. The lights were on in the hall and Michael noticed, too, that the sitting-room door was also ajar. Some inner sense told him instantly that something was wrong. He threw his hat down on a chair, and, passing Mary, walked quickly towards the sitting-room. As he reached it the door on the other side of the hall opened and Cynthia came out of Toogy's bedroom.

'So you're here at last,' she said.

'At last?'

'You understood it was urgent?'

Michael looked at her in bewilderment.

'What do you mean?'

'You got my message?'

'What message?'

Cynthia looked at Mary.

'Didn't you tell him?'

'I . . . I . . .'

Mary's explanations were lost, but Michael had no time for them.

'What is the matter? Is it Toogy?'

Cynthia nodded. He went past her without a word and into Toogy's room. She was in bed and the doctor, whom Michael knew well and who was an old friend, was sitting by her bedside. He got up as Michael entered and came towards him.

'What is the matter?'

Michael was aware that his voice was trembling and he felt suddenly desperately afraid as a child might.

'I'm glad you have come,' Dr. Howard replied.

Michael looked at Toogy. Her eyes were closed and her face seemed almost as pale as the pillow on which her head lay.

'What is it?'

'A very slight stroke following a heart attack. She has had these attacks before, as you know.'

'I didn't know.'

'I thought perhaps she wouldn't tell you. She didn't want to worry you. And she has been doing too much, of course.'

Michael moved to the bedside and knelt down.

'Toogy!'

He had to speak to her. For a moment there was no response and he spoke again.

'Toogy! I am here!'

Very slowly her eyes opened. She looked at him and tried to smile, but it was too hard for her. Michael took her hand in his and held it to his lips.

'Toogy, my darling. It's all right, I'm here.'

She made no reply, but he knew what she was trying to ask him.

'Yes, darling, it was a success. They all supported me; everyone who had said he would. Big things will be happening tomorrow. There were whispers as I left that the Prime Minister had called a Cabinet meeting at ten o'clock.'

Toogy did not speak, but he knew that she understood. He saw the approval in her eyes and then she closed them as if the effort had been a tremendous one. Michael kissed her hand and rose to his feet.

He walked across to the window, where breeze was blowing the curtains to and fro. He looked out at the river and it was as if the darkness of the night was reflected in him. There was an agony within him such as he had never known in his life before.

He felt Dr. Howard's hand on his shoulder.

'Don't worry too much, Michael, old boy. She should be better tomorrow. It is not as serious as it might be, but she will have to go slow for some time.'

Michael was suddenly aware that his hands were gripping the window-sill and his knuckles were white with the effort.

'That this should happen to Toogy,' he whispered.

'Yes, I know,' Dr. Howard answered, 'and we are all going to feel it, every one of us; you perhaps more than any of us. She is a wonderful woman.'

'She has been everything to me.'

'Yes, I know.' Once again the doctor pressed the younger man's shoulder. 'Come outside,' he said quietly. 'She will sleep now, and I don't want to disturb her.'

He led the way from the room and they crossed the hall to the sitting-room. Cynthia and Mary were there, and by the expressions on the two women's faces it was obvious that they had been having words. The doctor spoke to Cynthia.

'Miss Toogy will go to sleep now. I am not very anxious about her, but I think it would be wise for someone to sit up with her.'

Cynthia nodded.

'I will do that, of course.'

'No, I will,' Michael remarked.

Cynthia shook her head.

'That wouldn't be at all practical. Sleep here and I will call you if you are wanted. The doctor seems quite satisfied with her, aren't you, Dr. Howard?'

'I think she will be all right now,' he replied, 'but I knew she wouldn't rest until she had seen you, Michael.'

Michael turned to Mary.

'Was there a message for me?'

'Y—yes.'

'What she means,' Cynthia said, 'is that I telephoned your flat and because I gave her the message she didn't want to give it to you.'

Michael looked at Cynthia.

'What did you say?'

'I asked that you should come here as soon as possible. I didn't say Miss Toogy was ill, because I thought it might be a shock. But I did say Miss Toogy wanted you.'

Michael turned to Mary.

'Why didn't you give me the message?'

'I forgot. I was waiting up for you myself because I wanted to hear about the Debate, and then, as you know, I fell asleep. Miss Standish didn't sound at all imperative. If she had been more explicit it would have been better.'

Mary spoke angrily, and Michael made a gesture of despair.

'I might not have come, and Toogy was ill.'

'Miss Standish didn't make that clear,' Mary repeated.

Cynthia said nothing, and for the first time Michael's eyes met hers in understanding. She had known that he would have come at once whatever he had been doing. The mere suggestion that Toogy wanted him was sufficient; there was no need to make it a command where Toogy was concerned.

Cynthia had known this. Mary had not understood and never could understand a relationship which need not be expressed in superlatives. Michael sighed, but said no more.

'You are certain that there is no more we can do for her?' he asked Dr. Howard.

'Nothing I can think of, Michael. But I will come first thing in the morning; and if I think there is any anxiety, may I call in a second opinion?'

'Of course!'

'Mind you, I believe that she is going to be much better, but this is a warning, and a warning which can't be ignored. Miss Toogy has been doing too much for years; she never spares herself.'

'I think it was the journey to Melchester last week which made her so terribly tired,' Cynthia said. 'The trains were overcrowded and coming back she was unable to get a seat; she had to stand in the corridor the whole way. Then when she reached Paddington Station there were no taxis, so she came here by Underground.'

'Melchester?' Michael said. 'When did she go to Melchester?'

'Last Friday,' Cynthia answered. 'Didn't she tell you?'

'No, she didn't mention it. What did she go for?'

Cynthia looked at him in surprise.

'I have no idea. I thought it was something to do with you and the Constituency.'

'It was the day of the meeting of my Association,' Michael said, 'and they gave me a full Vote of Confidence. I was astonished at the time . . . now I wonder.'

He spoke as if to himself, and there was a moment's silence. Dr. Howard picked up his bag.

'Well, I must be going. You have got my telephone number, Miss Standish?'

'Yes, Doctor.'

'Just watch her and if there is anything that worries you in the very slightest ring me up.'

'I will do that.'

'I think I can get a nurse to come in tomorrow night.'

'There's no reason for that; I would like to help.'

'You can't be on duty both day and night, but you have done entirely the right thing and I know I can trust you.'

He smiled at her and opened the door.

'Good night, Michael; don't worry too much. I am sorry this has happened tonight of all nights. I shall read all you have said in the morning papers, no doubt.'

He went from the room and left Michael looking at Cynthia.

'What happened?' he asked.

She told him briefly how Toogy had come home tired, but apparently quite well. She had supper as usual and had got up from her chair to turn on the wireless.

'I expect it's too early for them to mention Michael,'

she said to Cynthia, 'but still one never knows. We will listen, shall we?'

She walked across the room; then suddenly as she reached the wireless she tottered and fell.

'At first I thought she had only fainted,' Cynthia said. 'I got her on to the sofa and shouted to Agnes to bring me some smelling-salts. When she didn't come round, I began to get frightened. Agnes telephoned Dr. Howard, and when he came he confirmed what I had already begun to suspect: that she had had a stroke.'

Michael put his hands up to his eyes.

'I can't believe it of Toogy. She has always been so active, so busy, and now . . .'

'Her heart has been bad for some time apparently,' Cynthia went on in a quiet, calm voice, 'but she didn't want you to know. She knew you would worry, and I think, too, she thought you would ask her to do less for you.'

'If you knew, you ought to have told him,' Mary said.

They both started when she spoke. Somehow both Michael and Cynthia had forgotten her presence in the room.

'Well, don't you think she ought?' Mary enquired of Michael when Cynthia didn't answer. He made no reply, waiting for Cynthia.

Speaking quietly, almost reluctantly, she replied:

'I didn't think it would be right for me, a stranger, to interfere between you two.'

'I shouldn't have called that interference,' Mary said quickly; but Michael silenced her with a gesture of his hand.

'You are wrong, Mary! Let us leave it at that, shall we?'

He went to the window, his back to the room and the two women. Cynthia looked at him and there was both pity and understanding in the expression on her face.

She said nothing and after a moment she opened the door and went out.

Michael did not move and Mary stood looking at his back, hesitating what to do. She made up her mind, crossed the room and slipped her arm through his.

'I am so sorry for you; so terribly, terribly sorry.'

'Thank you, Mary.'

He did not move or look at her, and she felt that his muscles were taut.

'I know how much you love Miss Toogy,' Mary went on, 'and I know how fond she has always been of you. She has been wonderful to you, Michael, hasn't she? But you have been wonderful to her, and . . .'

Michael felt his control snap suddenly.

'Can't you be quiet? Must you always say the obvious?'

He shook his arm free of Mary's and walked abruptly away from her. There was a cigarette box on the small table by the fireplace. He opened it and took out a cigarette. Mary stood where he had left her, her eyes slowly filling with tears.

'Oh, Michael,' she said at last. 'Why must you be so unkind to me? I only try to help, but you don't want my help. I would like to look after Miss Toogy, but instead there is a stranger here—a girl who will only try to harm you—and yet she is allowed to do all the things I would love to do for your sake.'

'Please be quiet,' Michael said.

'No, I won't,' Mary replied. 'You treat me so badly; you have always treated me badly. I am supposed to be your secretary, but Bill is there doing all the attractive things, driving about with you, going where you go, being with you, while I have to sit at home and do the dull part, type until my fingers ache, and be pushed out of the way like an unwanted servant when it suits you.'

'You need not do it,' Michael said sharply.

'Oh no,' Mary replied, her voice rising. 'Oh no, I

needn't do it. But why do I? Because I love you; because you have made me love you, and because you kept me from dying when I wanted to.'

Mary was almost hysterical. The tears were running down her cheeks, her hands were clenched together convulsively.

'Oh, Mary, for God's sake!' Michael exclaimed, throwing the cigarette he had just lit into the empty fireplace.

'Michael! Oh, Michael!'

It was a cry of desperation and Mary held out her arms. As she moved towards him the door opened and Cynthia came in. She stood for a moment in the doorway and then coldly she said to Michael:

'I think Miss Toogy wants you. Could you come for a moment?'

Her words seemed to vibrate in the small room, seemed to break Michael's tension and the feeling of horror he had experienced on hearing Mary's cry. Without a word he turned towards the door and was conscious as he went that Mary had crumpled up and flung herself sobbing into an armchair.

He hurried across the hall. Toogy was lying very still, but her eyes were open. He knelt down beside the bed and then bent and kissed her.

'Darling,' he said, 'Cynthia thinks you want me.'

There was no answer but Michael knew instinctively that Toogy was striving to speak. It was a tremendous effort, and impulsively he said:

'Don't, darling, don't force yourself. Everything will be better tomorrow.'

But she would not relax. He waited. At last a word came.

'Letter! Letter ... for ... you.'

It was so unlike Toogy's voice, so thick and slow, almost inarticulate, that Michael could have cried when he heard it. Steadily he replied:

'Yes, darling, a letter. One you want me to have? Is that right?'

She nodded her head very faintly and then once again tried to speak. Her eyes moved and he understood that the letter was in the room.

'You put it somewhere for me? Is that right?' Michael asked, and again he knew that he was correct. 'Now where can you have put it? In the drawer? In your despatch case? In your desk?'

All the suggestions were wrong, and then somehow he found the right question:

'In your Bible?'

He had often as a little boy seen the big Bible which lay beside Toogy's bed. She nodded very faintly now and he opened it. At the back he found a letter. It was addressed *'For Michael. To be opened in the event of my death.'* He took it in his hand and then, as the full impact of her meaning swept over him, he bent forward until his eyes were hidden against her shoulder.

'Don't . . . say that . . . Toogy. Don't . . . you are not going to die, Howard says you will be better tomorrow Don't frighten me.'

It was the cry of a child who feels lost, the cry of a man who understands the full depth of the love which has been given him. Very, very faintly he could hear Toogy's heart beating, and after a moment he raised his head and said with a brave attempt at a smile:

'I shall put your letter in my pocket, but I shall be giving it back to you tomorrow. I am not going to have to open it for many, many years, you know that. I cannot do without you, Toogy! There is so much to be done; so many things, and I couldn't manage them alone.'

Again he tried to smile, fighting the tears in his eyes.

'You are frightening me, but I am not going to let myself be frightened. It is like you to have planned everything, to have tidied up all the ends. You have always been so practical, Toogy dear, but this time it is a case of

"Wolf, Wolf!" You are not going to die; I want you. I want you too much.'

It seemed to him as if she tried to reassure him, but there was something in her eyes which frightened him. They were such wise eyes which had known and seen so much. They had known so many things by instinct. No one without a super-normal intelligence could have done all Toogy had done in her life for other people.

'Toogy! Toogy, my very dear!'

Again it was a cry of fear, and there were tears on Michael's cheeks as he bent forward to kiss her.

It was nearly an hour later when he came from the room. Cynthia was waiting for him outside.

'Is she all right?' she asked.

He nodded. Somehow he felt as if he could not speak. For the past hour he had said so many things. He had talked to Toogy, who could not talk to him, but who he knew could understand. He had had a sense of urgency upon him, a feeling that if he did not speak now he would be too late. When he started to speak he had been driven by fear—fear of what he might learn in silence, fear of the loneliness which seemed to be closing in upon him in the shadows.

Then gradually the peace and understanding which always came to him when he was alone with Toogy swept away his fears and he became conscious only of love, his love for her and her love for him; of the happiness and of the perfect moments which had been his since he was a child.

All his memories seemed to be resurrected at that moment and crystallised into speech so that he must tell her all she had meant to him.

So Michael had talked, but at the same time he had felt there was really no need for words. Toogy, who had understood so much all her life, would understand one thing more—his unchanging need of her.

But he had gone on talking, whispering to her, recalling reminiscences of the past, anticipating what the future would bring. And then at last the brightness in her eyes was dimmed, her eyelids dropped in slumber and he knew she was asleep.

For the first time he was conscious of his cramped position and the weariness of his shoulders, which were twisted. He rose to his feet and saw that he still held the letter he had taken from the Bible. He thrust it deep into his pocket.

'Tomorrow,' he said to himself, 'I will put it back where it belongs.'

But he had known then as clearly and as if someone had said the words out loud that he would not do so.

With cramping pains in his legs Michael turned towards the door, shutting it very quietly in case Toogy should be wakened. In the sitting-room he poured himself out a drink. Cynthia was sitting in an armchair and instinctively she sensed his discomfiture as he looked around for Mary.

'I have sent her to bed. She was tired and upset.'

'Oh, quite right,' Michael approved. 'She gets so worked up.'

His thoughts were still with Toogy. And then suddenly, though Cynthia said nothing, he was aware of what she was thinking. Hadn't he told her once that David would not have fallen in love with her without encouragement? Embarrassed, he said quickly:

'Won't you have a drink?'

'No, thank you. I have had some coffee to keep me awake and now I am going to Miss Toogy.'

He turned now to look at her and saw for the first time that she was dressed comfortably in a long warm dressing-gown with wide sleeves, not unlike a monk's robe.

'You will be all right?' he asked. 'Can I carry anything into Toogy's room for you to rest on?'

Cynthia shook her head.

'I will sit in the armchair. I don't want to be too comfortable or I might go to sleep.'

'Perhaps it would be better if I stayed up with her?' Michael suggested.

'No, of course it wouldn't,' Cynthia replied. 'The doctor has given me all instructions, and besides you have got to get some sleep. There is a lot for you to do tomorrow.'

'How do you know? I mean . . .'

'Miss Toogy told me what you were going to say,' Cynthia answered. 'You were a success?'

It was not a moment for prevarications, so Michael nodded.

'Good, that will please her. She believes in you.'

'I know that.'

'That is why you must never fail her; never, whatever happens.'

'What do you mean?' Michael said sharply.

But he knew only too well what Cynthia meant. She was voicing his own fears, voicing what was more than his own fears—an inner conviction which would not be denied. It seemed to him at that moment that everything was out of focus and a little strange. Cynthia was looking at him.

There was only one light on in the sitting-room, but he could see the expression in her eyes. There were dark shadows in the corners of the room; the curtains were drawn back and the night was dark through the open windows. They stood alone in a little oasis of light—he and Cynthia—the woman he hated.

She stood very still, and though he tried to be hostile to her the hostility had gone. Toogy liked her; Toogy trusted her; Toogy indeed was in her care. It was all beyond his understanding, and suddenly Michael threw out his hand in a gesture of appeal, a gesture such as a drowning man might make in hope of rescue.

'Tell me, Cynthia,' he said, 'she isn't going to die, is she?'

There was a moment's silence and then Cynthia's answer was surprising:

'We can always pray, Michael,' she said quietly, and the door closed behind her.

Her words were with him as he went to his own room. He undressed and as he got into bed he found himself repeating, 'We can always pray.' Somehow these were the last words he had expected to hear on Cynthia Standish's lips, and yet somehow they did not seem incongruous.

'I won't sleep,' he told himself, 'I shall lie awake in case they want me.'

But actually he fell asleep as soon as his head touched the pillow, and he did not awake until his curtains were drawn back with a clatter and he opened his eyes to see that Agnes was in the room. For a moment he was drowsy and then quickly the events of the night before came crowding in upon him. He sat up in bed.

'How is she, Agnes?'

'Miss Cynthia says she has not moved all night,' Agnes replied.

She spoke in a voice blurred and very unlike her usual sharp tones, and Michael, looking at her, saw that her eyes were red and puffy obviously with recent tears.

'Is the doctor here yet?' he asked.

'No,' Agnes replied, 'but he won't be long. He's never late when he says he will come.'

She went out of the room and Michael jumped out of bed. He put on his dressing-gown and slippers—everything he needed for the night was duplicated here and in his own flat—then he crossed to the dressing-table and brushed his hair.

A second later he was at Toogy's door. He tapped very softly and turned the handle. The curtains were partially drawn, and the pale sunshine was coming into the room. Cynthia, already dressed, he noted, was sitting by the bed. She was looking down at Toogy and her fingers were on her pulse. She saw Michael as she got to her feet and walked across the room. She did not speak but touched his arm. He followed her from the room.

In the hall she looked up at him with wide eyes.

'Michael, I'm frightened. She hasn't moved all night and her pulse is very, very faint.'

'Have you telephoned the doctor?' Michael asked.

'Yes, I rang his house twenty minutes ago and they said he was on his way here.'

'Why didn't you fetch me?'

'What can you do? What can any of us do? I may be unnecessarily alarmed. I thought she was asleep and then just now it struck me how still . . . how very still she is.'

Cynthia's voice quivered, and without thinking Michael touched her arm reassuringly and then went back into Toogy's room. Cynthia was right. Toogy was lying very still indeed.

It was hard to know if she was breathing at all. He sat down beside her and took her hand in his. It was cold, but there was just a faint warmth about it. Cynthia did not come into the room and Michael guessed she was waiting in the hall for the doctor.

He sat looking down at Toogy. Last night he had talked to her, now he had no words. He looked at the sharply etched nose, the broad brow, the deep-set eyes under their straight eyebrows.

Toogy's face was wrinkled, and yet he wondered if she had ever been more beautiful. She wore her wrinkles as proudly as any man might wear his decorations won in battle.

All through her life Toogy had fought, had battled against injustices, privations, misery and dirt; all through her life she had been a Crusader, and where other women had enjoyed soft and easy existences hers had been hard,

204

an uphill fight all the way. And yet neither she nor any-one else would have had it different.

Perhaps sometimes she had longed for a husband and children of her own. Once again the easy road was not for her. Instead she had Michael and the thousands of children who had passed through her clinic and the day nursery, and who owed her either consciously or uncon-sciously a debt of gratitude all through their lives.

How many people had she made happy? How many people had she saved from misery? It was a question nobody could answer, and yet somehow and somewhere such things are recorded.

'How wonderful she is!' Michael thought, and even as he thought it Toogy's fingers tightened on his. His heart gave a little bound of relief as he felt the pressure of her fingers. At the same moment he heard the front-door bell ring and steps crossing the hall to answer it.

'It's the doctor,' he thought as Toogy's eyes opened. She looked up at him and her lips moved.

'Michael, my darling!'

He sensed rather than heard the words, and then when he would have spoken, the sudden glory in her eyes ar-rested him. He could only stare at her.

She had been looking at him, but now she was looking past him. The sunlight in the room seemed reflected in Toogy's expression. There was a wonder of a joy too ecstatic to be expressed; then her eyes closed and her fingers dropped from Michael's.

He heard the door open behind him. He did not move, but a voice which he hardly recognised as his own vibrated through the room:

'Toogy is dead!' he said.

13

Sitting in the car in a small *cul-de-sac* off the City Hall of Melchester, Bill Evans gave up trying to read in the gathering dusk and lit a cigarette.

Michael was attending a meeting and he had anticipated a wait of about two hours, but now the time was past and he began to wish that he had gone inside to listen as Michael had suggested rather than remain in the car. At the same time he always dreaded large crowds and had moments of feeling suffocated and breathless, especially at mass meetings.

As he smoked Bill found his mind going back over the events of the past weeks. So much had happened since Miss Toogy's death and even now the thought of her renewed the quick pain of loss.

Bill had known her only a short time, yet he had loved her whole-heartedly. She had meant so much to him, not only in her understanding and in her sympathy, but also in the fact that she gave him some inner strength and courage, even as Michael did, to go on trying.

The great crowds which attended Miss Toogy's funeral had been no surprise to Bill. They had indeed astonished many people, including the writers to the national Press, but Bill had understood where the secret of Miss Toogy's power lay.

It was not what she gave people through her welfare services, but what she ignited within themselves—a flame which, once lit, burned steadily and steadfastly.

Both she and Michael inspired people, not always to do great things, but at least to live up to the best that was in themselves. Bill had heard so many people speak of Miss Toogy after her death and all had said the same thing.

All expressed in different phrases the burning impulse Miss Toogy had awakened in each of them to do better, to reach a higher standard, to be, as one girl put it, 'good for a change'. But it was impossible for most people to put into words what they felt at losing Miss Toogy, and Bill was no exception. He had only been able to say brokenly to Michael:

'I shall never be able to forget her. She did so much for me.'

But he knew that Michael had understood and he realised, too, that Michael could only express his own feelings in much the same words.

It had been impossible at first for those who had lived so close to her to believe that Miss Toogy was dead. It had always been difficult to remember that she was getting old; she did so much.

Yet now she had gone and a sense of dismay seized those who remained behind when they realised the emptiness without her.

Fortunately much that had been a part of Miss Toogy remained. The day nursery was filled with children, the clinic with expectant and young mothers. Miss Smithers was grimly determined that nothing should be altered if she could help it and Cynthia Standish had taken on many of Miss Toogy's jobs, slipping into her place unobtrusively yet nevertheless inevitably when the occasion arose.

Bill knew, though Michael did not, that people still flocked to 253 Wharfside Road. There were old women in search of comfort for their souls or material benefits for their bodies; there were young women in difficulties with their husbands or sweethearts; men in search of a job; children who needed homes.

They had grown used to their pilgrimage up the long stone stairs to the flat at the top, and though there was no Miss Toogy to receive them now, there was Cynthia, whom she had liked and whom they understood she had chosen to take her place.

The word had gone round, travelling as swiftly as news travels in an Eastern bazaar, that Miss Standish had been chosen by Miss Toogy to carry on. There was nothing official about it, but they accepted Cynthia.

And only Bill guessed, when he came to the flat with messages or to fetch Michael's correspondence, what a strain it was on her. Once Cynthia asked his advice about an ex-serviceman.

'What am I to do, Bill?' she questioned, and he had known it was a cry for help.

'Shall I see the chap?' he asked.

'I wish you would,' she replied, and smiled at him gratefully. 'His tale sounds feasible enough, but still I am not quite certain about him. If what he says is right, we must get his local Member of Parliament to take his case up; but'—Cynthia hesitated a moment—'but I don't want to make a mistake.'

Bill had understood.

'I will see to it for you.'

Cynthia pushed back her hair from her forehead.

'That's very kind of you, Bill. There is so much to do and it has all come so quickly.'

He knew she was referring to Miss Toogy's death and impulsively he said:

'You are doing marvellously; no one could expect more.'

He had been surprised that he had not felt presumptuous when he said it. He had always felt rather afraid of Cynthia, but now her smile was grateful and friendly.

'I wish I could believe you,' she said.

'You are doing fine,' he asserted stoutly.

He had spoken entirely sincerely and Agnes had confirmed his judgment. As she showed him to the door, she had asked, with her little peaked face looking up at his:

'How is Mr. Michael?'

'Frightfully busy,' Bill answered. 'And it is a good thing; I was a bit worried about him at first. . . . I was afraid he would take it hard.'

Agnes had nodded.

'Of course, we all did.'

'But he is putting his heart and soul into his work,' Bill went on. 'He asks if you are all right, but somehow I don't think he wants to come back here . . . not yet at any rate.'

'Well, we're O.K.,' Agnes said sharply. 'We're getting along, and not too badly if it comes to that. Nothing will ever be the same, of course; but she'd have been the first to say we'd got to "carry on".'

It was an unusual speech for Agnes, and Bill could only mutter:

'You've got something there!'

Yes, Miss Toogy would have wanted them to carry on just as Cynthia was doing!

Bill's cigarette was finished and he chucked the stub out into the road. As he did so he saw someone come out of a side door of the building, hesitate, then walk towards the car. Although it was too dark to see her face at that distance, Bill recognised Mary's slim figure. He jumped out of the driving seat and went forward to meet her. She saw him and waved her hand.

'Michael will be another half-hour at least,' she announced, as soon as she was within earshot. 'He has spoken, but there are two Councillors to speak yet and there is a whole crowd of people wanting to ask questions. It was so hot in there that I couldn't stand it any longer, so I slipped away.'

'I don't blame you,' Bill said.

He opened the back door of the car, but Mary shook her head.

'No, I will sit beside you,' she said. 'I feel I want to talk to someone.'

'That suits me,' Bill answered.

He helped her in, shut the door and walked round to his own side of the car.

'Will you smoke?' he asked, offering her a packet from his pocket.

Mary shook her head.

'No, thanks, I don't really like it, and it gives me a headache when I'm tired.'

'And you are tired tonight?'

'Yes, I get fed up with these everlasting meetings. It is all right when Michael speaks, but the rest of them . . . Really, some of these men oughtn't to be allowed to get on a platform. It's cruelty to an audience.'

'I chose the better part when I preferred to sit out here,' Bill smiled, 'but I would like to have heard Michael. I can never hear him too often.'

'Nor can I,' Mary agreed.

There was a little throb in her voice, followed by a sudden silence, then quite suddenly she remarked:

'Oh, Bill, I'm so miserable.'

'Poor Mary! But why?'

He knew the answer, but still he thought it best to ask the question.

'Because I'm a fool,' Mary replied. 'A fool who has fallen in love with a man who doesn't love me. I'm not telling you anything you don't know already, am I, Bill? How could you be with us all these months and not know what I'm feeling?'

'I'm sorry,' Bill said simply.

'What's the point of being sorry?' Mary said miserably. 'I am sorry enough for myself, but I don't know what to do. You see, since Miss Toogy died Michael has hardly spoken to me.'

'He has not said much to any of us, has he?' Bill asked.

'That's true,' Mary answered. 'He has just worked and worked.'

'It was a frightful shock to him,' Bill said. 'He adored her.'

'Yes, I know; but I adore him, and where is it getting me?'

Bill was still for a moment, then he squared his shoulders and took a deep breath.

'Would you like me to talk to you frankly, Mary?'

She turned her head to look at him. In the dim light from the dashboard she could see the expression on his face.

'Yes, why shouldn't you?' she enquired.

'You might be angry with me,' Bill answered. 'You used to dislike me a lot.'

Mary smiled, a faint, rather quivering smile.

'I know, I was jealous of you. But I have got over that now, and you have been jolly decent to me, Bill. That's why I want to talk to you. There's nobody else I can talk to. When I go back to the flat at night I feel unwanted, out of place. Cynthia Standish doesn't like me, nor does Agnes. I want to get somewhere else to live—that is if I still go on working for Michael.'

'Don't you want to go on working for him?'

'Yes, in a way, and yet what is the good? It is agony to be with someone you love but who just treats you like a machine. That is all I am to Michael—just a machine.'

Her voice broke on a sob. To her surprise Bill reached out his hands and put them on her shoulders. He turned her round in her seat to face him, then he looked at her for a long moment.

'Answer me one question, Mary. What do you really want of Michael?'

'Want? I want him to love me.'

'And you expect him to marry you?'

'To marry me?' Mary echoed. 'Oh, I don't know. I hadn't thought of that.'

'Yes, you had,' Bill said grimly. 'And can't you see, can't you be honest enough with yourself to realise, it is asking too much?'

'Why is it?'

She stirred uneasily beneath his hands.

'Because Michael is far too big a person for you. Face it, Mary; don't kid yourself over this. He is too important for that. You are a sweet person, and some man would love you an awful lot; but not Michael, you are not strong enough for him.'

'Strong . . . enough? What does he want strength for?'

'Not the strength you are thinking of,' Bill answered, 'not muscle or anything to do with the physical body, but more the kind of strength Miss Toogy had. But never mind about that, we are talking about you. You want someone to look after you.'

'Well, why shouldn't Michael do that?'

'Because he would never have the time, and so the person Michael has got to marry must give as much as . . . no, more than she takes. You couldn't do that, Mary, you haven't got it in you.'

Mary shook herself free of Bill's hands.

'You are not very complimentary, I must say.'

'I was not trying to be complimentary at the moment; I was trying to show you that you are not the right person for Michael. There are other people for whom you would be the right person—a man who would love you and who would want to look after you and protect you if only from yourself.'

'Well, if there is such a man, I haven't met him,' Mary said sharply.

'Haven't you? Are you so certain of that?'

There was something in Bill's voice which surprised her. She had been staring ahead of her through the windscreen; now she turned to look at him.

'What do you mean by that?'

He put out his hand and touched hers as it lay on her knee.

'I am not very good at expressing myself, Mary.'

'What . . . are you trying to say?'

Bill took a deep breath.

'Oh, Mary, can't you . . . try and understand?'

Her eyes widened as gradually his meaning dawned upon her. Then, as she was still silent, his arm groped its way across the back of her seat and drew her close.

'You are so sweet and so pathetic, Mary,' he whispered, but still she did not speak.

He put his cheek against hers. After a moment, when she did not repulse him, he said quietly:

'It's cold comfort loving someone who doesn't want you. Let me try and teach you to love me, Mary. I'm not much of a catch and I haven't got any money, but I would work for you. You are such a little creature, I want to take you in my arms and hold you there. I want to kiss the unhappiness away from your eyes.'

Still Mary said nothing, and very, very gently and tenderly Bill's lips touched her cheek. He kissed her once and then again before he found her mouth. It was a kiss with no passion in it and her lips did not respond to his. Nevertheless he was encouraged and as her head fell back against his shoulder he kissed her again.

'When we were out in the East I used to dream of holding a girl in my arms,' he said. 'We all talked of love out there, and we all believed that when we came home someone lovely would be waiting for us. It has taken me many years to find you, Mary, but now you are here, close in my arms. . . . Oh, my dear, I cannot tell you how wonderful it is.'

His voice deepened and he held her a little closer, and now at last Mary spoke, her voice low and hesitant.

'I . . . don't . . . understand, Bill. I never thought you felt like this about me.'

213

'At first I was sorry for you,' Bill answered; 'and yet from the first moment I saw you I wanted somehow to take care of you. You looked too pale and frail to be earning your own living, to be grappling with Michael's vast affairs; and then gradually I found myself beginning to count the hours until I could see you again. Just to look at you, just to see your sweet little face, was heaven enough.'

'Oh, Bill, and I never knew!'

'How could I tell you? I knew you loved Michael.'

'I still love him,' Mary said quickly.

'Of course you do,' Bill answered. 'I understand that; I am not asking anything of you yet. Only remember I'm here and you need never be lonely again. You must never feel that nobody wants you.'

'Oh, Bill!'

Instinctively she cuddled a little closer towards him and again he sought her lips. This time there was a faint response and tenderly he kissed her eyes.

'You are so sweet, Mary,' he whispered. 'Oh, darling Mary, you are so sweet.'

His mouth was against her cheek, and bending his head he kissed the pulse beating in her throat. Now she stirred and her hands fluttered a little, but still she did not draw away from him. His breath was coming quickly now, and looking down into her face he saw that her lips were parted.

'Oh, Mary,' he breathed. 'Do you ever think that you might . . . ?'

She gave a little sigh as if she awoke from a dream.

'Perhaps, Bill . . . perhaps one day.'

Her answer was scarcely above a whisper and she felt the tremor which shook him all over. Then he held her closer to him, so close that she felt she could hardly breathe. Once again his lips were on hers, but this time they were possessive, demanding, and she felt a flutter of excitement within her, her pulses racing. Instinctively she put up her hands to ward him off.

'No, Bill, no.'

Instantly he released her and she moved away from him, her eyes wide, her breath coming quickly.

'Oh, Bill!'

Her tone was not really reproachful, but he apologised.

'I'm sorry, Mary. I love you and you're so utterly desirable.'

He took both her hands in his and raised them to his lips. He kissed her fingers and then turning them over kissed the palms long and lingeringly. He felt them tremble beneath his touch and when he raised his head her eyes were shining. He bent forward impulsively, but what he would have said Mary never knew.

At that moment Michael, accompanied by another man came striding down the street.

'Ah, here's my car,' they heard him say. 'Good night, Major Whitlock, and thank you for a splendid meeting.'

'I expected great things from this evening,' the other man answered. 'By the way, Sir Norman Baltis said that he would like to take the Chair next Friday.'

For a moment Michael was very still and then he answered:

'Is that . . . er . . . necessary?'

'Necessary?' Major Whitlock asked. 'It is an excellent idea, and one which came from Sir Norman himself. After all, the majority of people present will be from the Baltis works.'

'Yes, I see.'

Michael's voice was still vaguely perturbed.

Major Whitlock laughed.

'I wish I knew—but I suppose you will never tell me —how you managed to convert Sir Norman overnight, as it were. From being openly opposed to you he is now one of your most ardent supporters. If you will forgive my saying so, as far as we are concerned it was an amazing achievement.'

Michael said nothing and there was something in his silence which made the Major feel embarrassed. Quickly he held out his hand. 'Well, good night and good luck.'

'Thank you.'

Michael got into the car.

'Are you all right, Mary?' he asked. 'I saw you slip away and thought it very wise of you.'

'Yes, I'm all right, thank you, Michael.'

There was something new and tremulous in her voice as though she could hardly bring herself to answer him conventionally.

'Well, home, Bill,' Michael said. 'Goodness, I am tired!'

'I'm not surprised,' Bill replied. 'But I'm glad to hear it was a good meeting.'

'First rate!'

Michael leant back against the cushioned seat and closed his eyes. The car started and no one spoke again until they reached the house.

'You will take Mary on to her lodgings, won't you, Bill?' Michael asked. 'I wish you could stay here, Mary, but I suppose we must observe the conventions.'

'Of course,' Mary replied, 'and I am very comfortable as it happens.'

'I am glad,' Michael said. 'See you in the morning.'

'I'll be round at nine o'clock. Good night.'

'Good night. Are you staying here, Bill, or at home?'

'At home; my father wanted to see me.'

'I understand. Good night, then, and thank you for waiting so long.'

'Good night, Michael.'

The car drove off and Michael inserted the key in the door. There was a light burning in the hall and he saw that on the table there was a pile of letters for him. He picked them up and took them into the dining-room. There were some sandwiches laid out ready for him and a bottle of beer.

He ate absent-mindedly as he opened his letters, sorting them into piles—those which he must answer personally and those which could be given to Mary in the morning. Many of them were still letters of condolence and he read them hastily, almost as if he were afraid to let their meaning sink too deeply into his consciousness for fear that it would wound him too severely.

At last the letters were finished and so were the sandwiches. He got up and went into the sitting-room. Everything in the room was just the same as when Toogy had arranged it when they first came to Melchester; even her work-basket was on a stool beside her favourite chair. He stood looking down at it, his face shadowed, his eyes great pools of pain. Suddenly he flung back his head.

'Oh, Toogy, you are with me still, aren't you?' he asked.

His voice vibrated in the room, disturbing the silence and seeming to Michael to echo and re-echo within the narrow confines of its four walls. Then there was silence; a silence in which he held his breath, in which he waited, though he was not certain for what. Suddenly he knew.

Toogy was there, her presence and her personality were warmly, closely with him. She was beside him as she had always been, her love just as strong to help him as it had been in the past. Michael put up his hands to his eyes and when he took them away again the expression on his face had altered.

'I knew it,' he said aloud. 'I knew you could never die.'

He was whistling as he went up to bed, and he slept calmly and dreamlessly as an exhausted child. He was awakened by Mrs. Gubbins banging about in the kitchen below him; and when she brought him an early-morning cup of tea and the newspapers, he was sitting up in bed writing letters.

'You're early, sir,' Mrs. Gubbins remarked.

'It's a lovely morning,' Michael replied, 'and I have

got the dickens of a lot to do.'

'Well, it seems to suit you, I must say,' Mrs. Gubbins remarked. 'Can you manage two eggs for your breakfast?'

'Yes, and some bacon if you have got it,' Michael answered.

Mrs. Gubbins put down his cup of tea with a clatter which spilt some of it into the saucer.

'There, I do like to see a young man with an appetite. I can't understand those la-di-da young fellows who can't eat a decent breakfast. They'll be no use at anything, that's what I say to them, neither at work nor play, and there's many a woman as will bear me out in what I says.'

'Get along with you, Mrs. Gubbins, you are putting ideas into my head early in the morning,' Michael ordered.

She chuckled with laughter and went downstairs to get his breakfast.

A moment or so later he heard the postman's knock and the clatter of the letter-box. He got up, put on his dressing-gown and went downstairs to collect the mail. There was the usual pile of correspondence and he turned the envelopes idly over, thinking he would leave most of them until after breakfast, when one big grey envelope addressed in spidery writing caught his attention. He frowned and opened it. He knew who it was from before he saw the heading on the notepaper. The letter began:

'My dear Fielding,

'I understand from your secretary that you are free tomorrow, Tuesday, evening. I think it is time that we had a talk. Will you therefore come to Claverley at seven o'clock and stay for dinner?

'Yours,
'Norman Baltis.'

Michael stood staring at the letter. The moment had come then which he had been dreading, the moment when he must talk with Sir Norman and acknowledge him as his father.

When he read the letter which Toogy had given him before she died, he could hardly believe its contents. He read it and re-read it again and again before he could be certain that he had not been mistaken and that his eyes had not deceived him.

She had written clearly and frankly, as might be expected of her. It was all characteristic of her, too, that she should expect Michael to approve of all that she had done.

'I saw no reason to tell you this before. When you were a little boy I planned to tell you about your parents when you were twenty-one, but the war came and your twenty-first birthday was spent in the East and there was every chance then that you would die without ever knowing your father's identity. It didn't seem to me to matter very much. We had managed so long without him and there was no doubt at all that he made your mother very unhappy. Then to my astonishment, when you came home, you were drawn almost like a magnet to Melchester.

'Life is a queer thing, Michael, and what we call coincidence is in my opinion inevitably the workings of fate. You belonged to Melchester and Melchester wanted you. It was inevitable in its own way, and it was fate, too, that the one person who should make things difficult for you was your own father. I knew then that the time had come when I must speak, when I must tell him the truth. I went down to see him. It is difficult to put into words what happened at that interview. I can only tell you that I was sorry that I had kept your secret so long; and if ever a man was punished for his sins in the past, your father has been.

'*He wanted a child, longed for a son more than for anything else in the whole world, and although he had one, he has never known him. It was his suggestion that you should not be told at once, but that he should wait until my death. There was a delicacy and an understanding in this which I want you to appreciate. Who knows when I will die?—perhaps it will come to me quickly; perhaps it will be many years—but I want to record Norman's decency in this matter because I am ashamed to say that I did not expect it of him.*'

There was very little else in the letter; words of love and encouragement, words of love which any mother might write to a son whom she adored.

Sir Norman could not have anticipated for one moment that Toogy would die so quickly. As she had said, Michael thought, it was decent of him to leave Toogy her adopted son for her lifetime.

It must have been a hard decision for him to make, as he had wanted a son of his own so much and would doubtless want to acknowledge him.

But for Michael it was all most uncomfortable and he had an impulse to avoid the meeting at all costs, to go back to London; to put off the evil hour until a more opportunt moment.

Then, even as he contemplated flight, he felt that Toogy was laughing at him. She would call him a coward, wouldn't she? Besides, what was there to fear? Was he, Michael Fielding, afraid of one frail old man whose life was nearly finished? Yes, Toogy was laughing at him. He thrust the letter into his pocket and threw the others down on the hall table.

'All right,' he told Toogy in his heart, 'I will go, but you will jolly well help me over this. I feel as shy as any schoolboy.'

When he dictated his letters that morning Michael noticed that there was a change in Mary. She seemed more alert and she looked prettier than she had for some time. He had grown used to her miserable expression, her turned-down mouth, her dark reproachful eyes, which seemed to follow him round like those of a whipped dog.

This morning she was smiling and more than once she chuckled when some point in his letters amused her. He was half afraid to comment in case any personal remark invited a repetition of the scenes which he dreaded. But when his letters were finished, Michael said:

'You seem in good spirits, Mary.'

'I am. Perhaps the Melchester air agrees with me.'

She smiled, and somehow he had the impression that she had no desire to discuss herself further. Instead she opened the engagement book.

'You are lunching in the City,' she said. 'You have a meeting with the Governors at five o'clock. Sir Norman Baltis telephoned yesterday and asked if you would dine at Claverley tonight. He said he would write.'

'Yes, he has. Will you telephone him and say I will be there at seven o'clock?'

'Yes, is there anything else?'

'Nothing I can think of at the moment. You will be here all day, I suppose?'

'Yes,' Mary answered. 'You can telephone if you want anything.'

'Thank you, Mary.'

He wished he knew what it was which was making her so different, but he dared not show his curiosity. Instead he went out of the house to the car, where Bill was waiting for him. Mary smiled to herself as she watched the car drive away; then she started to type her letters.

It was not long before she was interrupted by the telephone. Three or four local calls came through and then there was one from London.

'Hold on,' the operator said. There was a click and Mary heard Cynthia's voice.

'Hullo, is that you, Mary? Is Michael there? I wanted to speak to him.'

'No, I'm afraid he isn't. Can I help you?'

'No, I don't think so. When will he be coming back from Melchester?'

'I don't exactly know. Not until next Monday at the very earliest.'

'Oh, bother! I hoped he would be coming back today.'

'Oh no; as a matter of fact he is dining with your god-father tonight.'

'With Uncle Norman? Whatever for?'

Mary sensed a criticism in Cynthia's voice and bridled instantly.

'As a matter of fact I think Sir Norman wants to have a quiet, personal talk with him. He is a great supporter of Michael in these days, you know.'

'I didn't know. Surely that is very surprising?'

'Oh, not really. Michael converts people so easily that Sir Norman is only one of many.'

'But he was fanatically against Michael.'

'Only for a very short time. Now he is fanatically for him. It is the way these things go.'

Mary spoke in a superior manner, delighted for once to be able to put Cynthia in her place.

'I can't understand it,' Cynthia said.

'You must get Michael to tell you all about it,' Mary suggested, and added: 'Is there anything more? We are terribly busy this morning.'

'No, nothing, thank you,' Cynthia answered.

Mary put down the receiver. It was no use, she told herself, she didn't like Cynthia and would never like her. It was gratifying to know that Michael did not like her either and that apparently she knew very little about his affairs.

'Bill and I can look after him,' Mary said aloud, and somehow coupling herself with Bill gave her an inner glow of satisfaction. He was kind and nice and it was very pleasant to have someone about who thought one was wonderful.

She thought of his kisses last night and the way he had held her close for one long passionate moment when they reached her lodgings.

'I love you, Mary,' he had said. 'This is the most wonderful night of my life.'

She surrendered herself to him for a moment, but when she moved within his arms she was immediately free. There was something a little heady in the knowledge that she was loved.

'Good night, dear Bill,' she said, 'and thank you.'

'It is I who should thank you,' Bill answered.

She kissed him again and then, half afraid of his response, had opened the door of her lodging and stood inside listening to his footsteps going away. She heard the car drive off and only then had she realised that her heart was behaving in a most curious way.

'What does it mean?' she asked herself. She couldn't be in love with Michael and Bill. Was she in love with love? She didn't know; she only knew that she was no longer alone or lonely.

All through the morning as she was working Mary found her thoughts slipping away to the night before. The more she tried to question herself about her own feelings, the more unreal it all seemed. And yet she was happy!

Spring was blooming within her heart where it had been Winter before. At one o'clock, just as she was going to her luncheon, the telephone rang. She lifted it up impatiently.

'Hullo!'

'Mary!'

It was Bill's voice at the other end.

'Oh, Bill!'

'I had to ask you how you were.'

'Where are you speaking from?'

'From a call-box. I have just dropped Michael at his banquet and now I am off to get a bun and a cup of tea myself.'

'Oh, Bill, eat a proper lunch. It's bad for you not to eat properly.'

'Do you mind if it's bad for me?'

'You know I do! I want you to get well.'

'I am well. I am better than I have ever been in my life before. Mary, did you mean what you said last night?'

'What did I say?'

'You said "perhaps". It's the most wonderful word I have ever heard in my life.'

'Oh, Bill! What things you say!'

'Not half the things I'm going to say, if you will only listen.'

Mary laughed.

'What are you laughing at?'

'Us! Not unkindly, but because it's rather exciting.'

'Oh, Mary, I love you so.'

The operator's voice interrupted them.

'Your time's up. Another fourpence, please.'

'I am afraid I haven't got it,' Bill said. 'Good-bye, Mary, see you this evening.'

'Good-bye, Bill.'

They were cut off. Mary sat for a long time, staring out of the open window, her lips parted, her eyes shining.

14

Michael looked at Claverley with a queer feeling in his heart. This was his home! This was where he should have been born and where he should have been brought up.

Somehow the house, white against its setting of green trees, looked more beautiful, more entrancing, than ever, and he asked himself whimsically whether his quickened appreciation of its beauty was due to this new knowledge of how closely it concerned him personally.

He dreaded the interview that lay ahead of him and yet at the same time he felt that the section of his mind which always responded to adventure and excitement was a little thrilled because of the drama which was unfolding.

Very, very slowly Michael drove the car up the winding drive. The evening shadows were creeping across the lake, the great trees were mirrored on its surface. In the centre on a tiny island there was a small stone summer-house or temple.

It was all rather unreal in its peace and beauty, and with an effort Michael forced himself to think of the great factories less than half a mile away, of people journeying home in overcrowded buses, of children who lived in overcrowded dwellings or down dark alley-ways and who had no playground but the streets.

'I must not be sentimental about Claverley,' he said out loud; nevertheless, as he parked his car and went up the broad steps to ring the bell he knew that he loved the place.

The butler led him through the hall into a room he had not seen before. It was obviously the library, for the walls were lined with books and there were big leather armchairs and a fine collection of sporting prints hung around the mantelpiece.

'I will tell Sir Norman you are here, sir,' the butler said. 'I think he is in the garden.'

Michael looked round the room. He sensed this was Sir Norman's own room and he saw a great pile of papers and letters on the desk. It was essentially a man's room, severe, entirely lacking in the graces and soft feminine touches which only a woman can give. For the first time Michael felt sorry for his father.

Had he been lonely all these years without a wife and without the knowledge that he had a son? Could industry, however successful and progressive, take the place of the human needs of affection and family lift? Even as Michael asked himself the questions, the door opened and Sir Norman came in.

Michael went forward to meet him, his hand outstretched, but both men were conscious of the tension as their fingers touched and they murmured, each in his turn, conventional greetings. Sir Norman picked up a big silver cigarette-box and held it out to Michael.

'Won't you smoke?'

'No, thank you, not at the moment.'

Sir Norman put down the box.

'Shall we sit down?'

The two men seated themselves, and as they did so Michael saw how tired Sir Norman looked. His face was drawn and rather white, and he remembered that his father was the same age as Toogy. Impulsively he took the initiative.

'This must be rather embarrassing for you, sir.'

'It is.'

Sir Norman's voice was gruff. He glanced at Michael for a moment and then he looked away.

'You see . . . it is not easy for me to apologise—never has been—and now I feel I have got to apologise to you for the things which happened before you were born.'

'I hope you won't do anything of the sort, sir.'

Michael spoke quickly, and Sir Norman made a little gesture with his hands.

'Yet the fault was mine; I know that now. I have known it for many years as a matter of fact, and certainly no man has been more punished for his mistakes.'

'I am sorry about that,' Michael said.

'Are you? I wonder!' Sir Norman commented. 'Susan seems to have made a good job of bringing you up.'

'I can understand that. She always was a fine person. If I had had any sense I should have married her myself. Perhaps I oughtn't to say that to you.'

Michael laughed.

'Why not? But I don't think she would have married you. Toogy was one of those people who were destined to do the work she did.'

'You believe in that? In destiny I mean?'

'To a certain extent. I think that when there is a really important job to be done someone is detailed to do it, but at the same time I believe we can each of us make of ourselves what we will.'

'I believed that once,' Sir Norman said slowly. 'It was because I believed such things that I achieved as much as I have.'

'A great deal, if I may say so, sir.'

There was a moment's pause and then Sir Norman said quietly:

'I could have done so much more had I known about you.'

'It is not too late.'

Sir Norman sighed.

'It is for me. I am an old man, Michael, and old men

find it difficult to adjust themselves to new ideas. A sudden shock, a great surprise, knocks one a little off one's balance at my age.'

He paused for a moment and then he continued: 'I have always wanted a son so much and I always bitterly regretted that I had no family.'

'You don't blame Toogy, sir, for not telling you?'

'No, no, of course not! She had given her word to your mother. When she told me, we decided that for the moment things should go on as they were. You were doing great things and Susan did not wish you to be upset or in any way diverted from your plans. I suggested that it was best that we should keep silent unless . . .'

'Unless?' Michael prompted.

'. . . Unless either of us died. Neither of us had at that moment the slightest idea how soon that might happen.'

'None of us had,' Michael said; 'she seemed so well, so active, but she was doing too much. She always did. It was impossible for her to spare herself.'

'Yes, yes, I know,' Sir Norman said.

'And now what are we going to do?' Michael asked.

'By "we" do you mean you and I?' Sir Norman enquired.

Michael nodded.

'That is for you to say, my boy. I have been thinking about it a great deal. I have been trying to see things from your point of view.'

He said the last words a little shyly as if it were an effort for him to admit his own unselfishness, and Michael, with a flash of that intuition which made him so beloved by those he led during the war, understood far better than Sir Norman could have told him exactly what those few words revealed. He bent forward in his chair.

'I would like to do what you want, sir,' he said, and for the first time the two men's eyes met in understanding.

There was a short silence, a silence in which father and son began to get to know each other, and then, speaking almost gruffly as if to hide the emotion in his voice, Sir Norman said:

'As a matter of fact, Michael, it is not what I want at this moment that matters. You are the person most deeply concerned. I understood from Susan, and from other people, too, that you are in the midst of a great campaign to save this country. The people who follow you know you as Susan's adopted son; let things remain as they are for the moment. When you have succeeded, it will then be the time for us to make changes or prepare announcements.'

Sir Norman had not spoken easily and Michael knew that it had been a tremendous effort for an obstinate, autocratic old man to subdue himself and his own interests to something he did not really understand. It was a fine gesture, and Michael responded to it. He got to his feet and held out his hand.

'Thank you, sir,' he said. 'I am very grateful.'

The hands of the two men touched for the second time and now there was a warmth in their grasp and a vibration between them which drew them closer one to the other. For a moment they said nothing, they just stood smiling at each other, and it seemed as if Sir Norman grew younger. His shoulders were squared and his eyes were bright.

'I am proud of you, Michael,' he said at last.

'Thank you, sir, but I have not begun as yet.'

'No? Well, maybe there is a long way to go. If I can help in any way ...'

'I shan't hesitate to ask you, sir.'

Sir Norman drew a deep breath of pleasure.

'Would you like to look over the house?'

'I would love to see it.'

There was a pride in Sir Norman's bearing as he turned to lead the way, and Michael, following him, felt at peace and satisfied. Things had not been so difficult as he had feared. In fact any apprehensions that he might have

229

had about this meeting were now laid at rest.

He knew in that moment that he and his father would become friends. They had much in common, for Michael knew at last from where he had inherited his drive and determination.

They went slowly round the house, for there was much to see. Over the years Sir Norman had collected many things that were both valuable and beautiful. At the end of the long picture gallery he paused.

Sir Norman stood looking up at a full-length picture of a woman wearing a grey dress and holding a bunch of roses. It was a picture typical of the period and there was something very lovely in the clear-cut features and in the way the sitter held her head high so that one was conscious both of her pride and her breeding.

'Your mother.'

Sir Norman spoke the words harshly, but Michael saw that his eyes had softened.

'I am so glad to see the picture, sir,' Michael exclaimed. 'Toogy only had a photograph, and not a very good one. It was taken before she was married.'

'That was painted immediately we returned here after our honeymoon,' Sir Norman said.

Both men looked at the portrait in silence, then Sir Norman drew his gold watch from his waistcoat pocket.

'Five minutes to eight,' he said gruffly. 'Dinner is at eight.'

They walked down the gallery without speaking, each man thinking his own thoughts, yet both conscious of a companionship which needed no expression. It was only as they reached the hall that Sir Norman said:

'There will be sherry in the drawing-room, and by the way, my god-daughter has asked herself to dinner. She rang up from London and said she particularly wanted to dine here tonight.'

'Do you mean Cynthia, sir?'

'Yes—Cynthia. She told me she is working in Susan's old place.'

'Yes, she is.'

'She should do well. She has got plenty of guts, that girl.'

It was impossible for Michael to say that he wished Cynthia had not come to Claverley. Nevertheless he felt annoyed as he went into the drawing-room and found her talking to Miss Helen. Both the women had changed, Miss Helen into a dress of black lace and Cynthia into a diaphanous gown of white chiffon which made her appear very young and ethereal.

'How are you, Michael?'

She held out her hand and smiled at him disarmingly, but Michael was not to be appeased. Somehow he felt that Cynthia had come here simply because she knew he was to be present. He had no proof of this, but Cynthia certainly laid herself out to be kind to him.

She was not provoking as she had been in the past and there was no longer a veiled double meaning beneath the friendliness of her conversation. She was just unaffectedly charming, and more than once Michael felt that he must steel himself against her charm, because despite his preconceived ideas of her nature and character it was hard for him not to be attracted by her.

She was very lovely, there was no doubt about that, and she was sweet to Sir Norman in a way that delighted the old man.

'Why have you suddenly taken to good works, Cynthia?' he teased her. 'Don't tell me you are tired of the gay life, for I shan't believe it.'

'Nevertheless, it is true,' Cynthia answered. 'And I can honestly say, Uncle Norman, that I am happier than I have ever been in my life before.'

There was a ring of sincerity in her voice which quite startled Michael.

'You intend to stay on in Dockland?' he asked.

231

'Of course,' she replied. 'I feel as if the people whom I am trying to help are a sacred trust left to me by Miss Toogy.'

It was difficult for Michael to speak to her cynically after that, and yet he told himself that he must not forget David. How could he trust this woman? How could he, when he remembered David's bitterness and the way he had died?

Michael was glad when dinner was finished and they returned to the drawing-room. Miss Helen poured out the coffee and Sir Norman persuaded him to have a glass of port.

'There is not much of this vintage left,' he said as he held his glass up to the light.

'Would you like me to play to you?' Cynthia asked.

Michael, remembering another night when she had played, felt that he could not bear it. He loved music and there was something within him which responded to it, something over which he knew he had no control.

Desperately he tried to think of an excuse to prevent her going to the piano. He looked out of the window.

'It is such a warm night,' he said, 'it seems a pity not to take a stroll outside.'

'But of course,' Sir Norman replied, 'and another time I want to show you the gardens.' He opened the long french windows which led on to the terrace outside and they all went out. 'You won't be cold, will you, Helen?' he said to his sister. 'Would you like me to fetch you a wrap?'

'No, thank you, Norman. It is lovely out here in the moonlight.'

Her words were almost an understatement. Daylight had faded, but it was not dark. The moon was creeping up the sky and there was a promise in its silver light of a great brilliance later on. The first evening stars were glittering over the trees and in the soft hush there was only the occasional note of a bat to be heard.

232

'The lake looks nice, doesn't it?' Sir Norman remarked, and Michael replied:

'It is beautiful. I was wondering this evening as I came up the drive about the little building on the island.'

'Oh, that's the most thrilling story in the whole of Claverley, isn't it, Uncle Norman?' Cynthia interspersed.

'Won't you tell me about it?' Michael asked, speaking not to her but to Sir Norman.

'As Cynthia said, it is a very interesting story,' he answered. 'It was built originally as a summer-house, or perhaps the original owner wanted just to add something artistic and decorative to his plans for the garden, but his son who inherited Claverley, the second Lord Claver, was of a very jealous disposition. Moreover, he married a very beautiful and very notorious young woman.

'I should imagine from her pictures that she gave him plenty of reason for jealousy; anyway, determined to prove her infidelity, he announced that he was going to Rome on a visit.

'Preparations were made for his journey, but secretly he prepared the building on the island as a hiding-place for himself.

'I can't help thinking that the Mistress of Claverley was very incurious or was too busy enjoying herself to notice that there were workmen on the island. Anyway, His Lordship said good-bye and set off for Dover.

'He changed horses at the first stopping-place and came back at dead of night. He was rowed over the lake, where he installed himself in the summer-house.

'History relates that he was there a week before his suspicions were confirmed; then coming back to the house, and climbing in through his wife's bedroom window, he killed her lover before her very eyes.'

'It is a horrid story,' Miss Helen ejaculated.

'Is that the end?' Michael asked.

'By no means,' Sir Norman replied. 'Mad with rage,

233

the irate husband dragged his unfortunate wife down the stairs and forced her into the boat on the lake. He took her to the summer-house and hanged her from the ceiling by the ribbons on her night-gown.'

'They say her ghost can still be seen there,' Cynthia added; 'anyway, no one on the estate will visit the island at night, will they, Uncle Norman?'

'Perhaps some of the old employees won't,' Sir Norman answered, 'but I think all the young people laugh at such things as ghosts.'

'And what happened to the murderer?' Michael enquired. 'Was he brought to justice?'

'No, he escaped the hangman. He went abroad and lived there, and was succeeded some years later by his brother.'

'I feel his exile from Claverley must have been a punishment in itself,' Michael said.

'But surely the punishment hardly fitted the crime,' Cynthia argued. 'Think of his poor wife dying in the summer-house.'

'Deservedly so,' Michael replied grimly.

'Poor Lady Claver,' Cynthia sighed. 'I cannot help feeling sorry for her, and if she still haunts the place it shows that she is repentant and sorry for her sins.'

'And if she doesn't, I suppose it proves that she still glories in them,' Michael said, an edge on his voice.

Cynthia looked at him.

'I am sure she is sorry,' she said softly.

'We shall never know for certain unless we see the ghost,' Miss Helen said. 'And personally, I never see ghosts.'

'But I do,' Cynthia exclaimed; 'I am almost certain I saw one when I was a child. Do you believe in them, Michael?'

'I don't know,' Michael replied. 'I had a very extraordinary experience once in Burma, and after that I would hate to say definitely that there aren't such things.'

'You are obviously psychic,' Cynthia said, 'just as I have always been convinced that I am. But this is wonderful! We must go and look for the ghost. There will be a full moon tonight, and it is well known that ghosts are always to be seen when there is a full moon.'

'I am afraid I have got far too much work to do to spare the time to go looking for ghosts,' Michael said quickly.

'Oh, but you must see the place where the Mistress of Claverley died,' Cynthia insisted. 'You will have time to work afterwards. We will go now! It is early, but there might be the faintest glimmer of a ghost—one never knows.'

'No, I think we will leave it until another time,' Michael answered, realising too late what Cynthia was scheming. But, ignoring him, she turned to Sir Norman.

'Don't you think it is a good idea, Uncle Norman? Make him come! These politicians only believe what they can see and touch. It would be an education for Michael if he saw the ghost. He might even be a little sorry for the lady who had to pay so drastically for her fun.'

Sir Norman laughed.

'Go along, Michael, Cynthia is longing to show you the spot on which the crime was committed. You will find the key in the hall, my dear.'

Cynthia slipped from the terrace and Michael turned hastily to Sir Norman.

'I really must be getting home, sir. I have got a pile of work waiting for me.'

'Well, this little expedition won't take you long, and Cynthia is set on it,' Sir Norman answered good-humouredly. 'She is a nice child, and it must be dull for her staying here with a couple of old fogies like Helen and myself. You must help us to make her visit an enjoyable one.'

He paused for a moment and said, 'All work and no play, my boy . . . You know the rest?'

Michael knew only too well that Sir Norman was trying to be kind. He was bringing two young people together—in fact throwing them together—so that they should enjoy themselves. It was impossible for him to explain that he did not want to go to the island with Cynthia, and equally impossible for him to refuse to go with her. She came running back with the key in her hand.

'I have got it, Uncle Norman.'

'Good girl!'

Sir Norman turned to Michael.

'There will be a whisky-and-soda for you in the library when you get back. Helen and I will be sitting there, for I have some work to do.'

'Very good, sir.'

Michael could do nothing but follow Cynthia down the garden path, which twisted through high rose bushes until it came to a flight of stone steps leading down to the lake. A boat was at the bottom of the steps and Cynthia jumped in, the soft folds of her chiffon dress billowing out around her.

'Are you a good oarsman?' she asked, and her voice was light with amusement as if she sensed his discomfiture.

'I have not rowed for some years,' Michael answered, 'so if I upset you it will be your own fault for trusting yourself with me.'

'I am not afraid. I won a cup at school for swimming and I know every inch of this lake. You need not be worried that I shall be caught in the weeds and come floating back to you like Ophelia.'

Michael pushed the boat out from the side and started to row steadily, the oars breaking the still surface of the water. Cynthia put her hand over the side.

'How quiet it is,' she said softly. 'I feel as if we were moving in a dream.'

'I shall soon have to wake up and get back to work,' Michael answered.

'One is never in a hurry in dreams,' Cynthia replied, 'only in nightmares.'

'I think I am always in a hurry,' Michael said.

'Meaning that this is a nightmare?' Cynthia answered. 'How ungallant of you!'

There was a slightly mocking note in her voice which he did not miss. At that moment they reached the island.

'There are the steps,' Cynthia said, 'and you can tie the boat up beside them.'

He did as she told him and then stood steadying the boat so that she could disembark. She stood up in the bows and held out her hand to him. He was forced to take it to steady her while she stepped from the boat.

Her fingers felt cold in his, yet somehow he sensed they quivered a little as if she was nervous. Despite every resolution he felt a strange excitement—or was it anger? he asked himself—rising up within him.

The steps led them to a grass path which encircled the tiny island. Their feet made no sound and Cynthia's white dress against the dark shadow of the summer-house made her appear like a ghost herself.

At the same time it was easy to distinguish the outline of her face and the shining wideness of her eyes. She looked back at Michael as she fitted the key in the door and he saw that her lips were parted.

The door leading into the summer-house swung open. Michael followed Cynthia. Anticipating that they would have to feel their way, he felt in his pocket for some matches; then he gave an exclamation.

The moon was pouring in through the windows of a small round room. It diffused over the whole place a silver light which was magical and enchanting.

Michael stood looking around him. For a moment he fancied that there were ghosts lurking in this lovely place: not unhappy ghosts, not the ghosts of those who had died violently, but ghosts of happy people who lived at Claverley and loved there.

Generation after generation would have come to the summer-house when they wanted to be alone. They would have come into this small room, to whisper their vows, plight their troth, perhaps to snatch a kiss when the vigilance of their chaperons was relaxed. Emotions leave an impression on the walls of a place.

The summer-house at Claverley seemed to Michael to hold the impressions of many people. He could feel them, he could sense them, he could almost hear them, and his heart seemed to be beating as theirs had beaten . . . quicker and quicker. . . .

He felt a movement by his side. Cynthia moved across the floor, her shoes making very little sound on the wood. She stood against the window and now her profile was outlined in silver, so that Michael could see her little up-turned nose and rounded chin.

She turned away and yet he knew she was over-whelmingly conscious of him as he of her. Her heart was beating too. He could see the tumult of her breasts moving beneath the white chiffon which covered them and one hand crept up to the whiteness of her throat.

She turned a little and the moonlight was on her face. She was so lovely that it was difficult at that moment to remember anything but her loveliness. There was a wild-ness in the atmosphere. There was something wild and ecstatic, too, in Cynthia's eyes as she looked at him.

'Michael!'

She hardly breathed his name, yet her voice seemed to pulsate in the moonlight.

He strode across the room to her.

'Why are you doing this to me? Why? Why?'

'Michael!'

She spoke his name again and he saw her lips move, so softly, so gently, that he sensed rather than heard the words she whispered:

238

'I . . . love . . . you.'

It was then that something seemed to snap within him, something which he had held bridled and controlled broke from his restraining grip. He put out his hands and seized her shoulders.

'I hate you!' he said. 'Don't you understand that I hate you? You brought me here and what happens now is your own fault. I hate you, but . . . I want you!'

His hands tightened on her shoulders until the very pain of it made her cry out. It was that cry of weakness which broke Michael's last semblance of control. He bent down and took Cynthia in his arms.

Just for a moment he looked into the darkness of her eyes, and then his mouth was on hers. He kissed her savagely and even as he did so felt flame rising within himself, igniting him, searing its way madly through his body and into his mind.

He kissed her again and again, bruising her lips, feeling her body tremble and quiver in his arms.

'I want you, Cynthia,' he heard his voice say, and his lips were on her eyes, her neck and her hair.

His passion consumed him. It was the fierceness of a tempest lashing him with its fury and its power. Again and again he kissed Cynthia. The fragrance of her skin and of her hair was in his nostrils, the softness of her mouth was against his lips. His hands felt the subtle warmth of her skin.

'I want you—now! You are mine!'

His cry was one of triumph, that of a conqueror supreme in his victory.

He raised her in his arms. He had forgotten everything at that moment, forgotten the world outside, even his ambitions and his plans had gone. He was wholly and utterly primitive—a man who held the woman he desired. to take her and make her his whatever forces were against him.

'I will master you,' he said almost brutally. 'I hate

239

you but I will break you as you have broken other men.'

It was then that Cynthia fought herself free. She reached the floor, evading Michael's arms, which would have recaptured her. There was a tearing sound as he caught at her dress and she wrenched it from his hands.

He heard her give a cry which was half a sob as she ran through the open door and he lost her.

For a moment he stood in the middle of the room, half believing she would come back, before he followed her. He came out of the summer-house on to the shadowed steps and saw her a little way to the left of him, standing at the edge of the water.

'Cynthia!'

He called her name and was conscious that his voice was still vibrant with passion. As he spoke. she turned her head, looked at him with what seemed to him to be an expression of fear, then dived into the water. He heard the splash as she broke the surface.

'Cynthia, Cynthia, what are you doing?'

Even as he called he saw that she was striking out for the shore. She did not turn her head and in the water he could see her white dress trailing out behind her as if she were a Rhine maiden.

'Cynthia!'

He called her name once again, but still she did not answer, and he could only stand watching her go while the heat of his passion ebbed slowly away and a cold logical reasoning took its place.

She swam quickly and he saw her disappear on the other side of the lake into some overhanging bushes. He went back to the summer-house.

The moonlight was still shining into the little room. He stood very still, the silver rays touching him like gentle fingers. And then he knew there were ghosts all round him; ghosts who were laughing at him; ghosts who had in their turn lost what they most desired.

Roughly Michael turned from the room, slamming the door behind him and putting the key in his pocket.

Slowly he rowed the boat back towards Claverley. It seemed to him as he went that the night was very dark.

'Oh my God,' he asked himself. 'What have I done?'

15

Michael drove home with a cloud of depression such as he had never experienced before encompassing him to the point of despair.

He hardly knew what he had said to Sir Norman and Miss Helen, who were waiting for him in the library. They had asked him where Cynthia was and he murmured some reply about her having gone to bed. They both thought Cynthia had been too shy to accompany him to the library after their ecstatic moments in the moonlight.

It was obvious that Sir Norman and Miss Helen were fostering what they imagined was a tender romance between the two young people. It was with the greatest difficulty that Michael prevented himself from speaking the truth and telling them that he had insulted Cynthia and that she had fled from him in disgust.

Driving slowly homewards, he told himself over and over again that such an insult was justified and she had invited it; but he could not convince himself for one moment.

The naked truth was that he had behaved like a brute and he was ashamed. Worse than that, he realised that the avalanche of his own feelings gathering speed revealed to him all too clearly what he had been afraid to admit before. He loved Cynthia!

Yes, that was the truth, and he was forced to acknowledge it. He loved her desperately, madly, passionately and eternally, and nothing that his logical mind could tell him could alter that.

Over and over again he repeated to himself the word 'David', as if it were some talisman which would exorcise the heat of his blood and the ache of his desire for the woman whom David had loved. But it was no use.

Nothing he could say could alter the beating of his heart or the emptiness of his arms, which told him all too clearly that this was not something which had happened suddenly but that it had been there for a long time.

He admitted now that Cynthia's face had haunted him, her beauty had been with him at all times, deny it as he would. He had thought of her not once but a thousand times a day; and though he had shied away from the thought, it had nevertheless been there, persistent and reccurring, until its very familiarity ceased to warn him of the danger.

Now it was too late! He knew now that she would haunt him for ever. He never could forget her or the warmth of her body within his arms.

Again and again he recaptured that moment when he had pressed her lips and felt his heart throb in response; and though he hated himself for what he had done, at the same time he knew that he could never forget the wonder of it.

'Cynthia! Cynthia!'

The whole night seemed to be full of her. He remembered every expression in her eyes, the way her hair grew back from her forehead, the soft pulse beating in her throat, the exquisite gestures she made with her hands and the almost breath-taking sweetness of her smile.

He loved her! Of course he loved her! But the whole thing was hopeless, doomed from the beginning because

243

of a young man who had died with her name on his lips in the wilds of Burma.

Desperately Michael tried to recapture his sense of horror; but persistently to his mind came instead Mary's voice pleading with him for his love, her arms outstretched, her eyes beseeching him.

Were Mary's and David's cases parallel? It was difficult for him to say they were not, and yet he felt that there would always be that barrier between him and Cynthia—a barrier erected long before he ever saw her.

It was heart-breaking that while he acknowledged the barrier he knew that he would still love Cynthia to the end of his life.

There would never be anybody else, he knew that now, and it seemed to him as surely as if she had said so in so many words that Toogy had chosen her for him. But even Toogy, clever and wise though she was, could not understand that, if he allowed himself to ask Cynthia to be his wife, he would always feel that David's blood was on his hands—David, who had died for love of her.

It was all hopeless, impossible! And Michael, drawing up outside his little house, had a sudden wild desire to drive away, to go on driving until he found a ship or maybe an aeroplane which would take him away from everything and everybody.

He wanted to be in the wilderness; in the empty spaces where a man could be alone.

Deliberately, because he must force himself to behave conventionally, Michael stepped from the car, took the latch-key from his pocket and inserted it in the lock. The light was on in the hall and there was a pile of letters waiting for him.

He took them up and went into the sitting-room. Bill who was staying the night with him, was sitting in an armchair reading a newspaper.

'Hullo, Michael!'

'Hullo, Bill,' Michael replied. 'I thought you would be in bed by now.'

Bill looked up at the clock over the mantelpiece.

'Why, it's not late, is it? It has only just gone half past ten.'

Michael stared at the clock, half disbelievingly. Only half past ten! It seemed to him that a century of time had passed since dinner. He had lived through so much; he had experienced enough emotion to last many people a lifetime, and it was strange to find that the hands of the clock had moved slowly and methodically. He felt a century older, and yet it was only half past ten!

'There's a letter for you on your desk,' Bill was saying. 'A despatch rider brought it about half an hour ago. He said it was urgent, but he was not told to wait for an answer.'

Michael took up the note and recognised the handwriting. It was from a great statesman, a man who had served the country valiantly during the war and who had retired from public life, but not from wielding great influence within his Party.

Michael opened the envelope. Inside there were a few lines in small, neat writing. He read it slowly:

'My dear Fielding,

I thought you should know at once that there will be a General Election in October. The Prime Minister will make the announcement tomorrow morning. You have both our gratitude and our support.'

Michael drew a deep breath. So it had come—the action he had been expecting, the moment which he had instigated several months previously! Without a word he held out the note to Bill.

'Good news?' Bill questioned as he took it.

He read the letter and gave a cry of joy.

'Michael, this is wonderful! This is what you have

245

worked for! Now at last we shall all have a chance to save England.'

'Will it ever be as easy as that?' Michael murmured.

'You are not doubtful, are you?' Bill asked. 'It doesn't sound like you! It is all you have worked for; surely you are not afraid in the moment of victory?'

'No, I'm not afraid,' Michael said; 'I am only seeing how much there is still for us to do, how much courage and fortitude we shall need before we finally win through.' He threw out his hands in a sudden gesture. 'It is all so slow, Bill; the Party machine, the General Election, while the world waits.'

'And yet real Democracy is worth waiting for,' Bill replied.

Michael walked across to him and put his hand on his shoulder.

'Thank you, Bill, that is what I wanted you to say. Democracy—the freedom of mankind! We must never forget that is the true foundation—the reason for our every action.'

'And a new Government . . .' Bill began.

'We need more than that,' Michael interrupted. 'No Government can change man's soul; the souls of men change Governments!'

He sat down in the armchair opposite Bill. For a few moments there was a silence, each man deep in his own thoughts, and then suddenly and unexpectedly Michael said:

'Bill, have you ever been in love?'

Bill started and flushed a little.

'Yes, Michael. I want to tell you about it. That's one of the reasons why I was waiting here tonight . . . if you aren't too busy to listen to me.'

'Of course I'm not too busy,' Michael said, but it was obvious that Bill's reply was a surprise to him.

'You see, Michael,' Bill said shyly, 'I'm in love with Mary. I have been for some time, and this afternoon she

. . . she promised to marry me.'

'Bill!' Michael's cry was one of complete astonishment; then he jumped to his feet and held out his hand. 'I am delighted!'

Bill took Michael's hand and looked at him with the frank, level gaze of a man who will make no pretensions.

'I love Mary, Michael, but she is not really in love with me—not yet. She loves you, as you well know.'

'But, Bill . . .' Michael protested.

'Wait a minute,' Bill said. 'I knew that, of course, before she told me about it. It doesn't matter, Michael. Mary is not the right person for you, as I have told her. I can look after her and I shall look after her. I shall be happy to work for her and in time I shall make her love me and make her understand how well suited we are to each other.'

'And you will succeed, Bill,' Michael said.

'Yes, I know I shall,' Bill said confidently. 'You see, I understand Mary, far better than she understands herself. She has been starved of love; starved, too, of many of the things which make life beautiful. It has been the same for me. We are going to face things together and somehow nothing is going to matter because neither of us will be alone.'

There was nothing for Michael to say. He could only put his hand on Bill's shoulder and know that he would understand how much he was trying to express. After a moment's silence Bill said hesitatingly, as if he were half afraid to voice his thoughts:

'Everything has come right for me, Michael, thanks to you, and I only hope that you, too, will be happy.'

'I think that is unlikely,' Michael said drily, and with a sudden bitterness in his voice.

'Why?' Bill asked; and he dared to add, 'Cynthia Standish is a wonderful person, and . . . I think she loves you.'

His words were a blow. For a moment Michael could

not answer, could not find the words in which to reply; it occurred to him that Bill was being impertinent to mention anything so intimate and personal.

He felt like telling him to mind his own business; but the look of anxiety on Bill's honest face and the expression of affection in his eyes told Michael that it was friendship that had prompted his remark. Bill was fond of him, genuinely fond of him, and wanted his happiness.

Taking a cigarette from his case, Michael turned it over in his fingers. At length he said slowly:

'Do you remember David?'

'Of course I do!' Bill answered.

He was puzzled by the question, but was obviously prepared to do his best to answer anything that Michael put to him.

'I was very fond of David,' Michael said in a deep voice.

'I think we all were,' Bill replied, 'and he was a good pilot.'

'You knew him even better than I did,' Michael said, 'for you shared a hut with him. You would say, wouldn't you, Bill, that he was a fine person?'

'Tip-top,' Bill answered enthusiastically. 'I liked him enormously and we got on awfully well together. He was a real good sort as far as men were concerned; his only trouble was the other sex.'

Michael, who had been leaning back in the armchair, sat up suddenly.

'What do you mean by that?' he asked, and his voice was imperative.

'Oh, merely that women were somewhat of a failing with David,' Bill replied; 'rather by way of being his hobby. He was always involved with some woman or other. Don't you remember that brawl in Bombay when we all got ticked off? That was David's fault originally. He tried to snoop the girl friend of some local nabob, who went for him with a knife, and then of course we had to intervene. I have got a scar on my shoulder still as a memento of that "bit of fun".'

'But David didn't really care for the girl, did he?' Michael asked, and Bill thought that his voice was low.

'Not for that one,' he said, 'but there was a Wren he was crazy about at one time and then a little woman in Simla. I shall never forget what he was like on that occasion.'

'I didn't hear about that.'

'No, I suppose, as you were our Commanding Officer and all that sort of thing, David thought it better not to tell you. Besides, you would have been furious if you had known.'

'Why?'

'Oh, David tried to overstay his leave and we had the dickens of a job with him. In fact we had practically to shanghai him to get him on the train. Not that I blame him, she was a pretty bit of goods—golden hair, a skin like peaches and cream. She had a husband somewhere up on the North-West Frontier, but no one bothered much about him, least of all the lady herself.'

Michael got to his feet abruptly.

'Why wasn't I told about this?' he asked angrily.

'Told about it? Good heavens, Michael, you must have been the only man in the camp who needed any telling about David's love affairs. We used to get sick to death about hearing him rave about his various girl friends. We used to have bets as to how long each one would last; three months was the limit, I think.'

'I had no idea,' Michael said—'no idea.'

He walked across the room and threw open the window. He felt suddenly that he must have air.

'Poor old David,' Bill went on reminiscently, 'and yet one has no reason to be sorry for him. He had a hell of a good time! We were all of us pretty woman-mad out there, but David always managed to be more dramatic about it than anyone else. I remember hearing him tell a girl in Rangoon that he would kill himself if she wouldn't let him make love to her. She did, of course, and all was well.'

Michael turned away from the window.

'Thank you for telling me,' he said abruptly, 'but I wish I had known sooner.'

'Why? Does it matter so very much?' Bill asked, and then, sensing something was wrong, he added: 'You know, Michael, you were awfully serious-minded about lots of things, and perhaps that's why the chaps didn't always confide in you about their light-o'-loves. We had a feeling that you lived on a much higher plane than us.'

'That's rubbish!' Michael replied.

'Not really,' Bill answered; and then with a little twisted smile he added, 'We would have followed you to either heaven or hell, whichever way you led us, but sometimes we just liked to sit on the earth and enjoy ourselves.'

The clock on the mantelpiece struck eleven. Bill got out of the armchair.

'I must toddle off to bed now. It's the doctor's orders that I mustn't be late. Anything you want, Michael?'

'No, thank you,' Michael replied.

Bill shut the door behind him and Michael sat down at his desk. He drew out a pad of notepaper from the drawer and picked up his pen. Supporting his head in his hand, he stared in front of him. What would he say?

How could he put an apology of such magnitude into words? He never for a moment doubted the truth of what Bill had told him and it seemed to him that he had always known that there must be some explanation which would exonerate Cynthia and which would explain why she should have acted as she did.

But his mind had refused to believe his instinct and his brain had challenged the verdict of his own heart.

250

Now he knew the truth and the truth showed him his own self in a very unpleasant light.

He had sat in judgment, he had presumed to dictate to a woman he had never seen before how she should behave to a man who had loved her. He had believed that man to be sincere; but, even so, it was not for him or any other human being to tell a woman whom she should or should not love.

It was presumptuous and intolerable, overbearing and unjust. There were many other adjectives with which he could label himself, but his humiliation must somehow be conveyed to her.

What could he write? 'I love you.' 'Forgive me I love you.'

He had insulted the woman he loved and who he believed loved him. He had treated her abominably; worse than that, he had degraded her and himself by an exhibition of unbridled passion of which any decent man would be ashamed. How could he now say in words that he was sorry?

He must do something better than that, something which would not only bring him Cynthia's forgiveness, but so very much more. Michael could feel the tempo of excitement rising within him.

For the first time he was free to seek Cynthia, to woo her and to win her. For the first time the shackles which he had forged with his own hands had fallen away.

He wanted her, he needed her, and he knew that he could not live without her! This had been ordained from the beginning, he was sure of that; this was Destiny playing its part in his life, leading him towards a greater fulfilment.

Suddenly Michael knew what he must do. He went from the room impetuously and with the haste of a man going into action. He slammed the front door and jumped into the car. He turned it round and sped away up the road.

He had come home slowly from Claverley; he went back at high speed, the night air on his face.

The lodge gates were open and he drove through them without checking his pace. It was only as he neared the house that he slackened speed. He looked around him and finally stopped under the shadow of a great oak tree and turned off the engine.

The moonlight was on the lake, which lay like a silver bowl cupped beneath the pale beauty of the house; the windows were dark and there was no light in them save where the moonlight shone iridescent on the glass.

Michael approached softly, walking on the grass so that the sound of his footfalls would not be heard. What he was going to do he was not sure. He was only certain of one thing: he must see Cynthia this very night.

If necessary he was prepared to waken the whole household, but he would try other and more subtle methods first.

As he walked he remembered the conversation at dinner when Cynthia had said something about the fragrance of the rose garden coming in at her bedroom window. That gave him a clue. He knew from that on which side of the house her room lay for he had seen the rose garden on the two previous occasions when he had been to Claverley.

He moved forward on the grass until at length he stood in the rose garden looking up at the windows above him. There was no light in any of them, but the moon was full and after a second or so as his eyes travelled around the house he saw that one window was open.

He told himself that the other rooms whose windows were closed were most likely not in use. This, therefore, might be Cynthia's room.

He drew nearer until he stood directly beneath it. He could see that the curtains were drawn back; and after a moment, with a leap of his heart, he discerned that some-one was sitting in the window.

He was still for some time, but there came no movement from whoever it was within the upper room.

'I must take a chance,' Michael told himself, and very softly he whistled. It sounded like a bird's cry, but there was still no movement. He repeated it and then someone turned and bent forward.

The moonlight was full on Cynthia's face, shadowing her eyes and sharply defining her cheek-bones.

'Cynthia!'

Michael called her name. She looked down at him and he knew that she was surprised to see him.

'What do . . . you . . . want?'

'I must speak to you.'

'No . . . Michael.'

He could barely hear her voice, it was so quiet.

'Cynthia, listen, I have got to talk to you.'

'It is too . . . late. You must . . . go away.'

She was standing up now and he could see that she wore a robe of some soft material with lace sleeves which dropped back to reveal her arms. He felt that she was about to shut the window, and impetuously he called:

'Cynthia, you must listen to me. It is important—desperately important.'

She was very still and he knew that she was debating within herself what she should do. He felt that he could not risk her refusal. He moved forward quickly. There was a wistaria growing up the lower part of the house.

Without hesitation Michael started to climb it, catching hold of the gnarled branches and finding a foothold in the stone pattern of the wall. It took him only a few seconds to climb up to Cynthia's window, and then he reached out his hand and clutched the window-sill.

He raised himself to the window level and looking up at Cynthia saw that both her hands were pressed against her breasts.

'Michael! You might have . . . killed yourself!'

He threw his leg over the sill.

253

'I have climbed worse things.'

He entered the room, brushed the dust from his hands and stood facing her. It struck him suddenly how very small she was and he could see she had been crying.

'Cynthia,' he said humbly, 'I have come to apologise.'

He could not read the expression in her eyes, but she inclined her head gravely, almost queen-like.

'Thank you, Michael.'

'Cynthia, forgive me!'

He took a step forward and with a pang in his heart he saw her shrink away from him.

'Cynthia, you have got to forgive me,' he pleaded, 'I understand at last. I have fought against loving you because I thought that I was being loyal to David. It is only tonight when I got home that Bill told me the truth about David. He wasn't what I thought he was and I was mistaken in my opinion of him.

'He is dead and there is no reason why we should ever speak of him again; but, Cynthia, I was terribly wrong. Whatever I thought of David, I had no right to judge you, no right whatever to accuse you. I loathe and despise myself for it. But you have got to forgive me. You have got to let me prove how desperately sorry I am; and most of all you must let me prove that . . . I love you.'

Michael's voice vibrated through the darkness of the room.

'I love you, Cynthia,' he repeated hoarsely; 'I need you so much, more than anything else in the whole world.'

He waited, but there was no answer. Instead Cynthia moved slowly and sat down on the window-seat. Her head was half turned away from him towards the garden. He could see the pucker of her brows and the soft droop of her mouth. Suddenly he was on his knees beside her so that his face was level with hers.

'Cynthia,' he whispered—'please, Cynthia, forgive me.'

There was something magnetic and compelling in his voice so that almost despite herself she turned her head and looked at him. Now the moonlight revealed the yearning in his eyes and the pleading on his lips.

She looked at him for a long moment and then with a sob in her voice she whispered :

'Oh . . . Michael!'

Very gently he reached out his arms and put them round her.

'Listen my darling,' he said, 'I love you with all my heart. I want you as my wife, only you can help me, and there are so many things for us to do together, if only you could love me too.'

'You know that . . . I . . . love you, Michael.'

Her voice was as deep as his and the magic of the moment ignited in them a joy which was beyond words. They could only look at each other, drawn together by a wonder and a glory which was not of this world. Everything that was false and unworthy dropped away and they saw the nakedness of each other's soul.

Cynthia was trembling, but still her eyes did not leave Michael's. There seemed to be a light within her so glorious, so lovely, that it illuminated the whole room.

'I love you . . .' she whispered, 'and it was knowing . . . you that made me see how empty and useless my life was . . . before.'

'You are perfect! The woman I have dreamt about all my life.'

Michael drew her closer and still closer to him. He could feel her heart beating wildly against his, and he saw in her parted lips and in the shyness of her eyes the first awakening of desire.

'I adore you! Oh, my sweet, you belong to me.'

The words seemed to burst from him, and then, as though the glory of the moment was too strong for them, human feelings broke the strain. With a little sob Cynthia turned and hid her face against Michael's neck. He held her fiercely and she heard his voice against her hair.

'You are mine, my darling—mine for all time and for ever.'

Cynthia threw back her head and looked into his eyes.

'For ever . . . Michael,' she whispered. Her voice broke. 'I love . . . you . . . I love you . . . more than . . . I can ever . . . say.'

His mouth was on hers, and then he was kissing her wildly, passionately, yet with a reverence which had not been there before, while the world seemed to vanish. They were alone—one and indivisible.

'Darling . . . my darling . . . I love you.'

It was only a whisper lost in an ecstasy which carried them towards the stars.

If you would like a complete list of Arrow books please send a postcard to
P.O. Box 29, Douglas, Isle of Man, Great Britain.